Other Books by Lane R Warenski

THE GRIZZLY KILLER SERIES

GRIZZLY KILLER: The Making of a Mountain Man
GRIZZLY KILLER: Under the Blood Moon
GRIZZLY KILLER: The Medicine Wheel
GRIZZLY KILLER: Hell Hath No Fury
GRIZZLY KILLER: Where the Buffalo Dance
GRIZZLY KILLER: Smoke on the Water
GRIZZLY KILLER: The Painted Skull
GRIZZLY KILLER: White Snake
GRIZZLY KILLER: The Trading Post
GRIZZLY KILLER: Spirit Talkers
Grizzly Killer: Spirits In The Wind

OTHER NOVELS

Trail Of The Vanished

Grizzly Killer:
Hell On The Horizon
(Grizzly Killer XII)

LANE R WARENSKI

WOLFPACK
PUBLISHING
— EST 2013 —

WOLFPACK
PUBLISHING
— EST 2013 —

Published in the United States by Wolfpack Publishing, Las Vegas

Wolfpack Publishing
6032 Wheat Penny Avenue
Las Vegas, NV 89122

wolfpackpublishing.com

Paperback ISBN 978-1-64734-274-6
eBook ISBN 978-1-64734-273-9

Grizzly Killer:
Hell On The Horizon

Dedicated to David and Douglas Anderson for their
unending support and belief that anything is possible.

Chapter 1

A Royal Battle

The stars were starting to fade with the coming light of a new day. Zach sat motionless, hidden in a thicket at the edge of the clearing as he waited for the coming dawn. The air was cold, here high in the Rocky Mountains. He could feel frost forming on his mustache from the moisture in his breath, but he didn't move. He knew there were elk in the clearing, he could hear them, although it was not yet light enough to see.

Jimbo was right by his side, the big dog knew he must not move. Jimbo had spent his whole life with Zach, he had been through this same scenario countless times since Zach had found him as an abandoned pup. His muscles were tense, he knew even more so than his master the elk were there in front of them.

Zach had found this small spring that seeped from the ground at the edge of the clearing the day before. There had been a small herd of elk bedded down in the forest nearby. Jimbo had started to chase the fleeing animals until a short whistle from Zach stopped him. He had hoped the dog hadn't frightened them so they would not return.

He had been cutting across this ridge on his way back to Blacks Fork, and his waiting wives, after setting his trap line. It was the first week of October, *naa-mea'*, the rutting moon to his wives people and the beaver fur was prime. Zach, his partners, and friends had been trapping for the last month, and they needed fresh meat in camp.

Zach had quietly left camp before any of the others had stirred. He wanted to be in this spot before light and had made it there a little earlier than he figured. The cold air of the early morning was starting to sink in with no movement for over a half hour now. He was seriously thinking about standing up and moving back deeper into the forest to get his blood pumping faster, but just then a bull elk bugled right in front of him. He could smell the strong musky odor of elk very strong on the gentle breeze as it shifted, blowing into his face.

Zach had approached the meadow and wallow from the downwind side. Although the breeze was very light, it was enough to keep his scent from the weary elk that he hoped were there. An almost imperceptible whine escaped Jimbo as the bull grunted and stomped the ground. Zach very slowly put his hand on the big dog to calm him.

The bull was close, it sounded only a few yards away, but still Zach could not see him. Another bull further down the ridge answered his challenge, and almost immediately the bull responded. He grunted and blew, then stomped the ground and bugled again.

Zach glanced up, moving only his eyes and could see only a couple of stars. As he looked back down, the shape of the magnificent bull came to him silhouetted against the lighter colored sage of the clearing. Zach watched in awe at the power of one of the largest bulls he had ever seen. His massive antlers stretched back over half the length of his body. He threw his head around, wielding his antlers like he held over a dozen long daggers. He thrust the daggers into a sage in front of him, ripping the bush from the ground and throwing it twenty feet into the air.

It was getting lighter by the minute. Zach could now see over a dozen cows scattered throughout the sage clearing. They seemed to be ignoring the temper tantrum the bull appeared to be having. It was light enough he could shoot anytime, but the magnificent bull had him mesmerized.

Zach had no intention of shooting the bull, his meat would be rank and tough. He wanted a yearling cow for the quality of the meat, and he could see three or four that he could choose from.

The other bull bugled again. This time he was much closer. The big bull trotted forward, then pushed his cows to the other end of the clearing before coming back to meet the approaching challenger.

The massive herd bull was only twenty-five yards in front of the thicket that was hiding Zach and Jimbo. Zach could see the muscles ripple along his back, shoulders, hips, and neck as his challenger broke out of the timber and into the clearing only seventy-five yards away.

The challenging bull was nearly as large as the herd bull. There was no doubt at all Zach was going to witness a violent fight of these two titans of the Rockies. They were fighting for the right to breed with the cows. At this moment, the only thing that mattered to either of them was winning the right to these dozen cows.

The herd bull stomped the ground and grunted before bugling once again, trying to frighten the challenger off by his display of power and size. The challenger didn't seem impressed or frightened as he trotted forward, accepting the herd bull's challenge.

They turned facing one another, now only a few yards apart. The herd bull suddenly lowered his head and charged the challenger. Their antlers collided with astounding force as each of the large bulls tried to get the advantage over the other.

Zach had witnessed elk fighting many times before. Every fall since he and his Pa had come to the mountains nearly ten years before, he had watched the bulls fight, but he had never been this close in the past. Their strength and power had always been evident, but now he could almost feel the force of their blows. He could hear them strain as they pushed against one another. The herd bull was a bit larger, but the challenger seemed slightly more agile. Zach watched, thinking they were very equally matched.

Five minutes had passed and neither of them appeared to be tiring. Then the herd bull's rear hoof slipped on the hard branch of a sage, and suddenly the challenger had the advantage. He pushed the bigger bull backwards right towards where Zach was hiding. They were less than ten yards away and Zach was figuring he would have to jump out of their way when the herd bull threw his head to the side, making the challenger lose his advantage. The two bulls separated, but neither turned away and fled.

The cows were now about seventy yards from the battling titans, and to Zach they appeared only mildly interested. The bulls clashed again, their impressive antlers crashing together with such force he couldn't believe they didn't break. This time it appeared the herd bull had the advantage as he pushed his challenger back.

The sage in the clearing was being ripped up and broken as the thousand-pound bulls fought. Zach could see blood on the shoulder of the challenger, where one of the herd bull's daggers had reached through the challenger's own antlers.

The fight of these royals lasted longer than any Zach had ever seen. He figured it had been almost fifteen minutes that the two mighty bulls had been pushing each other back and forth. More than once they had gotten way too close for comfort to the small thicket, he and Jimbo were hiding in.

With neither bull being able to get and keep an advantage over the other, it was pure exhaustion that finally ended the battle. The challenger broke off and ran back in the direction from where he had come. The old herd bull had won, but the victory had come at a cost. He was exhausted, so exhausted he didn't move. After watching his challenger run out of sight, the old bull laid down on the torn-up ground right where he stood.

Zach watched the old bull, lying only thirty yards from him. With the bull not moving he could see he had seven points on each side and one of his antlers had the ends broken off two of the tines. Zach wasn't sure whether they had broken off during this fight or some previous one. Since it was nearing the end of the rut, he was sure the old bull had been in several other fights keeping his herd of cows. He didn't believe any of the other fights would have been as intense as this one.

Zach moved his attention from the old bull to the cows, but he couldn't bring himself to shoot one of them. The majestic old bull had fought so hard to keep them, Zach couldn't take even one of them now. He stood up and the bull slowly turned his head to look at him but didn't have the strength to run. The cows all lifted their heads and watched, but none fled as he and Jimbo walked back into the forest and out of sight.

He had left Ol' Red in a clearing about a half mile away, and the sun finally peeked over the eastern horizon just as he stepped up into the saddle. He sat and watched as the golden rays of light shot out across the morning sky, bringing its brilliant light and warmth across the mountains.

Zach and his partners had spent the latter part of the summer and early fall with their wives and children at home on Blacks Fork. Their longtime friends, Grub Taylor, Ely Tucker, and Benton Lambert with their wives had also joined them for the fall hunt and to spend the winter.

After being away from home for the last year and a half, Zach, his wives and partners loved being home. Their horse herd had been getting fat and a bit lazy living in the big meadow rather than on the trail each day.

They all enjoyed the fact that Grub, Ely, Benny, and Little Dove were there. Now Grub and Ely had wives of their own, and Zach's little village had grown to six lodges. Two Flowers and Yellow Bird seemed just as happy as they could be with Grub and Ely. Yellow Bird was a couple of years older than Raven Wing, while Two Flowers was the same age. They had grown up together in the Shoshone village of Charging Bull. Buffalo Heart, Sun Flower, and Raven Wing loved hearing about everyone in the village since it had been several years since they had spent any real time in the village of their birth.

This summer at Rendezvous, Grub and Ely had taken the two of them as wives. It was the first time they had taken wives in the twenty-plus years the two old mountain men had been in the mountains, and to Zach and the others they both seemed happier than they had ever been.

Zach rode silently toward the small creek and the series of beaver ponds where he had set his traps. They had been actively trapping for the last three weeks and although they were all getting beaver, Zach could certainly tell the numbers were definitely down from what they were a few years ago. As he rode along he made a decision. They would finish out the fall over on the Bear River, maybe even go up to the creek where they had found the gold nuggets before going to Saint Louis a few years before.

Jimbo stopped on the trail right before him. Zach could see every one of his muscles were tense, but the hair down his back was not standing up, telling Zach whatever was ahead must not be dangerous. Zach strained to see through the scattered aspen when the glint of sunlight filtering through the brilliant yellow of the turning aspen leaves reflected off something ahead. The movement was evident as the large bull elk turned his head.

Zach watched as the nervous bull got to his feet. He was only seventy-five yards away and as he stood Zach could see blood on his shoulder. This was the challenger to the herd bull he had watched fight. He had come down the ridge this far and just as the herd bull had done, he laid down to recuperate from the mighty battle he had just fought.

Jimbo looked up, expecting Zach to shoot, but Zach just watched. The meat of this bull would be just as rank and tough as that of the herd bull. Zach knew there would be more opportunities to make meat. There always had been in these Uintah Mountains that had become his home. The big elk trotted away. If he was favoring his injured shoulder, Zach couldn't tell.

A hundred yards after the elk was out of sight, Jimbo stopped again. This time the hair down his back was standing on its end. Zach quickly checked the powder in the pan of his .54 caliber Hawken rifle he had bought right from the Hawken Brothers shop when they went to Saint Louis. Paying with gold he had found only twenty-five miles west of where he now was.

Jimbo started his low rumbling growl deep in his chest and then started to back up. Now Zach was concerned. There were very few things in this wilderness the big dog would back away from. The first was a grizzly. As he strained to see what was ahead of them, a porcupine came waddling down the trail toward them. Zach smiled at his big dog. Jimbo had learned his lesson with porcupines as a pup and he wanted no part of those painful, potentially deadly quills. Zach moved Ol' Red out of the game trail they were following and Jimbo followed suit as the fat critter waddled past them, paying them no attention at all.

A half hour later Zach could see the beaver pond where the first of his ten traps was set. A cow and calf moose were standing in the water along the far edge of the pond and he stopped, enjoying the view of the wildlife and spectacular beauty of this place.

He was just about ready to move on, when the cow raised her head, staring intently to the north. Only a moment later, two wolves trotted out of the forest right toward her and her calf. The wolves were after her calf. Zach wondered if they had a litter of pups to feed, but whether or not they had pups, a young moose calf would feed them all. First they must separate the calf from its very protective mother.

This was not the first time this cow had fought wolves. She led her calf out into deeper water, knowing the water would make it much harder for the wolves to attack. She stayed in the water herself. Keeping her large, powerful body between the wolves and her calf. Zach watched the wolves try time and again to pull the mother away by getting out into the water and trying to circle around her, hoping they would scare the calf out onto dry land. After several failed attempts, the pair of wolves moved on, hoping to find easier prey.

Zach rode along the pond's edge and to the beaver slide where he had set the trap. His float stick had not moved, so he knew the trap was empty. He waded out into the cold water and pulled the stake and trap. Then with dripping leggings and moccasins he mounted up and rode upstream to the next trap. By the time he had eight of the ten traps picked up, he did not have a single beaver. He moved on to the next and just before he reached the dam, he heard the slap of a beaver's tail hitting the water. A moment later there was a second slap, as the pair of beavers warned of the approaching danger.

There was a beaver in the last of his ten traps. He skinned it and rolled up the plew knowing wolves, a bear, coyotes, or even a badger would make quick work of the carcass. After he tied the rolled plew on the back of his saddle, he looked upstream. It had been a couple of years since he or Running Wolf had followed this creek up to its source. He longed to see what he would find higher up, but that would have to wait. Maybe next spring, once the creek was free of ice, he would make the ride. Right now he needed to find Running Wolf, Buffalo Heart, Benny, Grub, and Ely. If they were going to move over to the Bear River and the Gold Hill, they couldn't waste any time.

Chapter 2

Warriors are Coming

Star and Gray Wolf were trying to catch a squirrel while the twins, Jack and Little Moon, had uncovered a stink bug and were teasing it with sticks. Shining Star, Yellow Bird, and Two Flowers had hiked up to an upper meadow, gathering roots while they could still dig in the soft mountain soil before it froze solid. Sun Flower, Raven Wing, Morning Song and Little Dove had stayed with the children, making warm winter clothes for all of them.

Sun Flower was the first to see the four warriors riding across the meadow. The sun was dropping into the western sky and making it impossible for her to see the pattern of dress while they were still over a quarter mile away. She did not know if they were friend or enemy. She dropped her awl and deer hide, picking up her .36 caliber long rifle. Saying loud enough for the others to hear, "Get the children, warriors are coming."

As the others got the children, Sun Flower stepped to

the edge of the stream. She didn't shoulder her rifle but it was cocked and in plain view of the approaching men. These strangers were still a hundred yards away when they stopped and the one in the lead raised his hand in the universal sign for friend.

The women were all nervous. With the sun behind them, all they could see were silhouettes of the four riders. The leader could not only see the women were alone but that they were very anxious about their presence. He dismounted and took his bow from over his shoulder and slowly set it on the ground. He then handed his reins to another of them and now being unarmed, except for the knife in his belt, he started toward Sun Flower at a slow walk. He could plainly see the rifle in her hands, which she was holding like she knew how to use it. When he thought he was still far enough to dive out of the way if she shot, he stopped and asked in sign if he could approach.

Sun Flower never took her eyes off him as she asked the others, now speaking Shoshone, "Do you think they are truly friendly?" It was her sister that spoke, "I cannot tell who they are." Then Star said, "Momma Sun Flower, I think they are friends, I think they are a long way from home."

Sun Flower set the butt of her rifle on the ground, and she could see the relief on the warrior's face. Raven Wing stepped up beside her sister and signed back to him, "Who are you and what do you want."

"I am White Crow, we are Bannock, we are looking for three young hunters, lost now for many suns." Raven Wing signed, "White Crow, you may come in alone." He nodded, then looked back at the other warriors for a brief moment before slowly walking forward.

He had only walked a few more steps before they all recognized the dress. The Bannock tribe were considered by many to be a part of the Shoshone nation, and were allied with the Eastern Shoshone, which most of these women were.

White Crow stopped on the western side of the river, thirty feet from where Sun Flower and Raven Wing were standing on the east side. He had known all along, from the teepees and the women's dress they were Shoshone for the afternoon sun was in his favor. These Bannock warriors had been surprised when they first saw the horse herd in the big meadow and then the Shoshone teepees along the river, as they continued their search for the three missing hunters.

Sun Flower looked at her older sister and when Raven Wing nodded, Sun Flower said, speaking Shoshone, which she was sure these Bannock warriors would understand, "Come into our village White Crow, as friends you and the others are welcome." White Crow smiled he had been taken back by the beauty of these two Shoshone women. He knew they were sisters, they looked too much alike not to be. Just as the other three were approaching the river Zach, Running Wolf and Grub rode up over the low ridge on the western side of the big meadow at a fast gallop.

Zach had seen the tracks of the four horses and was getting back to the women as fast as they could, not knowing who was this close to their families. Ely, Benny, and Buffalo Heart were a couple miles behind, coming from a different direction. They were taking their time, not knowing anything was out of the ordinary.

Zach pushed Ol' Red into a hard run, Running Wolf and Grub followed suite when they saw the strangers moving across the river. The Bannock left their horses in the big meadow along with their weapons, showing the women they meant them no harm. But the four strangers became very alarmed when they saw Zach with Running Wolf, and

Ely coming at them at a dead run.

Growling Bear panicked and grabbed Raven Wing, holding her in front of him as a shield against the fast approaching riders and the giant gray dog that was charging at them. As Sun Flower picked up her rifle, Coyote Talker stopped her, holding her firm. White Crow yelled, "No, release them!" But it was too late for Growling Bear. Little Dove was already swinging a heavy black iron frying pan and hit him in the back of his head. Growling Bear's legs buckled, and he hit the ground with his eyes wide open, but only the whites were showing. He never moved and everyone there thought he was dead.

Just then, Zach and Running Wolf slid their mounts to a stop. Zach jumped off ready for battle. But it took only a brief moment before they saw no one but Growling Bear was in any danger. Coyote Talker released Sun Flower holding up his empty hands, showing he meant no harm.

Raven Wing knelt beside the downed Bannock warrior and found he was still breathing. The back of his head was already swelling and with his eyes rolled back into his head she wondered if he would survive.

Zach took a quick glance at the other three warriors, knowing Running Wolf and Grub would have them covered, he knelt down beside Raven Wing. Little Dove felt bad for hitting him as hard as she did, but she remembered the men that came into their camp up on the Sweet Water a couple of years before when they had killed Meadowlark. She had every intention of killing this warrior that had grabbed Raven Wing, and everyone there believed she had. Zach looked at Raven Wing and saw the worry in her eyes. At that moment, she did not believe her medicine was strong enough to save this Bannock warrior.

Zach looked up at Little Dove. She was still holding the heavy black iron pan. Her lower lip was quivering slightly and everyone there could see how bad she felt. White Crow rushed toward them but a vicious growl from Jimbo stopped him in his tracks. With only a slight movement of Zach's hand, Jimbo moved from his path and let White Crow come to his fallen companion.

As White Crow knelt beside them, Zach, speaking Shoshone, said, "Your friend is very lucky that Little Dove hit him, if the great medicine dog would have reached him first he would already be dead. Now maybe, just maybe he has a chance." Zach pointed to Raven Wing and continued, "This is the great Shoshone Medicine Woman, Raven Wing, and if anyone can save him, it is she." Raven Wing looked skeptical as she said, "I will do what I can but it will be up to the Creator of all Things whether he lives or joins his grandfathers in the great beyond."

Zach could see the event weighed heavily on this Bannock Warrior. Sun Flower then said, looking at Zach, "Grizzly Killer, these Bannock hunters are looking for three young hunters lost for many days. Their leader is White Crow, I do not know the names of the others." As Zach and White Crow both stood looking at one another, Little Dove set the heavy frying pan down and she and Morning Song rushed forward to help Raven Wing.

Jimbo, along with the rifles of Grub and Running Wolf, had kept Coyote Talker and Yellow Horse from moving. Now, Zach called Jimbo to him and Grub and Running Wolf lowered their rifles and dismounted. Zach could see the relief on the two warriors' faces. A half hour later, introductions had been made and the six of them were seated around a small fire. The women had Growling Bear on a buffalo robe lying next to the larger cooking fire. White Crow told them it was an honor to finally meet the great white warrior Grizzly Killer. Just then Shining Star, Two Flowers and Yellow Bird came down the trail into camp.

They were carrying baskets woven from cattail leaves carrying the roots the three of them had been digging much of the day. They stopped when they saw the strangers in camp but before anyone had said anything, Ely, Benny, and Buffalo Heart came trotting across the big meadow.

Introductions were made, and the women, all but Raven Wing and Little Dove, started fixing a meal. Star and Gray Wolf cautiously approached their fathers. Luna staying right between them. The beautiful white wolf had been their protector, and she wasn't going to leave their sides with strangers in camp.

While the women prepared their meal, Running Wolf got his ornately carved pipe and the men passed the pipe around as White Crow told why they had come so far. It seems the three lost hunters were very young and had ventured way too far, trying to prove they were men, while still only boys. White Crow told them he had led a hunting party up the river the white trappers call the Weber. The boys had come to care for the horses, but while the men were hunting, they had gone off on their own and had not been seen since, that was five suns ago. They had tracked them this way until a storm had washed away all sign.

A moan was heard by the fire as Growling Bear regained consciousness. The men all stopped talking as White Crow rushed to his fallen companion. Growling Bear's vision was blurry and the pain in his head was severe, he remembered where he was, but he had no idea what had happened to him or why his head hurt so bad.

Raven Wing brewed her willow and aspen bark tea, and although Growling Bear was unsteady and groggy, with White Crow's help he sat up to drink the bitter brown liquid.

As the sun set, Growling Bear was alert, which surprised them all. They could all see his dark eyes were not the same, and Raven Wing told them he must rest quietly for a couple of days, maybe more. After a brief discussion, Zach and all of his partners offered to help look for the lost Bannock boys, while Growling Bear recovered. It would cost them a few days of trapping, but they all knew the lives of three boys in their early teens was more important than another dozen or two plews.

The next morning Growling Bear's vision had not cleared. The pain in his head had changed from the sharp stabbing pains to a severe dull ache. Raven Wing had been up with him most of the night, as had White Crow. They had him drink more of the bitter tea every couple of hours. Part of the time he could hold it down, part of the time his stomach rejected the bitter liquid.

After talking about the lost boys well into the night, it was decided they would ride back to the last place White Crow had seen their tracks, just a couple of hours east of Weber River, along a creek just south of the canyon of many echo's. They took supplies for three or four days and decided Grub would stay in camp with the women. Since Ely was the best tracker any of them had ever seen, they all wanted him out looking for sign.

Grub didn't mind staying behind, he knew how important the women and children were to all of them and it was an honor to have all of these men trust him to keep them safe. Though they all knew safety in the wilderness was just a relative state.

It was a hard day's ride through some rough country to reach the spot where the boy's tracks were last seen. They made a small fire and set rabbits to roasting. Coyote Talker and Buffalo Heart had shot several with their bows and arrows as they rode through the afternoon.

Long wispy clouds glowed bright orange, making the western horizon look like the whole world was burning as the sun dropped below the distant western ridge. Naa-mea', the rutting moon was now a week old, and the air at night was cold. Scattered junipers grew on the hills along this creek, growing out of a white chalky dirt. It was Ely that first called this Chalk Creek.

They gathered a supply of firewood from piles left by countless spring floods along the creek and figured they would keep the fire burning through the night. Morning brought a covering of frost on their bed rolls and the warm fire and hot coffee felt very good to them all.

They rode out in two's scaling the steep chalky hills, they would signal the others with a rifle shot if any sign of the boys was found. The creek had already been checked by White Crow and his Bannock hunters as they had followed it east, and through the mountains all the way to Blacks Fork. That was the only direction the men did not cover.

It was early afternoon when Ely, riding with Yellow Horse first spotted tracks cutting across one of the white chalky hillsides several miles to the southeast. At first they thought it was made by elk, the loose dry dirt would not hold the shape of the tracks. Since they had nothing else to follow, Ely followed this trail. Less than a half hour later the trail topped out on the ridge and they could plainly see the hoof prints of a horse.

Ely fired a shot in the air, although he believed they were too far from the others for the shot to be heard. He sent Yellow Horse back to find the others and let them know they had found a track. Even though Ely had no way of knowing, he believed this single track had to be left by one of the young hunter's horses.

From there, the tracks were easy enough for Ely to follow. An hour later the tracks crested another ridge and there they were once again lost. This time trampled into the dust by what looked to be two or maybe three dozen elk. The far side of the ridge was covered in thick aspen and below that was a large basin nearly a mile across. It was covered with oak brush and a few scattered pines.

Ely zig zagged down into the basin, carefully watching the ground for the distinctive mark of the horse's hoof print. He was just coming out into the open when something caught his eye. He slipped out of the saddle and carefully moved the dry grass aside to reveal another horse print in the rich mountain soil. He looked ahead and in his mind could see the trail the young man had followed. Then half-way through the basin everything changed. There were a dozen sets of horse tracks surrounding the single track he had been following.

Chapter 3

Trail of the Lost

Grub climbed up on the ridge above Blacks Fork and sat in the warm afternoon sun. He thought about Ely and the others wondering where they were and if they had found any sign of the missing young men. He watched the women, all busy doing various chores outside the teepees, and the children playing by the stream. Suddenly Star looked up the hill at him and waved. He wondered how she knew he was watching her. He then smiled and wondered how he had known how he had been watched so many times in the past. It seemed a person could feel the eyes of another, whether man or animal watching them and figured the little girl was no different.

As he watched this idyllic scene below, he thought about how much his life and the life of his partners had changed. He had been content living the life of a bachelor in this wilderness. He had always believed he had everything he had ever wanted. Now he wondered how he could have been so wrong all off these years. He watched Two Flowers sitting by the fire, making a pair of fur lined moccasins for the coming cold weather. He looked at Shining Star, whom he had once called the most beautiful woman he had ever seen and meant it, and wondered what his and Ely's lives would have been like if they would have taken wives years sooner.

He looked at Star and Gray Wolf and then the twins. Grizzly Killers daughter with her dark hair and bright blue eyes was going to be as beautiful as her mothers, and he wondered if he had a daughter what she would look like. He then laughed to himself knowing he was too old to be thinking like that.

His eyes looked to the west, and again he wondered where his partners were. Had they found any sign of the missing boys? Growling Bear had been quiet, Grub didn't think he had spoken more than a half dozen words since the others had left. The lump on the back of his head was very pronounced and although he seemed grateful for the care he was receiving, Grub suspected there was a hidden hatred for the woman that had done that to him. Even now, Grub had his rifle in hand and wasn't letting this hurting Bannock warrior out of his sight.

*****

Once again Ely dismounted to better study the tracks. As he carefully studied the area it became clear, the rider of the horse he was following had been taken prisoner. He could see where the young man had put up a fight, but it appeared to have been brief. A dried drop of blood on a blade of grass made Ely believe the young man had been injured. How bad, he had no idea.

The hard ground and storm of a couple days ago made it hard to tell when the young man was taken but Ely knew whoever had taken the boy had a three or four day lead on them. Ely knew the trail of a dozen horses would be easy enough to follow, but why would they take a boy only fourteen summers old? He believed this was one of the boys but where were the other two?

He looked at the surrounding hills and wondered if they had been taken as well, from someplace he had not found?

He waited there for the others to arrive. But it was nearly sunset before he saw the long ears of Ol' Red crest the ridge and start down into the basin. The others rode into the basin two at a time. Running Wolf and White Crow were the last ones there.

When Zach heard what Ely believed happened, he figured he knew the reason for taking the boy. He didn't say anything hoping he was wrong, he needed to wait for Running Wolf.

A small fire was burning as Running Wolf and White Crow dismounted, and Coyote Talker was already telling White Crow what had happened. Running Wolf got an angry look as he put his hand on White Crow's shoulder and said, "Slavers." Zach's fear was confirmed. Many Indian tribes made slaves of their captors. And many Ute villages were no different. It had been the slave trade that first brought horses to the Ute people. The Goshute and Shoshone people that live in the vast desserts of the great basin to the west had always been easy targets for taking as slaves. Many were marched all the way to Santa Fe where they were traded to the Spanish for horses, iron knives, and other European goods.

Running Wolf looked at White Crow, Coyote Talker, and Yellow Horse saying, "I believe this young warrior was taken by Ute Slavers. Some of my people trade slaves to the Spanish for horses." Zach could see the anger in the eyes of these men and added, "We do not know for sure the attackers were Ute Running Wolf," Zach added. With a sad expression, Running Wolf answered, "No Grizzly Killer, not for sure, but in this place who else would they be? I do not think Shoshone would have taken a young Bannock warrior."

They all knew that boys of twelve and fourteen summers were not yet warriors, but they called them such to show respect. As angry and upset as White Crow was about the situation, he appreciated the gesture and the help of Grizzly Killer and his partner. Coyote Talker was more suspicious, especially of Running Wolf's apparent willingness to help against his own people.

Ely stepped forward, he could read the body language and facial expression of Coyote Talker. It was plain he was younger and much quicker to anger than White Crow. Ely said, "I figure there is about an even dozen of 'em and if they is moving with slaves, they ain't gonna be moving fast and that there trail is gonna be easy enough to follow. We can move a whole lot faster than they can dealing with slaves on the trail." Running Wolf added, "As late in the year as it is, they may just take them back to their village and use them themselves until next spring, then take them south."

White Crow asked, "Do you think they have taken all three boys? It is plain to see only one of them was here."

"Don't know what else to think, White Crow," Ely said. "We ain't seen no sign of the other two, I figure we best just follow these here tracks we can see 'til we know different."

"Who do you think it is that has taken them," Zach asked Running Wolf.

"I don't know, maybe the Sahpeech, or Pahvant, but this is too far north for the Pahvants. We will find out when we catch them."

Coyote Talker, still angry, said, "You lie, it is probably your own people." He then turned to White Crow and nearly shouting said, "He is Ute, you cannot trust him, they will probably lead us away from them and we will never see my brothers again!"

Zach stepped forward, but Running Wolf held up his hand to stop him. White Crow could see the anger in all of their faces over the words of the hot headed Coyote Talker. Running Wolf was calm as he looked at Coyote Talker and said, "Coyote Talker, I know you are upset and angry, I would be too, and if you would prefer to go after and rescue your brothers on your own we will leave and let you. I am a Uintah Ute, and no one from my village has taken slaves for trade since I was a child. I do not believe any person has the right to own another. You say you have heard of the great white warrior Grizzly Killer, if you have, you know he is a man of his word and so am I, if you will allow us to help, we will find your brothers and you can all return to your people with your heads held high."

It had been eight years since Zach and Running Wolf had first met. Over that time they had grown closer than most brothers. Zach had never been more proud of his partner than he was right then. He reached out and put his hand on Running Wolf's shoulder and looked at White Crow and asked, "Well White Crow, what's it gonna be? Does Coyote Talker speak for all of you, or would you like our help." White Crow looked embarrassed as he looked up into Zach's sky-blue eyes and then at Running Wolf, "Please forgive Coyote Talker, Running Wolf, two of the young men are his brothers, and we would very much like your help."

Running Wolf looked at Coyote Talker who was staring at the ground, it was plain to see he was embarrassed about his outburst but his pride was not going to let him apologize for what he had said. It was then that Ely stepped forward and said, "Coyote Talker, we can all see you are a proud young warrior. Pride can be a very good thing, as long as you do not let it get you killed." Then with a brief glance at White Crow he continued, "I am a tracker, but it ain't gonna take no tracker to follow this here trail. When we get close enough that Jimbo gets him a snout full of scent, we are only gonna need to try to keep up with that there big dog. For now, I figure the trail is too old for Jimbo to pick up the scent. All these here horses need rest except mine. We have been resting here for hours. I am gonna ride on ahead and go as far as I can. You all let them there horses rest through the night and catch up to me after daylight. Don't worry none about being spotted, if there is anything to worry about, I will leave you all a sign."

Without further delay, Ely jumped up on his horse and headed southwest, following the well-beaten path left by what he thought was nearly twenty horses. Ely knew very well, the danger they were riding towards. His eyes, trained by a lifetime in the wilderness, never stopped moving as he rode and the sun set behind the western mountains.

Even though he had never been through this land before, Ely Tucker knew the wilderness. He rode with confidence, but behind that confidence was a weariness that had kept him alive much longer than most had survived the Rocky Mountains. As twilight faded, stars began to dot the sky and Ely slowed his trusted gelding, but he knew the horse could see the ground much better than he could, and he rode on.

The trail was now angling south by west and for several miles now had been going steadily downhill. By the time the half-moon reached the western mountains, Ely figured he had gone far enough for tonight. The slavers, and he believed Running Wolf's assessment, had been following a tiny little creek and he had dropped out of the pine and aspen into a much dryer landscape. Juniper and sage dotted the hill sides. Before the moon had set, he believed they were heading into what he believed was a broad valley below.

A quick glance at how far the big dipper had moved around the north-star, told Ely it would be getting light in another three hours. He didn't bother with a fire and he had eaten a couple pieces of jerky while riding. He laid out his bed robe in the soft needles under a large old juniper. As he closed his eyes a lone wolf howled somewhere in the broad valley below, but Ely was asleep before the mournful sound had faded into the surrounding hills.

*****

The Stars were still shining brightly but the moon had set when Zach first opened his eyes. Jimbo raised his head and looked at his master as though the dog had heard Zach's eyes opening. Zach looked at his huge dog and wondered if he had. He then listened to the sounds of the early morning, just as his Pa had taught him all those years ago. He could still hear the words his Pa had seared into him, *"When you wake up son, never move a muscle 'til ya listen to the sounds all around. If all is quiet, you'll know danger is near, and your movement might let that danger know where you are. But if the sounds are normal, you know it is safe to move."* Zach smiled as he listened, remembering the lessons his Pa had taught him was always pleasant memories. Even though he knew if danger was close, with Jimbo's keen senses, his dog would let him know long before he would be able to hear. Never the less, Zach listened to the sounds of the very early morning. There was a slight rustle in the brush not far away, which he guessed was a rodent rummaging through the grass looking for seeds. Way off in the distance, a pack of coyotes sounded like they were hot on the trail of a rabbit. Only a moment later the high pitched squealing of a rabbit in distress, caught by a bobcat, coyote, or fox, shattered the calm of the morning.

Zach sat up and looked out into the darkness, he wondered just where Ely was and how far ahead these slavers really were. He knew owning slaves was common practice for both white men and Indians, but he didn't believe anyone had the right to force another person into slavery. Unlike other white men he had heard talk, Zach knew the Indians and the blacks that were forced into slavery were men, just like he and his partners were.

He stood and spoke loud enough for everyone to hear in near perfect Shoshone, "I figure the horses are rested boys, we best be on our way. No telling how far ahead Ely is by now."

Coyote Talker jumped to his feet, surprised it was a white man that was the first of them ready to go after his brothers. Zach knew the young Bannock warrior did not fully trust him. It was plain for everyone to see he didn't trust Running Wolf at all. But as proud and impertinent as he was, Zach could see he fully trusted White Crow.

Zach liked White Crow, he along with his partners, could see the concern White Crow had for the missing boys. Even more than that, Zach could tell he was intelligent, cunning and strong. He was a man that would be cunning and wise in battle, one that would not let his own pride cost the lives of any of his men.

Even though it was cold they did not restart the fire, and the sky was just starting to turn gray along the eastern horizon as they started out. Zach could plainly see Ol'

Red warm breath as he saddled the big mule. He then told Jimbo to find Ely, and as the big dog headed out, Zach turned to the others and said, "Now we just have to keep up with him." Some of them chewed on a piece of Jerky as they headed out, but Zach was concentrating on following the trail of Jimbo. As intelligent as the big dog was, he had never seemed to grasp the idea that Zach and Ol' Red could not go under the brush and low branches of trees the way he did.

As the gray of dawn faded into the light of the coming day, Zach followed Jimbo up over a ridge only partially covered with trees and brush. From the top of this ridge he could see a large wide valley below. This was new country for Zach, Running Wolf was the only one of them that had been through here before, and that had been many years before. As they rode down the ridge, the land got drier and junipers replaced the pines, aspen, and oak brush.

Running Wolf told them the trail was leading to the Yambow, what the Utes called the large wide valley below. The Yambow, he told them, was the usual summer home to a Ute village but he did not believe they would be there this late into the fall.

The sun was only a couple of hand widths over the horizon when Jimbo found where Ely had finally stopped and spent the night. Zach was mildly surprised Ely and gone this far before stopping and it was plain to him White Crow, Coyote Talker, and Yellow Horse were as well.

White Crow asked, "When will your friend wait for us?" Zach shook his head and said, "He may not wait for us. I suspect as long as he knows we can follow the trail, he will keep right on after them."

They reached Weber's River and stopped to rest the horses. After they had cooled down, they let them drink their fill. Here the river valley narrowed, and the trail followed along the edge of the hills on the east side.

Zach had not seen Jimbo for nearly an hour. It was unlike the big dog not to check in more often than that, and he wondered why. What had the dog found to keep him away for this long? Of the many possibilities, Zach hoped nothing had happened to Ely. He knew Ely was one of the most capable men in the mountains, but he also knew how dangerous this wilderness can be. Zach had always believed his Pa was the best man in the wilderness that had ever lived. He didn't even make it a year before that grizzly had killed him.

Running Wolf, Benny, and Buffalo Heart could see the concern on Zach's face as he stared south. It was Running Wolf that asked, "What is it my brother?"

"Jimbo, he hasn't checked back for quite some time," Zach replied. Benny said, "Maybe he caught up with Ely." Zach then turned to Benny and Benny could see the worry in his eyes. "Ely can take care of himself Grizzly Killer," Benny continued. Zach nodded as he said, "I know Benny, but so could my Pa."

Chapter 4

On the Bank of the River

Jimbo was nearly five miles ahead of Zach, with the scent of Ely and his horse getting stronger with each closing mile. But there was a new scent on the trail now. It was the scent of man and horse. The big gray dog followed with more urgency now. His instincts telling him his friend may be in trouble, so instead of going back to Zach he was pushing ahead, farther and faster.

Ely dismounted, leaving his horse below the crest of the hill in front of him he cautiously crawled to the top. There were much fresher horse tracks in the trail he was following. Tracks made by two horses that were at least a day newer than the main group that he figured the stolen Bannock boy was with. Figuring this may be two more of the slavers trying to catch up with the others, Ely was being mighty careful.

By studying the tracks, Ely believed he had gained nearly two full days on the slavers. They were moving even slower than he figured they would. These new tracks that were on top of the older ones were moving much faster. To Ely, it was obvious the two new riders were trying to catch up to the others.

*****

Little Bull and Gray Deer had hidden as they watched the enemy warriors capture Brave Fox. These boys had never seen Ute warriors before, and they had no idea who this enemy was. They waited and watched, both afraid and ashamed that they were too afraid to help their friend and brother. Little Bull was just over a summer behind Brave Fox, and Brave Fox was six summers behind Coyote Talker, the oldest of the three brothers. They hid in silence as the Ute slavers bound Brave Fox's hands and put him on the back of his horse. It was a particularly mean looking man that took the reins of Brave Fox's horse and led him out of sight.

Gray Deer was fourteen summers old, the same age as Brave Fox, and a year older than Little Bull. All three thought of themselves as warriors. Believing all they lacked was the experience of Coyote Talker and the other men. Little Bull was as quick to anger as his oldest brother, but he was afraid. The fear he felt made him ashamed, he didn't believe a real warrior would feel any fear.

Gray Deer was much more even tempered than Little Bull, and he put his hand on his friend's shoulder and said, "We cannot help Brave Fox, there are too many of them. We must go back and find White Crow and Coyote Talker and the others, together we will free Brave Fox." Little Bull fought back tears as he thought of his brother being led away, then nodded, knowing Gray Deer was right. He did not want to admit even to himself how frightened he felt. Having Gray Deer suggest they go back for help was a great relief.

Once again neither boy wanted to admit it, but it soon became apparent they were lost. After Brave Fox was taken, they rode in circles trying to the find the trail back to their camp. One ridge looked just like the next and they circled until after dark. Scared, exhausted, and alone in an unknown wilderness, the two young men stopped and built a fire. Vowing they would find their way back the next morning. They were so tired neither of them ate even the dry pieces of jerky they carried. Gray Deer added a couple of arm sized branches to the small fire and before the flame had even died down from the initial flare up, both boys were asleep.

Little Bull was restless, he dreamed of the unknown warriors taking his brother over and over again. He dreamed of finding Coyote Talker, and he was so ashamed he couldn't look his oldest brother in the face. Little Bull and Gray Deer both knew they alone could not have gone against a dozen enemy warriors, but that wasn't where the shame he felt came from. It was the fear he felt inside that made him ashamed. Even now he felt afraid, afraid of being lost, of not finding Coyote Talker, of never seeing Brave Fox again. He woke, he could feel something crawling down his cheek. He brushed it away, only to find it was a tear. Shame filled him again, he had never seen a warrior cry. He sat up and used a stick to stir a bit of life back into the fire.

As Little Bull watched the tiny flames flickering back to life, he vowed he would never be afraid again. He had no idea right then how he would stop the fear from overpowering his thoughts and mind, but he vowed to find a way. He would not live in fear of anything ever again. As

Little Bull slowly drifted back to sleep, he had no idea how that sacred vow, made of out fear, in this unknown place would set the course for the rest of his life.

The sun had just pushed above the mountains that towered above them, when Gray Deer woke up. He looked across the now cold fire at Little Bull and could see the streaks of tears that had ran down his dirt covered cheeks. He felt the weight of the world was on his shoulders, he was the oldest, and it was up to him to find their way.

There was no water where they had stopped, and they were thirsty and knew their horses would be as well. Neither of them had realized they had been riding in circles the day before and now were further from their original camp and the help they desperately needed than they had been when they decided to go back.

Gray Deer knew to find water they would have to follow the ridge they were on down-hill. Maybe all the way down to the valley floor to the west, so that was where he headed. They reached the river within an hour, not knowing this was the same river White Crow had led them along for several days. They found horse tracks along the river and since they had no idea at all where to find White Crow and Coyote Talker, they decided to follow the tracks. Neither of them realizing the tracks they were following were made by the Ute Slavers with Brave Fox and seven other women and children captives.

They pushed on, neither of them knowing who they were following, but hoping whoever it was would help them. They rode quickly, trying desperately to catch up. Neither believing they were anywhere near the warriors that had taken Brave Fox.

The river was very low this time of year and there was a thin film of ice forming around the rocks where there was little to no movement of the water. They had no idea how far they had traveled when the river turned to the east, heading up a large canyon coming from the high mountains above. The tracks crossed the river and continued south, now following a creek that was lined with beaver ponds.

The two of them rode ahead neither feeling confident they were doing the right thing. They slowed their pace, not being sure they really wanted to catch up, but not knowing what else to do.

Gray Deer stopped, and Little Bull rode up beside him. Gray Deer said, "I do not know if we are doing the right thing, Little Bull. Something does not feel right about it." Little Bull sat there in silence, staring at the trail before them. Trying to be as mature and experienced as Coyote Talker and White Crow, he said, "We should stop and build a fire and pray to the maker of all things for guidance." Gray Deer was surprised at Little Bull's words, never before had his younger friend talked like that. Little Bull was always impatient, acting before he thought. These words now were words that he thought would come from a village elder, not from his quick to anger young friend.

They stopped on a flat covered in dry fall grass and cleared a small area. Little Bull gathered firewood from along the creek as Gray Deer prepared a shallow fire pit.

Gray Deer sensed a change in Little Bull. He had no idea what was different, but there was something different about him. After the nearly smokeless fire was burning, the boys sat down. Little Bull laid a couple of sprigs of sage on the flames, just as he had seen the elders in the village do. As the smoke of the burning leaves swirled into the sky, the boys prayed. Believing the smoke from the sage would carry their prayers to the Great Spirit above, the maker of all things.

*****

Ely slowly raised his head just enough to see over the hill-top. Not knowing what to expect, he was being mighty careful. He wished his old partner was with him. Grub's eyes had always been a bit better than his own. Now, they were getting old it seemed that Grub could still see as a young man while Ely's sight seemed to get a little worse with each passing year.

Ely believed something was there, something nearly a mile ahead on the bank of the river. He believed he could see smoke. He was concentrating trying to make out what was there when suddenly he sensed a presence.

Ely reacted out of instinct. He started to roll to the side, hoping if an arrow was already in flight he could get out of its path. After two spins, moving as fast as he could, he stopped, and before he saw what was before him he was bringing his rifle up. There right at his feet was Jimbo, the big dog had his head tilted to the side wondering what Ely was doing.

He stared at the big dog for a minute, trying to calm down. Finally, in no more than a whisper said, "Where did you come from big feller, I didn't hear a thing." Jimbo rushed forward and licked Ely across the face, relieved he was alright. Ely rubbed his ears asking, "Where is Grizzly Killer? He must not be too far behind for you to be here."

Ely then looked ahead once again, he could see Jimbo staring at the trail ahead as well. Ely whispered once again, "Well big feller, what is it you see up ahead? Sure wish Grizzly Killer was here. He would know how to send you up there to have a close look see." The words had barely come out his mouth when Jimbo took off. He cleared the twenty foot wide creek in one bound and keeping brush between himself and the boys with their fire he silently ran toward them. Stopping only a hundred yards away.

Jimbo watched as they sat there waving the smoke over their heads. His instincts told him they were no danger, so he ran in his silent way toward them. Gray Deer was the first to see this huge wolf-like dog running at them and panicked. Trying to pick up his bow he stumbled and fell. Little Bull quickly jumped to his feet and turned to see what Gray Deer was panicked about. The sight of Jimbo made him freeze. Neither of them had seen a wolf as big as Jimbo. While Gray Deer was scrambling back to his feet, Little Bull was walking toward this huge vicious looking wolf or dog, Gray Deer wasn't sure which. He yelled at Little Bull, "Stop he could kill you, Little Bull!"

"Yes, but he won't." Little Bull replied. At that Jimbo's tail started to wag, and a minute later Little Bull was patting him on the head.

Gray Deer stood there in awe, his younger friend petting this huge strange dog or wolf, he still wasn't sure which. Finally Gray Deer said, "Little Bull, that is the bravest thing I have ever seen."

Ely, still behind the hill, could not tell from so far away the strangers were just boys, but it was obvious that Jimbo was making friends. Ely mounted up and rode forward, staying in plain sight the whole way. The boys did not take their eyes off Jimbo and didn't see Ely coming until he was nearly to them.

Gray Deer was once again surprised and now holding his bow, drew his arrow to full draw. Ely dove off the side of his horse just as Gray Deer's arrow hit and stuck fast into the cantle of Ely's saddle. Ely hit the ground and rolled as Jimbo lunged forward. With a vicious growl and faster than either of the boys could believe Jimbo had his powerful jaws on the lower limb of the bow. Ripping it from Gray

Deer's grip. Gray Deer jumped back and fell once again. This time Jimbo was right over him with teeth bared. Ely walked up to the boys and realizing as soon as he was close to them they were two of the missing Bannock, and said, "You best know who you is a shooting at boy, next time it might not be somebody as good natured about it as me."

Gray Deer's eyes were the size of a full moon, and both boys just stared at Ely as he called Jimbo away from the very frightened young man. Little Bull was standing there silently, but unlike Gray Deer, Ely could see no fear in his eyes at all.

Ely reached down to help the boy up, but Gray Deer didn't take his hand. Finally Ely stood up straight and turned to Little Bull and said, "I figure you two is looking for White Crow and Coyote Talker, ain't ya?" He then realized they couldn't understand him and then repeated everything he had said in Shoshone.

Little Bull was the first to speak, asking, "You know my brother?"

"If your brother be Coyote Talker, I know them for sure. Him, White Crow and the rest of them oughta be coming along any time before dark."

The relief was so evident on the boys' faces, Ely kind of smiled. He reached down and offered his hand again to Gray Deer. This time the frightened young man reached up and took it. Once he was on his feet Ely said, "This here is the great medicine dog, Jimbo, and my name is Ely.

Little Bull asked, "You say my Brother and White Crow are coming here?"

"They is a coming alright, just not sure how far behind me they is. Could be a couple of hours and could be closer to a full day. Grizzly Killer, Running Wolf, Buffalo Heart, Yellow Horse, and my partner Benny is with 'em. We'll wait right here 'til they catch up." He turned to go back to his horse, then turned back to Gray Deer and said, "Son, you want to come and get your arrow out of my saddle?"

The fright had left Gray Deer, and now he felt embarrassed for having reacted the way he did. But Ely turned back to him and said, "You is right boy for not trusting somebody you don't know. I should have let you know I was a coming in. But you best not be shooting at somebody unless you know you're gonna get them, cause most people will shoot back, and they might not miss."

Gray Deer thought about what Ely had said while he was prying the arrow from the saddles rawhide covered hard wood cantle. He knew this hairy faced white man was right. If Ely had shot back, he would most likely be dead right now.

Ely turned to Jimbo and said, "Maybe you best go find Grizzly Killer and bring him here." Both boys watched with their mouths open as Jimbo spun around and bounded away. In only moments he was out of sight. Little Bull asked, "Does that wolf dog really understand you?" Ely smiled as he looked at the two boys and said, "Well now, I ain't saying he does or he don't, but that there is the smartest dog that was ever born, and whether he can understand the words or not, he knows just what you want him to do."

Ely got out an old beat up coffee pot and filled it with water and after setting it on the edge of the fire and adding a few more sticks to it he sat down and asked the boys, just what had happened.

Little Bull started out telling of the three of them deciding to go hunting after the men had all left camp. They went farther than they had realized and got lost. Both boys looked down at the ground after admitting they were lost and Ely could tell how embarrassed they were and he said, "Boys, if there is man that says he ain't never been lost in this here wilderness, well that man simply ain't telling the truth." He hoped hearing that might help them feel a little better.

They went on telling this hairy faced stranger what had happened and now was even more lost than they were before. They told him that the warriors that had taken Brave Fox were at least a day and a half away and they did not know where they were or which way they are going. Hearing they didn't know surprised Ely. He said, "Well boys, you is right on their trail." Hearing that, the boys looked at on another, and Ely could see the doubt in their minds.

As the boys told him what had happened, he had roasted a handful of coffee beans and now started to crush them. As he poured the crushed up, coffee beans into the nearly boiling water, he told the boys that he had followed these tracks from the place where Brave Fox was taken. Again the boys looked down, ashamed. They knew they should have known that, it was their fear that made them forget their early training.

When the coffee had boiled for several minutes Ely pulled it off the coals and Little Bull asked if he was a medicine man. They had only ever seen a medicine man brew things like Ely had just done.

They each tasted the bitter black coffee and Ely smiled as he watched them try not to make a face at the taste. He told them it was something they had to get used too. Ely relaxed as they waited for the others to catch up, he drank his coffee and asked questions about their people. He learned of a severe drought in the lands north of the great lake of salt. The drought had forced the hunters to these far mountains to find game where there was more water.

The afternoon passed quickly, Ely enjoyed learning about the Bannock. They were a people he had seen at Rendezvous but had never been into their lands. He liked these two young men and after spending just a couple of hours with them he believed they would both grow into good warriors and would make their village proud.

The sun had disappeared behind the western horizon when Jimbo came running back to Ely. The western half of the sky was ablaze with color. The long wisps of clouds glowed like the dancing flames of a fire. Both boys jumped back in fear as Jimbo, in his excitement, rushed to them. Even though they realized he was just as friendly as could be, his size and fierce look startled them.

Although Ely still could not see Grizzly Killer or the others, he knew they would not be far behind the great medicine dog.

Chapter 5

The First Storm of Winter

The light was fading fast and Zach was beginning to wonder if they would catch Ely before having to stop for the night. He knew their horses could all use the rest, and so could the men. It was evident Coyote Talker still wasn't sure about being with Zach and his partners. Coyote Talker felt a heavy responsibility for his younger brothers and just wasn't sure he could trust these men. The white trappers and especially this Ute whom he did not know. He could see they were on the trail and he knew his concern for his younger brothers was affecting his judgement and was very glad White Crow was with him.

Coyote Talker had taken on the role of teaching them to be Bannock warriors. Their father had been killed by the Black Feet while hunting along the river of many falls, four days north of their village. It was a role Coyote Talker had taken very seriously, it had been Coyote Talker that had convinced White Crow to let the boys come along. The older warrior had agreed it would be a good experience for the three of them. But now, Coyote Talker blamed himself that this had happened, and anger was the only way he could express himself. At first he had been angry at the boys, then himself for bringing them along, then at White Crow for agreeing. Now Coyote Talker was just angry. Angry at everyone and everything, even though he knew his anger was irrational, he could not help the way he felt.

They had stopped to rest the horses about two hours before sunset, but now, Zach started looking for a place to stop for the night, the horses needed to rest again. The red in the western sky was fading fast as Zach led them through a stand of cottonwoods, and then he saw the fire along the river only a half mile ahead.

Jimbo came running back to him and from his excitement Zach knew that it was Ely at the fire. As they got closer, he could plainly see there were others at the fire as well and he stopped making sure they weren't riding into trouble but as Zach stopped Ol' Red, Jimbo ran forward and then Ely stood and shouted, "Well, is ya coming in or ain't ya!" Zach urged Ol' Red forward and as they got closer Coyote Talker kicked his horse into a lope. Zach was still thirty yards from the fire when Coyote Talker jumped from his horse and rushed to the boys.

Neither Little Bull nor Gray Deer would look up at the older but still young warrior. Both ashamed they had gotten lost and Brave Fox had been taken. Both knew they were in serious trouble. When Coyote Talker saw Little Bull he knew immediately, it was Brave Fox that had been taken.

Finally, after a minute of awkward silence, Little Bull stood and faced his oldest brother. Knowing he would be punished and wondering what that punishment would be. He believed he deserved whatever punishment his brother or White Crow felt was just. Instead of anger, the volatile Coyote Talker pulled Little Bull to him and with a firm hug showed him how glad he was to see him.

Gray Deer was a year older than Little Bull, and he felt responsible for them getting lost. He had not said a word when White Crow approached and was surprised at their leader's tone and his words and he said, "Gray Deer, it is very good to see the two of you." Gray Deer looked up into the older warrior's eyes with a surprised look. Zach was watching the scene, as was Ely, Running Wolf, and the others. The love these warriors felt for the young men was very evident.

Yellow Horse, Buffalo Heart, and Benny took care of the horses. They cooled them down for twenty minutes and then let them drink their fill before hobbling them on tall dry grass just across the river.

Ely knew just how the boys were feeling, he had got to know them pretty well in the few hours they had been together. He looked at Zach but when he spoke it was for Coyote Talker and White Crow, "Grizzly Killer, I caught up with these two youngsters 'bout midday. They was hot on the trail of them slavers." It was Little Bull that spoke up them, "No we weren't, we were lost."

Ely smiled at the young man and asked, "Was you two not following this here trail or weren't you?"

"Yes, but we didn't know we were following those that took Brave Fox." Little Bull said.

"Well, you would have found out just as soon as you caught up to them now wouldn't ya."

Everyone there could tell what Ely was trying to do. Zach, Running Wolf, and White Crow were all smiling. Finally, White Crow walked over to the two boys and asked, "You know you did wrong by leaving camp don't you?" Both boys nodded while staring at the ground. "Then we don't need to talk about that anymore." White Crow said, he then turned to Little Bull and continued, "Little Bull, I am proud of you for standing up and telling the truth. But is it not as Ely has said?" Both boys looked up into White Crow's face and nodded again. After a long minute of silence White Crow said, "Let us sit and council around the fire. We will make a plan to get Brave Fox back." Coyote Talker added, "And make those that took him pay."

Running Wolf was the only Ute in the group and he knew exactly what Coyote Talker meant. He did not believe there was a way to keep blood from being shed.

Running Wolf did not know for sure, but he believed by the direction of travel, it was warriors from the Sahpeech band of Utes that had taken the boy. He knew they would not give up their captive without a fight. This was not the first time he and Grizzly Killer had trailed a Sahpeech Warrior.

Black Hand, the feared Sahpeech war chief, had taken Shining Star from their Ute village eight years before. He had been determined to make Running Wolf's beautiful sister his wife. Black Hand's reputation as a great warrior was known throughout the mountains, but he lost his life challenging Zach to a knife fight. Even though Running Wolf knew these warriors had nothing to do with his sister being taken, since that day he had felt no kinship with the Sahpeech Utes.

As the horses grazed on the dry fall grass the cold of the fall night settled upon the land. They all sat around a crackling fire as the boys told of what had happened. They had lost track of how far they had gone following a herd of elk further and further into the mountains. By the time they realized they were not going to catch up to the elk they had no idea where they were. They had split up to try and find the trail back to camp and had agreed to meet when the sun was in the center of the sky in the canyon where Brave Fox was taken. Gray Deer and Little Bull reached the rendezvous spot just in time to see Brave Fox taken by the twelve strange warriors.

Both boys were staring at the ground, ashamed once again they had not tried to help Brave Fox. Everyone around the fire could see the shame the boys felt. It was White Crow that first said, "It takes more than bravery to be a good warrior, it takes wisdom as well. Wisdom to know when to fight and when not to fight. Even Coyote Talker and myself or even the great white warrior Grizzly Killer that sits before you now could not have taken on that many enemy warriors. If you two would have been killed or taken, we would not know what had happened. Sometimes it takes more courage not to fight than it does to fight."

This time it was Gray Deer that said, "We were afraid, it was not courage that kept us from helping Brave Fox it was fear."

Ely now spoke again, "Sometimes courage and fear can be so close together they is the same thing." Both boys looked up at him and Little Bull asked, "How can they be the same thing?" Zach then looked at White Crow before speaking, he knew it was not his place to council the boys, but when White Crow gave a slight nod Zach continued, "Fear is not something to be ashamed of, it is something to be embraced. I have never met a warrior who is without fear. It is how we use the fear we feel that makes a great warrior. The fear you felt kept you from making a very bad decision. Do both of you not see how foolish it would have been for you to go against so many enemy warriors? So the fear you felt helped you make the right decision, so now we can all help Brave Fox."

White Crow had been watching Coyote Talker as well

as the boys as Ely and Grizzly Killer had spoken. He had hoped the volatile young warrior was picking up some of the wisdom of these two white men, whom he had grown to trust and respect in a very short time.

Speaking as much to Coyote Talker as he was to the boys, White Crow continued, "Take heed to the wise words of these men, for they speak the truth. It always takes more courage to do what is right than to do what we feel in our hearts."

White Crow had watched Coyote Talker grow into a warrior. He had watched him change after the death of his father. He was fearful that Coyote Talker's need for revenge on the men that had taken Brave Fox would affect his judgement, and even with the help of Grizzly Killer and his friends, they would still be outnumbered. He knew it would take much more than courage to get Brave Fox from his captors, it would take wisdom as well, and now more than ever he believed these men he had just happened upon had more than enough courage, wisdom, and integrity to get Brave Fox back.

A warm breeze was blowing from the south as they rolled out their robes around the fire for the night. By morning the wind had shifted direction, and they all knew, as daylight first broke, that a storm was blowing in.

Bright yellow leaves from the aspen and cottonwoods along the river were being whipped from the trees by a bitter cold north wind. They rode on, grateful they were heading south with the wind to their backs. By midday Ely found where the slavers had camped for the night and by studying the tracks, he figured these slavers had eight captives. Ely's ability to track and read sign had even impressed Coyote Talker by now. He had never seen anyone that could tell so much by looking at two or three-day-old tracks.

They continued now with their bed robes wrapped around their shoulders to fight off the bitter wind, and by midafternoon sleet had started to fall. They all knew with even Ely and Jimbo tracking, there would be no tracks to follow if they were covered by several inches of snow.

As the creek, like Weber's river before, turned east, coming from the mountains, the trail led them south. They reached another river and followed it to the southwest through hills covered with thick oak brush and maple. Choke cherry bushes and wild plums, service and buffalo berries grew in abundance along the river, but with each passing mile the trail became harder to follow.

The sleet turned to snow as the temperature dropped throughout the afternoon. The first major storm of the season was bearing down on them. As the sun dropped behind more towering mountains, they reached another large valley. Zach had never been here before, he had wanted to explore this country but had never taken the time to do so. It seemed the mountains went on forever. He knew of the Great Salt Lake and vast deserts to the west. He had been at Rendezvous when Jedediah Smith and two companions had made it back from the Spanish lands far to the west. But right now, with the first winter storm upon them and a Bannock boy to rescue, he couldn't think about the far distant lands he was yet to see.

The trail was gone when Ely stopped along the river and they prepared to spend a cold miserable night. Their only protection from the wind and snow being a stand of cottonwoods with a few leaves still clinging to their branches.

They soon had two fires burning, and as the yellow flames danced into the cold snow filled air, they all sat in silence. They hadn't taken time to hunt during the day so cold jerky and pemmican along with hot coffee was their supper.

Zach could see the frustration and worry on the face of White Crow. He knew this experienced Bannock warrior did not know what to do. He still had his village to provide meat for. After all, that was the whole purpose of this trip. But he knew it wasn't right to abandon the boy either. Was the life of the boy more important than the wellbeing and safety of the entire village?

Coyote Talker was beyond frustration, and anger was the only way he knew how to deal with it. They could all see he was having a hard time controlling the anger he felt. Little Bull had stayed close to him throughout the day, but now he and Gray Deer were keeping their distance, not knowing what the volatile young warrior would do.

Ely commented, "Them their slavers ain't moving fast but they is moving mighty steady following this here river. With their tracks now covered with snow and no sign of this here storm letting up I figure we just follow the river come morning." As heads slowly nodded their agreement Running Wolf spoke, "No Ely, they will move off the river and follow an old trail over the mountains to the south." Everyone was thinking about the words of Running Wolf when Coyote Talker's anger and frustration got the best of him. He screamed, "No! Ely is right, they will follow the river. This Ute only wants to lead us away from the trail." Running Wolf knew Coyote Talker was frustrated but he was tired of Coyote Talkers continual distrust and said, "I do not have to be here Coyote Talker, I could be back in my warm teepee in the arms of my wife. You go ahead and follow the river, it will lead you through a narrow and rocky canyon. It will be treacherous with snow on the ground. Then you will reach a valley many miles across. In the valley, the river runs into a very large lake. There will be a village maybe two or more of Timpanogos Utes. They will either be along the river or near the lake's shore, but you will not find your brother among them. The Sahpeech will follow a trail that leads through the mountains to their homes in the south. If I am wrong and it is the Pahvant Band, they will probably follow the same trail through the land of the Sahpeech on their way to the southwest."

Coyote Talker could see everyone around the fire were seriously listening to the words of this Ute and shouted out again, "We cannot trust him, he is a Ute! He will lead us away from my brother."

It was White Crow that spoke next, "Coyote Talker, I do not believe Running Wolf will lead us wrong. He knows this land and the Ute people. You have heard the stories, just as I have heard how Running Wolf and Grizzly Killer helped the Shoshone fight the Blackfeet on the shore of Sweet Lake several summers ago. I believe his heart is true and we should follow him." Coyote Talker stared at the older White Crow for a long minute, defiance written on his face. White Crow knew his defiant young friend and was silent, giving Coyote Talker time to process his words. Everyone was watching as Coyote Talker finally slumped his shoulders and he looked down into the flames of the fire. That is when White Crow continued, "It is already past the time to meet Painted Hand and the others. We must use our time wisely in getting Brave Fox back, but we must also think of the hunger in our village."

Zach could see the emotions of the young Bannock were more than he could control. He also believed he was torn between the responsibilities he felt. Coyote Talker finally looked up from the fire and said, "You are right, White Crow, but I cannot abandon my brother."

Zach gained more respect for him in that moment than he had in the days they had been together. To Zach, family was the most important thing in this world and he knew then that Coyote Talker, even with his temper, was a man of honor.

Running Wolf could see what Zach saw in Coyote Talker and said, "I give you my word Coyote Talker, I will lead you to your brother." Coyote Talker looked at him and asked, "But why? You are Ute."

Chapter 6

Leaving the Trail

The early winter storm blew across the Uintah mountains with a vengeance. Grub stared across the big meadow as he stood outside his teepee. It was still snowing and was hard to see the far side. The horses were all standing with their rumps to the wind, he was sure they were as cold as he was. A buffalo robe was wrapped around his shoulders as he stood and wondered about his partners and friends.

Yellow Bird was bent over the fire blowing life into the small glowing ember in the fist size ball of tinder she had struck the spark into. Two Flowers had just set an armful of twigs down as the tinder caught. The two women carefully added small twigs until they had the fire going.

Growling Bear was in a lean-to next to the fire. The injury to his head was worse than anything he had ever experienced. He still felt nauseous when he sat up, and the pain in his head did not seem to ever let up. He had grown very appreciative of Raven Wing and her bitter tea. Even though at times his stomach would reject it, when it stayed down his head felt a little better.

Growling Bear knew why Little Dove had hit him, it was his own actions that had caused it, but he still felt a resentment toward her. He was very grateful to everyone else in this tiny village of Grizzly Killer, they had treated him as one of their own. Even the white trapper was friendly and willing to help with anything he needed.

His vision was very blurry most of the time but would clear from time to time. Each day that passed saw his vision improving. The white wolf was always between him and the children, even this morning with the new fallen snow, the white wolf stood between him and each child as they hurried out of their teepee's to relieve themselves. The wolf would watch him, like she could sense the resentment he felt for Little Dove. Even though he believed he was hiding the resentment he felt, it was like the wolf could feel his own feelings. He knew he would never be able to hide his thoughts from the green-eyed wolf.

Coals were just starting to form in the fire and Raven Wing was there, setting a pan of water next to the larger coffee pot. This morning she added several other ground up plants to the tea and even a spoonful of their precious sugar. Once the tea had steeped for a few minutes, she poured it into one of their tin cups and helped Growling Bear sit up. He hesitated before sipping the hot liquid, remembering the bitter taste, then took a big gulp. A smile formed on his face as he tasted it, the bitterness had been replaced with a sweetness he had never tasted before. Raven Wing smiled at the look on his face.

Growling Bear could not believe a medicine woman could be as young and beautiful as Raven Wing was. In fact, he couldn't ever remember being around women of such beauty. He thought many times how lucky the men of Grizzly Killer's village were.

Little Dove stepped out of her and Benny's lodge just as a gust of the bitter cold air blew snow from a pine bow above her lodge. The snow hit her on the back of her head and went down her back. Growling Bear's vision was clear enough this morning he could see what happened, and a smile formed that he tried to hide from Raven Wing.

*****

Zach sat up, knocking the snow from his buffalo robe. Jimbo had not left this morning for his usual morning hunt. The big dog was still curled up at his feet. Jimbo shook the snow from his own coat, then stretched his cold stiff muscles. Although it wasn't yet light, Zach could tell the clouds were still dark and gray overhead.

Coyote Talker was the next to rise and started on the fire. The night had been long and cold and the dancing yellow flames of a warm fire was very welcome to them all. As the first light filtered through the clouds, the world around them had been transformed with a blanket of white. The heavy cloud cover was hiding the mountain peaks, but the snow had nearly stopped.

They were camped along a river that Running Wolf said ran into a very large lake on the far side of the mountain. Zach believe this was the same river he had heard Etienne Provost describing at Rendezvous, as he and his brigade of trappers from Santa Fe was the only white men to have explored this part of the country at that time.

The smell of the boiling coffee, along with the smoke from the fire was filling the air around them as Coyote Talker went to White Crow and said, "I have not slept thinking about what you said last night White Crow. With this storm our village will need meat now even more than before, and we are still many days from getting back there. I cannot abandon my brother, but you and Yellow Horse must take Little Bull and Gray Deer and go back. After I find Brave Fox, I will go with Grizzly Killer and the others back to their village and get Growling Bear before we return."

White Crow looked the young warrior in the eyes, he had never been as proud of him as he was right then. He wondered what had changed, the anger seemed to be gone, replaced by the wisdom of a much older man.

As White Crow and Yellow Horse with the protesting boys rode north back toward Weber River, they had no idea when they would see their volatile young friend again. Both Gray Deer and Little Bull still felt guilt over Brave Fox being taken and both wanted to stay with Coyote Talker. It was White Crow that looked at both boys and said, "I too do not wish to leave the trail, but we have other responsibilities. Do not the two of you think that not obeying has caused enough trouble?" Both boys stared at the ground, ashamed once again. Neither liked it, but they would not disobey again.

White Crow wasn't sure why, but he had grown to respect and trust Grizzly Killer and the men with him as much as he had ever trusted anyone. He felt sure if Brave Fox could be saved, these men would do it.

With eight inches of new snow there was no trail to follow. Running Wolf pointed to a canyon many miles to the southeast and said, "The ancient trail leads through that canyon, then across the mountains and into the land of the Sahpeech. It may take several days to reach there. We must try to catch them before they reach their village, or there will be too many of them and we will have little chance of getting any of the slaves back."

Zach pointed toward the canyon and Jimbo led the way

bounding through the new fallen snow. Unlike Zach and the others, Jimbo loved the snow. The cold didn't seem to bother him at all. Although their progress slowed with the snow, they still made good time until they reached the mouth of the canyon. Here the seldom used trail was clogged with oak brush and maple. The sides of the canyon were too steep to go up and around the brush in the bottom.

They were only two or three miles into canyon still fighting their way through the brush when Ely's sharp eye spotted a freshly broken branch. Coyote Talker asked, "How do you know an elk or deer to not break the limb?" Like a patient father, Ely took a moment to explain that any wild animal would not be so far to the side of the trail, that only a man on a horse trying to ride around or fighting with someone could have broken that branch. He showed him the way the broken end was turned, showing the direction of travel of the horse that had broken it. He explained to Coyote Talker that in the spring of the year it is possible to tell about how long ago the twig was broken by the drop of sap on the end, but there was little sap to form a drop this late in the year.

They pushed on fighting for every mile. Benny and Buffalo Heart, knowing this search may take many days or even longer, knew they would need meat and dropped behind saying that would meet them at dark.

By late afternoon their horses were exhausted, fighting their way through brush and snow, which had become deeper the higher they went. Even Ol' Red, being bigger and stronger than any of the horses, was tired. Zach stopped in a grove of pines on one of the few semi-level places he had seen since entering this canyon and didn't figure they had made more than ten or twelve miles during the long hard day.

They were sitting around the fire all silent in their own

thoughts when they heard the hoof beats of Benny and Buffalo Heart's horses fighting their way up the nearly nonexistent trail. A wolf howled on the ridge high above as Buffalo Heart came into sight, he had a yearling buck deer tied over his saddle and was leading the tired animal.

During the day, Ely had found several other broken twigs, which made them all confident Running Wolf had led them on the right trail.

By now, Coyote Talker truly believed Running Wolf and the others were helping him. He had given up trying to understand why, but he could feel their friendship. His anger was still there, but now it was aimed toward those warriors that had taken his brother, not at these strangers that were trying to help. He was glad Little Bull was out of harm's way. He didn't believe he could ever go back if both his brothers would have been lost.

They sliced up the liver and heart of the young buck and put the slices on willow branches over the fire. They were all so hungry, cold, and tired, the meat had barely got warm when they pulled it from the flames and ate. Then, after making sure the horses had plenty of willow leaves and grass, they could scrape down to, they each curled up under their buffalo robes, as close to the fire as they could get.

They had taken turns adding wood to the fire through the night, and as the early dawn started to turn the eastern horizon gray Zach could see the sky was clear, a bitter cold gripped the bottom of the canyon, but the fire was still burning, with a very welcome warmth.

While venison cooked over the fire the horses were all saddled. Zach slipped several times as he climbed up the side of the canyon to get a better view of what lay ahead. He could see less than a mile as the steep canyon walls twisted their way to the south, steadily climbing higher.

Running Wolf had just been a young teenager, like the boy they were trying to rescue, the last time in had been through this canyon. Many Ute Bands had gathered for a bear dance in the huge, broad, and open valley to the east of this canyon they were fighting to get up now. He remembered it was at that bear dance, in the spring that Black Hand first wanted to take Shining Star. But Running Wolf's beautiful sister had her heart set on another. Now Running Wolf remembered with bitterness the chase that he and Grizzly Killer made several years after that bear dance and pow-wow.

After Shining Star's first husband had been killed, Black Hand had come to their Uintah Ute village to ask for her hand. With most of the men out hunting it had been easy, after Shining Star had rejected his offer for him to simply take her. Just as these warriors had taken the Bannock boy. A couple of days later when Running Wolf, Zach, Sun Flower and Raven Wing arrived at the village on Rock Creek. The two of them headed out to rescue Shining Star.

Black Hand would not give the beautiful woman up. He was the war chief of the Sahpeech, and he did not believe he could be beaten. That belief had cost him his life, for he challenged Zach to a knife fight.

That chase and fight had taken place a big day's ride to the southeast of this canyon they were struggling to get up now. This time, Running Wolf knew there was not going to be just one warrior to fight but a dozen of them, maybe more.

Jimbo led the way with Ely, the tracker, next. With only one way to go in this narrow canyon, no one needed Running Wolf as a guide until they reached the top.

The clear skies and cold air made fighting through the snow, now two feet deep, a bit easier than it had been the day before, but the slow progress they were making was frustrating them all.

By midmorning the bitter wind had stopped in the canyon and the warmth from the sun could finally be felt, but their climb through this long and winding canyon was far from over.

Ely spotted a few more broken twigs, one he stopped and studied for a couple of minutes. A smile formed on his face as he turned and announced, "One of them there captives is a real thinker. This here branch was busted and left for us to find. There just ain't no way brushing by it could have busted it like that, no siree, somebody is leaving us a sign."

Coyote Talker rushed forward, he looked at the branch and smiled, Ely could see the recognition on the sign. Coyote Talker said, "It is a game we play as youngsters in our village. It has always been the way we learn to track. I am sure that Brave Fox is alive, and it is he leaving us the sign."

That news lifted everyone's spirits but did nothing for the exhausted horses fighting through the two feet of snow and steep canyon. Ely's horse had been breaking trail all day and Zach moved forward now, believing the strength of Ol' Red breaking trail might mean a couple of more miles before the horses were too exhausted to continue.

When they reached the pass at the top of this canyon, Zach guessed they had come fifteen maybe twenty miles from the valley below and it had taken them two full days and the horses were exhausted. They were now looking out over a huge shallow valley that ran for miles and miles to the south and east. The valley, like the canyon they had just come through, was covered with a blanket of snow.

The sun shining through the now clear October sky had warmed the air throughout the afternoon. They made camp on the edge of a stand of aspen along a creek, about a mile past the summit.

The wind had nearly stopped now, and the bitter cold they had been fighting was gone. Zach had seen these early storms come through the mountains many times in the years he had made them his home. He hoped this would be like most of them, and a week or two of warm dry weather would follow.

This rescue of Brave Fox and the other captives was taking longer and leading them much farther from home than any of them had thought it would. But they were committed and each one of them knew they must see it through, although nothing was ever said about it.

As the sun set on the exhausted men and horses, an elk bugled, answered only a moment later by another across the way. It reminded Zach of the magnificent bulls he had watched fight just a few days before. Now that few days seemed long ago.

Morning once again brought warmer temperatures, and the snow was settling and even starting to disappear on the south-facing slopes. The broad valley before them was surrounded by high rolling hills covered with aspen and pine. They weren't the high towering peaks, with the unpassable shear rock faces like high above Blacks Fork, but they were still formidable obstacles. They followed a creek leading to the southeast and just before midday that creek flowed into a small river.

Running Wolf told Zach, "This is the same River that runs into the Duchesne. We crossed it rescuing Shining Star, many miles to the east." Zach remembered crossing the river and the trail over the mountains. He remembered taking extra mounts and changing often so Ol' Red and the exhausted horses could keep going. He remembered what happened when they finally caught up to Black Hand and feared this time, it would be a much bigger battle.

Chapter 7

Making Meat

They camped that night on the edge of a large stand of aspens, there were a few pines mixed in among them. Zach could see that not far above them the pines overtook the aspen and became a dark timbered forest. Just before dark a bull elk bugled several times, he listened but did not hear an answer to the bull's challenge.

As he turned to walk back toward the fire, a lone wolf howled way off in the distance and Jimbo suddenly appeared next to him. Even after all these years he marveled how a dog that big could move so silently through the forest.

The next morning when Zach opened his eyes and watched Jimbo run out into the aspen and pine forest looking for a cottontail or grouse to satisfy his hunger, the bright stars looked close enough to touch.

There was mud around their fire pit where the fire from the night had completely melted the snow. He stirred the coals and found a still glowing ember. He added small dry twigs to it and with a gentle breath, he blew life back into the fire. Once the twigs were burning, he added larger sticks and soon small logs.

The others were all stirring by now. Benny and Buffalo Heart cut thin strips of venison from the deer and set them to cooking over the fire. Zach walked to the edge of the aspen and looked out over the open expanse of the valley before him. Running Wolf walked up to the side of his partner and Zach asked, "Will we follow the same trail now?"

"No my brother, from here we must turn to the southwest, climb out of this valley and follow another creek until we reach the old Spanish Trail."

As hard as it had been for Coyote Talker to believe these men were helping him, he did believe them now. He still had no understanding why, but they were. Now he looked at each of them with a respect like he felt for White Crow. He had watched Ely closely and believed he was a better tracker than anyone he had ever seen. He wondered if even old Crooked Foot, the best tracker in their Bannock village, could have picked up this trail and followed it through the snow like Ely had.

He stayed close to Ely, hoping he could learn to see the trail as well as this old trapper could see it. He watched Jimbo's interaction with Grizzly Killer and could easily see why he was called the great medicine dog. For the big dog truly seemed to know just what Grizzly Killer wanted him to do without being told.

Coyote Talker had been around dogs all of his life, but in his village if they weren't used as pack animals they were eaten for food. This was the first time he had ever seen a dog that was treated as part of a family and in the few days they had been together, there was no doubt in his mind that Grizzly Killer and the great medicine dog had very powerful medicine.

The sky was clear and with the rising sun it promised to be another beautiful fall day. Zach hoped they had gained enough on the warriors they were following that the trail would be easy to follow in the wet ground. When he mentioned that to the others Ely said, "I don't figure you best get your hopes up Grizzly Killer, I suspect them there pole cats we are a following knows they is being followed. Don't know for sure, but I figure they have picked up their pace and I figure they is gonna make the trail even harder to follow." He then looked over at Running Wolf and asked, "If I am right Running Wolf, you know of any other trails they may take to throw us off?"

As Running Wolf thought, Zach could see the worry was very evident on Coyote Talker's face. After a few minutes of silence Running Wolf shook his head and said, "Only other trail I have been on is the one Grizzly Killer and I followed after Black Hand took Shining Star and that trail is a hard day's ride to the east. I believe if they do think they are being followed, they would head straight to their village for more help." Ely thought on that for a moment and nodded his head saying, "That does make sense, yes it does." It was Buffalo Heart that added, "What if they want to keep a fight away from the women and children of their village? I would not lead an enemy right to my village."

Zach had listened to everything that had been said. After a few minutes of silence he said, "Right now we are all just a guessing what they know and where they are going. I figure we best just let Ely follow and let their trail tell us where they are going." Benny then said, "Even if they do figure they are being followed, I never saw anybody be able to throw Ely off their trail."

Coyote Talker remained silent but Zach could see deep concern on his face and said, "Coyote Talker we will find your brother, you have my word we will not give up this chase until we have found him." Coyote Talker nodded, but everyone around the fire could see the worry and that he had not taken a single bite of the strip of deer meat he held in his hand.

Ely added, "You best eat that there meat, I suspect you is gonna need all your strength when we do catch em'. We best quit jawin' about it and get saddled up. It's gonna be light mighty quick."

As they were mounting up, Jimbo came back from his morning hunt with feathers stuck to his nose and lips. He didn't wait for Zach's hand signal, he just ran out in front of Ely and they headed south, turning away from the creek toward a canyon that led down from this large open valley to what Running Wolf had said led to the trail the Spanish used in their search for gold.

*****

Shining Star stood by the riverbank looking across the big meadow. Their horse herd grazed lazily on the dry fall grass. She wondered where Grizzly Killer was, and what he was doing. Sun Flower walked up alongside of her and reached for her hand. No words were spoken by Zach's wives, none were needed. Just knowing they both had the same concerns for their husband was enough.

Sun Flower and Shining Star loved each other as sisters, they had grown as close as Sun Flower and Raven Wing. Star, Jack, and Little Moon believed each of them was their own mother.

Grub watched the two of them and could see the concern they had. He too was concerned. It had been many days now, and he wondered what could be taking them so long. He knew how good of a tracker Ely was. He didn't believe three boys good elude his partner even if they were trying and he didn't believe three lost boys would be trying. No, Grub was convinced they had found some other trouble, but he kept his concerns to himself.

He poured himself a cup of coffee and put on his usual jovial smile and said, "Sure is a purty morning, ain't it girls? All six women turned and smiled at him, his happy-go-lucky attitude always brightened their spirits. Two Flowers came to him, reached up and moved his unruly mustache and beard aside and kissed him. That simple show of affection made the other women miss their husbands even more.

It was Little Dove that finally asked, "What could be taking them so long?" She wasn't asking anyone in particular but it was Grub that answered, "You know boys, they must a got themselves mighty lost, but don't you fret none Little Dove, you know Ely can track a squirrel through a downpour and with Jimbo with 'em, they is gonna find them boys and be back."

Growling Bear's head still hurt where Little Dove had hit him. His vision blurred on occasion, but the blurriness and the terrible aching was getting less each day. He had grown to appreciate the bitter tea that Raven Wing mixed for him several times a day. It relieved the worst of the pain. He had even started to feel less hatred for Little Dove as she was going out of her way to make him comfortable each day.

Growling Bear longed to be with the others, even feeling the effects of his head injury he was tired of being laid up and not with White Crow, Coyote Talker, and Yellow Horse looking for the boys. It had been several days and had stormed since the others had left. He knew there was no way he could find them, but even at that he had thought about trying.

He had watched these women, he had never seen a group of women as beautiful and wondered what they saw in these hairy faced white men they were with. Growling Bear had seen a few other white trappers but had never known any of them before. He had watched this old trapper the others left with the women, the one they called Grub, and even he had grown to like him. He always seemed to have a smile on his face and seemed to make the women smile whenever he spoke to them. The children treated him as their grandfather like the children of his own village would a village elder. As bad as Growling Bear longed to be with White Crow and the others, he really didn't mind being among these beautiful women and this likable old white man.

Grub could see the longing in Growling Bear to be out with the others and since they needed meat asked the recovering warrior if he felt good enough to go on a hunt. Growling Bear smiled and nodded. Even though another wave of dizziness hit him as he stood, he recovered quickly and was surprised as Little Dove brought him his bow and quiver of arrows.

Yellow Bird and Two Flowers brought the two men their horses and within a few minutes the two of them were out of sight heading up the Blacks Fork trail.

Only a couple of miles above the top end of the big meadow, was an area of small openings on the ridge separating Blacks Fork from Smiths Fork and each time Grub had been through that area he had seen sheep. He hoped today would be the same. He stopped and explained to Growling Bear what he was planning. The two of them would separate and meet once again in a clearing at the top of the ridge. Growling Bear nodded, and the two men split up.

It felt good to Growling Bear to be hunting once again. Although his vision was not yet back to normal and the dizziness would come and go. He believed he could take a sheep, deer, or elk. Whatever presented itself to him, he would be ready.

He reached the edge of the first clearing and slid off his horse, tying him to an aspen. The trail he was following was covered with sheep tracks, and he believed he would be better able to get in arrow range on foot.

He was moving very slowly, watching each step when another wave of dizziness came over him. He leaned against an aspen until the dizziness passed, and as his vision cleared the pain he had been fighting once again shot through the back of his head. Even though he had stopped blaming Little Dove, he knew it was his own action that had caused her to hit him. He still resented being hurt by a woman. It would have been bad enough to be hurt by another warrior, but for a woman to do that was humiliating to him.

He ignored the pain in his head as he started forward once again. He could smell sheep and knew they were very near. A sudden gust of wind blew more of the few remaining leaves from the aspen, and he knew the breeze was in his favor. He waited there motionless for several minutes before taking another carefully placed step. Suddenly the loud report of Grub's rifle shattered the stillness of the forest. As the sound echoed through the canyon, it seemed to magnify the pain in his head. He closed his eyes against the pain for but a brief moment and when he opened them a dozen sheep were running straight toward him. He didn't have time to think, for Growling Bear it was just a reflex. He wasn't even fully aware of what he was doing when suddenly an arrow was in flight. It found its mark and its fine stone point buried into the chest of the first sheep running at him.

Another wave of dizziness hit him and he reached out for a tree. The forest started to spin around him. He wasn't aware of the sheep or that he had hit one of them. He was holding on to a tree, trying to make the world around him stop spinning. He wasn't aware he had dropped his bow. He had no idea how long he been holding on to the aspen, but suddenly the forest stopped spinning and as if appearing from thin air Grub was right there beside him. The pain in his head was severe, and he wished for a cup of Raven Wing's bitter tea. He looked at Grub and said, "Guess I wasn't as ready as I thought I was." Grub smiled and replied, "Maybe not, but you sure got that there ram dead center."

Growling Bear couldn't even remember shooting his arrow, as he looked past Grub at the young ram with half curled horns lying in the trail. His arrow buried half-way to the feathers in the center of the ram's chest. Grub could see the surprise of his face and said, "Growling Bear, if you can shoot like that in your condition, I am mighty glad we is friends."

Grub could see the pain in this young warrior's eyes and said, "We best get you back to Raven Wing, I will come back later and get that there ram of yours." But Growling Bear slowly shook his head and said, "No Grub, I have a sheep to gut."

"Growling Bear, you don't have to prove how tough you is, I already know 'cause you is still breathin'. I don't figure many men would have lived after taking a blow like you took." Grub replied. But Growling Bear, determined to care for the sheep he had taken, stepped forward and fell into Grub's arms.

The dim flickering glow of a small fire in the center of the teepee was the next thing Growling Bear saw. He was groggy and weak and he could hear voices outside but couldn't make out what was being said. The voices were speaking in the tongue of the white men.

The teepee entrance flap moved, and he could see the familiar faces of Little Dove and Raven Wing as they stepped inside. Raven Wing was holding a tin cup that he knew was her bitter brown tea. Both women knelt beside him and Little Dove said, with a smile and relief in her voice, "It is good to see you awake Growling Bear, we were worried."

Growling Bear, still confused about what had happened, wasn't sure whether he had been dreaming he and Grub had gone hunting, or whether they actually had. It was Little Dove that asked, "Are you ready for some broth from the sheep you shot." He looked surprised and looked at Raven Wing for answers. She smiled and said, "Yes, Growling Bear, you and Grub both shot sheep today. You however were not ready. Your head needs more time to heal." Little Dove then helped him sit up as Raven Wing held the warm cup to his lips. He had become used to the bitterness and taste of the tea, and it provided a soothing warmth as he waited for the effects of the willow and aspen bark along with several other of her healing plants took effect.

Sun Flower then entered carrying a wooden bowl of fatty broth. Her beautiful face was highlighted by the flickering flames as she handed the bowl to Little Dove. Growling Bear knew he could not get better care in his own village, and although he still felt some resentment for his injury, he felt very fortunate to be here, receiving this kind of care.

Chapter 8

Watchers

It was miles of open sage as they crossed the large valley heading for the canyon rim Running Wolf had pointed out. Jimbo was over a quarter mile in front of Ely when he suddenly stopped sniffing the ground. He was still there as Ely and the others reached him, Zach knew his dog had found the scent of something although he wasn't sure what that something was.

Ely held up his hand to keep the others back as he walked circles around the big dog. Coyote Talker sat on his horse, watching and wondering what the old white man's eyes were seeing. Finally, Ely stopped and knelt down, then burst out laughing. Still chuckling, he turned to Coyote Talker and said, "Come here son and see what that brother of yours left us." Coyote Talker jumped down and rushed to Ely as everyone else was dismounting. As Coyote Talker reached Ely, he was pointing at the ground. Three small pebbles were lined up in a row running parallel with the canyon, then one more pebble was set off to the west side.

Coyote Talker smiled, and everyone could see the relief on his face as he said, "Brave Fox is alive. This is a sign we were all taught as children. It means one or more of them have turned off to the west. If Ely is right and they suspect they are being followed, those that turned off may be watching us now."

Benny then spoke, "Buffalo Heart and I will go find out, if we do not catch up by tonight we will tomorrow. Zach nodded and said, "Wait, Ely and Jimbo can follow this trail, I will come with you. We don't know how many of them might be up there waiting." Ely nodded, then turned back to Coyote Talker and said, "If they catch your brother leaving sign, they may go mighty hard on him." Coyote Talker nodded, then said, "Brave Fox is young, but he is a Bannock warrior, he will show no fear."

Zach, Buffalo Heart, and Benny left the others riding to the rear. If anyone was watching them, they would think the three of them were quitting the chase and going back. Ely, Coyote Talker, Running Wolf and Jimbo were the only ones left to follow the trail.

Ely said, "If we is being watched we best not let 'em think we is catching up too fast. Let's give Grizzly Killer, and them a little time to scare out any watchers theys got a waiting for us. Let's start us a fire and cook up some a that there deer and have a cup a coffee giving 'em time to make sure our trail is clear."

Coyote Talker had never been a patient man. He was quick to anger and often acted before he thought. His first reaction was he would not wait, he would go on by himself if necessary. Ely could see the frustration on the young warrior's face and said, "Brave Fox has proved he is a man that can take care of his self. If we go rushing into a dozen or so enemies and they is expecting us, it ain't gonna be good, no sir that be a right quick way to get yourself dead. Now I don't know about you, Coyote Talker but I ain't ready to go under just yet and I don't figure that brother of yours is either." Coyote Talker stopped, he knew Ely was right, but that didn't make waiting any easier.

*****

Zach led Benny and Buffalo Heart back for nearly three miles before turning off their back trail and heading west. It was another couple of miles before they reached the tree line and once in the trees and out of sight they turned back to the south.

They spread out as they worked their way south, Zach believed they would find warriors watching their own back trail. What he didn't know is how many or how far behind the others they would be?

They rode with great caution, watching ahead as far as they possibly could. Zach was closest to the tree line and at the point of each small ridge would step off of Ol' Red and carefully study the land ahead before moving on.

He smiled when he was even with Ely, Running Wolf, and Coyote Talker seeing they had built a fire. He knew Ely was giving them time to find the warriors watching their back trail and stop them from riding ahead, warning the others.

Zach cupped his hands around his mouth and with the screech of an owl told the other two it was time to be mighty careful.

They moved another mile when Zach heard a squirrel chattering just above him. He stopped and watched, and only moments later he saw Buffalo Heart and Benny silently moving through the trees toward him.

Benny was the highest on the hill, and from a small clearing he saw what he believed were two warriors watching the canyon. They were obviously looking for anyone that might be following. They left their horses and Ol' Red there in the trees and headed toward the enemy warriors on foot. Only a quarter mile away Buffalo Heart broke off and whispered he would get to their horses so they couldn't ride ahead if any escaped. With a slight nod from Zach, Buffalo Heart left him and Benny. They give him a few minutes head start, then headed toward the two enemy warriors.

They were only a hundred yards above and behind them before they saw Benny had been wrong. There were four of them, not two. They had not all been together when Benny first saw them. Zach hoped their horses were all together. It would be hard to keep all four of them occupied to the point of not even one escaping to warn the others.

Zach wondered how close the others actually were. Would a gunshot be heard? At this point, he did not want to take that risk. He figured a lone white man walking up on four Ute warriors would not be something anyone of them would run from. So with Benny with his bow and Buffalo Heart hopefully holding their horses. Zach stood, and with a stumbling walk, looking like that of a totally exhausted man. Zach stumbled forward, make as much noise as he possibly could. Still, he got within seventy-five yards of them before he was seen.

He acted as surprised and scared to see them as they were to see him. At first they motioned for him to leave, but he stumbled closer, pointing to his mouth indicating he needed water. Finally, one of the four decided to force him to leave. He stepped forward and started to draw his bow when Zach's knife left his hand so quickly none of the four warrior even knew he had thrown it until it buried to hits hilt in the surprised warriors belly.

There was only a moment's hesitation before all three of the others were running toward Zach. He waited until they were nearly to him, then went to the ground and kicked the legs out from under all three of them. Two of them were surprised at how fast Zach had moved, but the third had seen Zach throw his knife and although he had hit the ground, he was back on his feet only a split second later.

Zach got to his feet with the swiftness of a cat ready to face what he knew was going to be a formidable foe. As he did, he kicked the closest of them who was still on the ground a crushing blow to the ribs, breaking several of them. He hoped that had taken another out of the fight.

In that amount of time the other had gotten to his feet, and now Zach faced two warriors with knives drawn and his own knife still stuck in the belly of the first unlucky Ute warrior.

Zach knew these warriors were Ute but did not know which band of Utes they were from. But from the direction they were heading he believed Running Wolf was right, they were from the Sahpeech band.

These two warriors knew they were facing a very dangerous man. They had no idea they were facing the greatest white warrior in the mountains, Grizzly Killer himself. What they did know is they were now facing an unarmed man that had just taken out two of their companions, and this man in front of them was about to die.

Zach was standing in the way of Benny getting a shot off with his bow. So finally Benny charged forward, screaming a war cry and startling one of the two warriors, who turned and ran. The other was focused of Zach, knowing he was unarmed this enemy advanced forward. Zach pointed Benny toward the fleeing warrior as the other charged Zach.

Zach's speed surprised the warrior once again. He had never seen a man as big as this white man move so fast. His blade missed by more than a foot, yet he felt a stinging blow on his right ear as he spun to face this white man again.

This time Zach could see some confidence was gone from his expression. He was hesitant to make another wild swing. While they were walking in a circle around one another, each waiting for the other to make a move, Zach removed his possibles bag and holding it by the should strap swung it at the unsuspecting warrior. As the warrior jumped back Zach felt a sudden sharp pain in his left leg as the warrior that was still on the ground with broken ribs threw his own knife at Zach hitting him in the leg. The throw was weak, although the knife penetrated it went in less than an inch. But with that distraction, the standing warrior charged again, this time cutting Zach on his right forearm. Again it wasn't a serious cut, but Zach was tired of this fight and knew he must end it now.

Feeling much more confident once again, the warrior charged only to find the white man wasn't there, he had moved again with unbelievable speed. But now, he felt a terrible pain in his left knee as Zach kicked him as he went past. He tried to stay on his feet, but his left knee would not hold him. As he fell to the ground, he felt another stunning blow. This time, to his left cheek, he hit the ground and didn't move. Zach's knuckles had broken his jaw and cheek bone, and although he was still breathing, he was completely unconscious.

Zach pulled the knife from his leg and walked over to the warrior that had thrown it. The look on his face told Zach he believed he was about to die. He looked even more surprised when Zach asked, speaking perfect Ute, if he was Sahpeech. The stunned warrior nodded and

Zach asked, "Where are you to meet the others, and how many slaves do they have?" The warrior's look turned to one of defiance, and Zach knew he would not get the answers he wanted.

Zach looked him in the eye and asked, "Do you know who I am?" As the warrior shook his head Zach continued, "I am called Grizzly Killer," at hearing that the warrior's eyes went to the grizzly claw necklace around Zach's neck. Zach continued, "I am here to return the slaves you stole to their homes. You can help me and live or you can fight me and die." The warrior looked into Zach's blue eyes and said, "I am not afraid to die." Zach nodded as he said, "No good warrior is, but do you want to die?" Zach could see the answer in his eyes, no living being, whether man or animal wants to die. Sounding more defiant now, he said, "I will not help you kill my friends."

Zach said, "I do not want to kill anyone, I just want the people you stole to go back to their own villages."

The warrior looked at him and said, "But they are nothing but slaves."

Zach looked the warrior in the eyes and said "They are people just like you and me. They are only slaves because you force them to be."

Zach could see his logic was lost on this warrior lying there helpless before him. He also believed what the warrior had said was true. He would die before helping Zach hurt his friends, and for that Zach respected him.

The warrior Benny chased ran to their horses, only to find Buffalo Heart waiting there. He shot one arrow at Buffalo Heart, just clipping his shoulder as an arrow from both Benny and Buffalo Heart's bows entered his chest. One from the front, the other from the back. He was dead before he hit the ground.

While Buffalo Heart led the four Sahpeech warrior's

horses toward Zach, Benny went to retrieve Ol' Red along with his and Buffalo Heart's own horses. Zach looked up as Buffalo Heart approached. A slight shake of his partner's head told Zach the fourth warrior was dead.

Zach knew these Sahpeech warriors would never catch up with the others. One was already dead, the one with the belly wound he didn't believe would live long. This warrior he was speaking with had several broken ribs, although painful, Zach believed he could make it back to his village. The other unconscious one Zach didn't know about. He had felt the bones break in his face under the force of his rock-hard knuckles, but he had no idea how bad he was really hurt.

Speaking the Ute language, so this wounded warrior would understand him, Buffalo Heart asked, "Do we let them live Grizzly Killer, or should I kill them now." Zach turned and looked into the eyes of the only conscious warrior. He could see the worried but defiant look in his eyes. Zach knew he was not afraid of death, but he could also see he did not welcome it either.

Finally, Zach turned back to Buffalo Heart and shook his head, saying, "Let them live for now Buffalo Heart. I do not believe they can do us any harm." As he looked back at the wounded warrior, he could see relief on his face and he said, "You will live this day, you have companions to care for. But know this, if we ever see you again, we will have no mercy."

The defiant young warrior answered, "Neither will Red Eagle. If you catch him, you will all die. But I do not think you will ever catch him and his warriors." Zach just smiled at the young warrior, and as he did his sky-blue eyes turned cold, like a terrible storm blowing in a blizzard in the heart of winter. It sent a chill through the wounded warrior, and he never said another word.

As Benny rode up leading Ol' Red and Buffalo Heart's dark bay gelding, the warrior Zach had hit started to come to. He moaned as he tried to open his eyes, but his right one was already too swollen. His hands instinctively went to his face and Zach turned back to the defiant one and said, "Your friends need help and you best remember what I said."

Without another word he jumped up on Ol' Red and the three of them headed back toward Ely, Running Wolf, Coyote Talker, and Jimbo, leading the four horses with them.

Chapter 9

Answer to a Prayer

Zach had not found out how far ahead of them Red Eagle and his band of Sahpeech Ute warriors were. But he had stopped the lookouts from getting words back to him about how many of them were following him. Upon their return, they told the others of finding the four Sahpeech warriors. After listening to their story Ely said, "You may have stopped them Grizzly Killer, but them not reporting back will tell this Red Eagle that he is indeed being followed." Zach nodded his agreement, as Running Wolf added, "But they will not know how many of us there are Ely. He may believe there are many more of us because none of his watchers make it back"

Coyote Talker put his hand on Benny's shoulder and thanked the three of them, but asked, "Why did you let them live?" It was Buffalo Heart that answered, "It is not our way to kill a helpless man, even if he is an enemy." Grizzly Killer added, "We kill only when necessary, not because we can."

"But they stole Brave Fox and others, they are enemies, they deserve to die." Zach turned to him and nodded, "What you say is true Coyote Talker, but it is up to the Great Spirit, the creator of all thing to punish them, not us." Coyote Talker looked into Zach's blue eyes, he did not understand this white man or his friends. But he could see an honest determination in those eyes and he believed Grizzly Killer would do whatever is necessary to free not only Brave Fox but every one of the slaves these warriors had taken.

He looked at Running Wolf, still wondering why this Ute was helping against his own people. Hard as he had tried, Coyote Talker did not understand why any of these men were helping him, but he was very glad they were. In a very short time, he had grown to respect and trust each of them, even Running Wolf the Ute. Although by now he had given up ever understanding their reasons.

By the time the sun was touching the western horizon, they had traveled several more miles. They were now climbing up out of this huge valley they had been in and although there were still no tracks or sign of man, Ely was sure he was on their trail. He said it was more of a feeling than anything he had seen, and as Zach looked ahead at the top of the ridge marking the southern edge of the valley like Ely, he could see the path ahead and he was sure it was the route Red Eagle was taking.

They camped just below the summit of the ridge. Zach was quiet as he always was after a fight. He had never liked killing, although he accepted it living in this wilderness. He watched the flames flickering from their small fire and the fat from the venison dripped into the hot coals. The flames took him back to the fight earlier that day and too many other men he'd had to fight over the years. Running Wolf, Buffalo Heart, and Benny had all been with Zach after many fights. They knew his quiet demeanor was the result of the fight. Coyote Talker had no idea why Grizzly Killer was quiet and acting sad, after all he'd had a great victory today.

Zach was sad because of the victory, he hated to see anyone die, to throw their life away because of foolish pride. He would never understand why most Indians tribes were warrior societies. They seemed to always be looking for a fight to prove their medicine was strong. He knew they did not understand his beliefs any more than he understood theirs. He had chosen to live among them, to fight alongside of them. It was a conflict he often felt within himself. He loved this life as a free trapper. He loved the wild mountains, his wives, and children. He did not want to change anything, except the death and killing that most of the tribes seemed to think brought them honor and power. Even though he wished it wasn't that way he had grown to accept it. He knew he would never like it, but he did accept it as just a part of his life. He knew that as long as strong men tried to force their will on the weak that he would defend the weak. That was the way he was raised, it was the way he believed. If those beliefs caused the conflict he felt inside, he knew he would deal with it now and in the future just as he had in the past.

After the venison strip were eaten Ely started a conversation about where they were going. He and Grub had spent their twenty years in the northern Rockies, he had no idea what lay to the south. He had never been this far from his lifelong partner before. He missed Grub's sense of humor, he even missed his constant talk and complaining about every little thing. He could tell Benny missed him too.

Ever since Grub, Ely, and Benny had reached Grizzly Killer's tiny village on the banks of Blacks Fork, there had been mountains in every direction for as far as their eyes could see. He believed this land of the Utes, or Utah as it was called, was all mountains. The northern Rockies are mighty big, but there were huge areas of flat lands, and they were the home of massive buffalo herds. So far all he had seen of the land of the Utes were mountains, there seemed to be no flatlands anywhere. When he mentioned that, both Zach and Running Wolf smiled. Running Wolf told him of his home in the basin south of the Uintah mountains and to the great flat desserts to the west. But in Ely's mind the land of the Utes was nothing but mountains, one after another for as far as he could see. Each day they traveled was the same, every hill or ridge they had crossed led to more mountains and beyond that even more. If this land had any flat land, he was going to have to see it for himself, for he had no idea where flats would fit in between all the mountains.

Running Wolf explained that the next day when they crossed the ridge they would be going down into a very large canyon. At the bottom of it is the trail the Spanish had used since the time of his grandfather's. They came north from Nuevo Mexico looking for the shiny yellow rocks the white man believed were so valuable. He told them some of the history of the Spaniards. How they had tried to enslave the Utes and make them dig for the gold like they had so many of the Indians ever since the conquistadors first came to this land. He told of their cruelty, of killing and cutting off the hands of those that would not submit to them. He told them how the Utes had fought back against the Spanish and being vastly outnumbered, the Spaniards had finally left the Utes alone. They brought other Indians north with them as their slaves. Indians that didn't outnumber the conquistadors.

Many Spaniards believe in slavery, he told them, that is why some Ute bands traded slaves to them for horses, guns, knives, and many other metal things that the Utes have no other access to.

But now, with trading posts opening in the mountains and supply trains coming to Rendezvous', most tribes had other sources of trade. Sources where they could get the highly sought-after goods that previously were only available from the Spanish.

This was not only new country for Coyote Talker, hearing this history of the Spanish and Utes was new to him as well. He thought back to the many stories told around their fires by the village elders of the battles with the Blackfeet. But could not recall hearing any stories like what Running Wolf was describing of the cruelty to the slaves of the Spanish Conquistadors.

Coyote Talker felt even more compelled to rescue not only his brother, but the other slaves as well. He did not want any of them to suffer their fate in the hands of the Spanish. The way he felt now started to make him understand just a little as to why Grizzly Killer, Running Wolf and the others were not just willing, but seemed eager to help him rescue his brother.

It was another cold, clear morning as Zach watched Jimbo run out into the darkness on his morning hunt. By the time he had the fire going, after finding one small ember in the bed of coals, he was shivering and rubbed his hands together over the rapidly growing flames.

Ely commented, "I figure I must have been wrong about how far ahead them there slavers is. I figured we would have found their tracks by now. That there snow has been mostly melted for the best part of two days and we still ain't seen hide nor hair of them there tracks." Zach asked, "You still figure we are on the right trail?" Ely nodded, "I reckon we is alright. I ain't seen no track but I keep finding little things, I figure that there brother of Coyote Talker is doing everything he can to leave us a trail."

Running Wolf had overheard them talking and walked over saying, "We will come onto their tracks today Ely, before we reach the old Spanish trail. I don't believe they could be any further ahead than that."

"I hope you is right." Ely commented.

As the stars faded with the coming dawn, several wolves started to howl. Jimbo seldom answered a wolf's howl, but the big dog went just out of camp, and they all stopped and listened as he howled back to his wild cousins. What none of them knew was in the big meadow, just across Blacks Fork from their teepees, Luna was howling into the early morning sky at the same time as her wild cousins and Jimbo that were over a hundred miles away.

*****

Two Flowers moved her naked body closer to Grub as she listened to the white wolf howling. She had heard Luna howl many times before, but this time was different. This sounded as if she was calling to Running Wolf, or maybe Jimbo. When the wolf was silent once again, she rolled up on top of Grub and they made love. Grub wondered at times if he could keep up with the love making of his wife, but then would smile and think how much fun it was trying.

When Grub and Two Flowers finally came out of their teepee, the other women were already up. Sun Flower was feeding the twins mush or porridge, as Grub called it. Star was sitting by the bank of the river, her arm around Luna. Both were staring across the big meadow.

Grub looked out across the meadow at the horse herd, as he did every morning. Only this morning something was different. He wasn't sure what it was, but after looking for several minutes it hit him: Thunder, the spotted stallion wasn't there. Thunder was always out there, watching over his herd of mares. This morning Grub could not see him.

He didn't say anything to anyone, he wanted to make sure he wasn't at the river getting a drink. It was Star that said it first, "Do not worry Uncle Grub, Thunder went to help Daddy and Jimbo find one of the missing boys."

Grub turned to see if the others had heard what she said. All of them were staring at her and he knew there was no need to repeat it. Shining Star walked over to her daughter, as did Raven Wing. The two knelt down by her and Luna, Shining Star asked, "What have you seen my daughter?" She looked up at her mother and then at Raven Wing and said, "I did not see anything, Luna told me Jimbo called out for help and since she could not leave us, Thunder went to help him."

Growling Bear heard everything that the little girl said and was shocked that all these people seemed to believe her. They appeared to believe the wolf had really talked to her. Sun Flower could see the doubt in his eyes and said, "It was hard for us to believe at first, but she has never been wrong. What she says will happen, happens. What she hears always turns out to be true. She is gifted beyond that of even Raven Wing. You may not believe her, many do not, but that does not change the fact that what she sees or hears is always true."

Growling Bear looked at her in disbelief, then he looked back at Star. Luna turned and stared into his dark eyes. It was only for a brief moment, but in that moment he felt something he had never felt before. He had no idea what it was he felt, and he did not know why, but he now believed every word the little girl had spoken.

Grub watched the horse herd closely for the rest of

the day, but Thunder was gone. None of them had any idea where Zach and the others were. They had no idea how Thunder would find him, but they all knew the spotted stallion had found him before and over great distances as well.

Grub wondered what the stallion could do that Jimbo couldn't do. He knew that Jimbo could cover as much ground in a day as Thunder could. He believed Jimbo could follow a trail better than any horse that was ever born. So, if by some unknown means the great medicine dog had called for help, what could the stallion do? Grub pondered on that throughout the day and as the sun set he still had no idea. All he knew for sure was the stallion was gone and the words of a five-year-old girl was the only clue as to where he had gone.

Raven Wing left Gray Wolf with Star, Jack, and Little Moon for the others to watch and headed up the river trail. It was midafternoon, and she was heading to a small clearing on the ridge a mile or so above their village. It was a place she went to meditate and pray. She felt she needed guidance from the one above.

Raven Wing, like Grub, could not understand what Thunder could do that Grizzly Killer, Running Wolf, Jimbo and the others couldn't. She wondered if they were in some kind of trouble and just where they were.

Once she reached the clearing, she rolled out an elk skin robe. There she knelt and tried to clear her mind of her worries and questions. She built a small fire and watched the tiny column of smoke twist its way to the sky. She knew the smoke would carry her words into the heavens, to the ears of the creator. She didn't know how long she had been there before she reached her arms toward the sky and asked the one above, the creator of all things, to help her husband and his companions. To help them find the lost boys and return safely back home. She asked him to let her know they were safe and how long they would be gone.

To Raven Wing this was a sacred place. She had prayed here many times. She always felt closer to the creator when she was here. She waited, kneeling on the elk skin for hours. She didn't feel the calmness she usually felt, and she did not receive any answers. The sun had set, and the light was fading fast when she finally rolled up her sacred robe and started back to camp.

The others had made a mutton stew of the meat Grub and Growling Bear had taken a couple of days before. Everyone there noticed Raven Wing was quiet. Star came over and sat by her and Gray Wolf asked, "What is the matter mama?" She just smiled at her son and said, "Nothing Gray Wolf, I am just thinking about your father." At that Star took her hand and said, "Aunt Raven Wing, Daddy and Uncle Running Wolf are fine, but they are a long way from here. Thunder won't find them until tomorrow night."

She looked down at Star and asked, "How do you know that, what have you seen?"

"I don't know, I just know it. I have not seen anything." Raven Wing put her arm around Star and hugged her. She was troubled, everyone could see that, especially her sister. Sun Flower knew her better than anyone, in some respects even better than Running Wolf did. She knew Raven Wing would share any visions or feelings she had, and because she had not shared, Sun Flower knew she was troubled for that very reason. She had not seen or heard anything accept what Star had told them.

Gray Wolf slept in Grizzly Killer's teepee with Sun Flower and Shining Star and the other children that night. Raven Wing did not expect to get much sleep. She was troubled, she wondered if she had done something wrong. Was the one above not happy with her? When she prayed she always felt better, whether she got answers or not, she always felt a calmness come over her. This time she felt troubled. Did that mean Running Wolf and Grizzly Killer were in danger or trouble? She didn't know, and that made her feel even more troubled.

She added wood to the small fire in the center of her teepee and sat down in front of it. She watched the fire and the smoke curl up through the smoke hole, mesmerized by the dancing flames. She had no idea how long she had sat there. She didn't realize she had fallen asleep when she heard her husband's voice. Then Grizzly Killer was talking with Benny and Buffalo Heart, then Ely was talking about following a trail. A moment later she could see them all sitting around a campfire. Coyote Talker was with them, but she could not see White Crow or Yellow Horse. She heard Jimbo whine as the big dog looked to the flames of the fire. She could feel his eyes upon her.

She made out that they were talking about only one of the boys. His name was Brave Fox but they never mentioned the other two. Then the word slaves and Sahpeech come up. She knew it was a war chief of the Sahpeech Utes that had taken her beautiful sister-in-law, and with Grizzly Killer rescuing her, he'd had to kill Black Hand and Shining Star had become his second wife. Soon the image faded into the darkness of the night. Raven Wing didn't awake until the sun had risen over the eastern ridge. She could hear all the others outside around the fire. Suddenly the teepee flap was thrown aside and Gray Wolf and Luna came rushing in. Sun Flower was right behind him trying to stop him from disturbing his mother, but as she stepped inside the little boy was already in his mother's arms. Raven Wing smiled up at her sister and the look of relief on Raven Wing's face told Sun Flower that she had gotten at least some of the answers she had been praying for.

Chapter 10

Bound, Hand and Foot

Jimbo ran out in front of Ely and was out of sight within seconds. That in itself wasn't unusual, but Zach knew his dog well, and Jimbo seemed to be more excited to be on the trail this morning.

The trail of Red Eagle was still no easier to follow. The early winter storm had wiped out any trace of their tracks, but Ely was finding other signs of their passing. A broken branch on a sage where he believed a horse had miss-stepped. A fallen aspen leaf under a sage hundreds of feet from the nearest aspen. Ely didn't believe it was happenstance that leaf was there, he believed Brave Fox or one of the other captives was leaving them a trail to follow.

They stopped only briefly at midday, they had only seen Jimbo a couple of times throughout the morning. The big dog had ventured much further ahead than he usually did. They were just mounting up from their brief stop when Jimbo came running back to them. Zach knew he had found something, he just didn't know what that somthing was. Zach jumped down off Ol' Red and Jimbo ran to him and he said, "Have you found 'em big feller. Take us to 'em." Jimbo spun around and took off once again. Everyone there was excited they all hoped Red Eagle and his captives were now close at hand.

By late afternoon they were still following the big dog. They had given up hope that their prey was close. There were still no tracks, and they knew if they were as close as they hoped there would be tracks. It was nearly impossible to hide the tracks of over a dozen horses, so none of them believed they were close. What was it that Jimbo had found? Zach knew his dog, he knew Jimbo had found something.

Throughout the afternoon Jimbo had stayed out in front but within sight. They could tell he was leading them to something he had found. They were nearly to the bottom of the canyon when Jimbo came running back again, but before the dog reached them Zach and Ely both saw a faint column of smoke in the bottom.

Coyote Talker was excited, he wanted to charge right in and free his brother, killing anyone that tried to stop him. It was Ely that made him listen to reason. In just a few days Coyote Talker had formed a bond with the old mountain man. Zach could see the respect Coyote Talker had for Ely each time he looked at him. He wondered if Ely reminded him of someone from his past. Whatever it was, Coyote Talker's quick temper was cooled by Ely's simple words, "Son, you figure you is good enough to take on a dozen warriors just by charging in. Why Grizzly Killer himself wouldn't try that."

The impatient and quick tempered young warrior stopped and looked up into Grizzly Killer's blue eyes as Zach said, "We will get you brother back, but we will not let you or any of us go under doing so." Running Wolf then said, "They are Ute, me and Grizzly Killer can go into their camp and talk to them. We will be welcomed at their fire, we will see their captives and their numbers."

Coyote Talker was suddenly suspicious. Would Running Wolf warn them, would he help them get away? Ely could see the doubt on his face put his hand on his shoulder and said, "Coyote Talker, no man, white or Indian has more honor than Running Wolf, I have known him for nearly twenty years, you ain't got nothing to worry about, we's is gonna get your brother back."

Ely could feel Coyote Talker was shaking, doing his best to control his anger. He knew he wasn't angry at these men around him he just didn't know how to focus that anger on just those that deserved it. Every muscle in his body was tense, his jaws clinched tightly together as he fought, getting his own inner demons under control. He not only wanted his brother back, he wanted Red Eagle and all of his warriors to pay for taking him with their lives.

It was Buffalo Heart that stepped in front of Coyote Talker, he didn't have Ely's patience. He looked the volatile Bannock warrior in the eyes and said, "I will not let your anger get any of my friends hurt, if you want to die, that is up to you, but as long as we are near you, if you cannot control yourself we will." Everyone took what Buffalo Heart said as a threat, including Coyote Talker. The Bannock knew he was wrong but could not let a threat go unanswered. He stood there in front of Buffalo Heart defiantly when suddenly a rawhide loop landed over his head and tightened, jerking him off his feet.

He landed hard on his butt, and suddenly there were many hands binding him hand and foot. He laid there furious, his anger totally out of control, but he couldn't move his hands or feet. He made threats, telling them all they would pay for this. Buffalo Heart knelt down and said, "You can do anything you think you need to once we have the captives back and are safe. Until then you will stay bound."

Coyote Talker felt as if he was going to burst. He was humiliated, which made his anger even more extreme, but he was helpless, his hands and feet were bound tight. He would kill Buffalo Heart if he was free, he swore he would kill them all if he was free.

Zach and Running Wolf both felt bad, but the volatile young warrior could not control his emotions. Zach knew it was not just his anger, his anger would pass much quicker than the humiliation he felt. His feelings took second place to the safety of them all. He knew Running Wolf was right, the two of them would be welcomed in any Ute camp.

Coyote Talker was still struggling against the rawhide rope Benny had lassoed him with, but to no avail. His eyes were bloodshot as he watched Grizzly Killer and Running Wolf ride down the canyon toward the smoke, with Jimbo trotting alongside the big red mule.

They approached the camp with caution, although they stayed in plain sight. There were five teepees pitched, which surprised both of them. They didn't expect Red Eagle to take the time for teepees. Soon they heard children's voices, and as they looked at one another a Ute woman dropped an armload of firewood and ran to the teepees, shouting. A moment later six armed women came forward.

Zach and Running Wolf both stepped out of their saddles. The women could tell Running Wolf was Ute by his dress, but the big hairy faced man they weren't sure about. Zach held up his hand in the universal sign for peace and said, "I am Grizzly Killer and this is Running Wolf of the Uintah band. We have come looking for information, may we come in and talk?"

The women whispered among themselves for a moment, then relaxed and motioned for them to come in. They sat down and were offered water. It was obvious to both of them there were no captives in this camp. They learned this was a hunting camp of Timpanogos Utes. The men would be back tonight. They learned that Red Eagle had indeed passed through here and followed the trail upstream toward the pass that leads them into the land of the Sahpeech, but that was nearly three days ago.

These women held great disdain for Red Eagle and his followers. They told them even their own chief had made them leave their village. They had seven captives with them. They had taken what meat was left in their camp when they came through. Leaving the women and children with nothing until the hunters returned. Zach and Running Wolf gave them what little jerky they carried with them and headed back up to the others.

Jimbo ran on ahead, letting them all know Zach was coming in. He was pleasantly surprised that Coyote Talker was sitting with his hands and feet free. It had taken over a half hour for him to calm down, and even then Buffalo Heart figured he was going to be in for a fight. Coyote Talker looked up at him and nodded, letting Buffalo Heart and the others know he understood.

Coyote Talker's anger had gotten him into trouble most of his life. He had tried to learn to control the anger rather than have it control him, but sometimes, like this time, it just got the best of him, and he lost control. Although his pride would not let him apologize, he was contrite and quiet as Zach and Running Wolf told them what they had found out.

Ely was surprised he had believed they were closer than three days behind them. They had much time to make up and if Red Eagle wasn't welcome in his own village, they would move on through the valley of the Sahpeech and probably head for Santa Fe. They all knew now this was going to take much longer than any of them expected.

They found Red Eagle's campsite of three nights before, about three miles above the hunting camp of Timpanogos Utes. They camped in the same place, and Ely found another line of small pebbles pushed into the still moist soil. Now there were tracks, the tracks of over a dozen horses would be easy to follow and they all knew, going forward, they would make much better time.

As darkness fell in this very large canyon of the old Spanish trail. Zach thought about his wives and little ones. He longed to be lying between his two beautiful wives. He could almost feel their naked bodies pressed against his own as he closed his eyes. He tried to remove the thought of his mind, knowing it would just get him frustrated and keep him awake. Jimbo curled up on the bottom of his buffalo robe as Benny added more logs to the fire.

Zach felt Jimbo get off the bottom of the buffalo robe and he opened his eyes, looking at how far the big dipper had moved around the north star he knew he knew it was still three or four hours until dawn. He wondered where the big dog had gone. This was a lot earlier than his usual morning hunt.

Zach never went completely back to sleep. He laid there under the warm robe, wondering where his dog had gone. He could hear the horses were as restless as he was, but none of them were acting as if danger was near, they were just milling around more than usual.

He was up and had the fire restarted just as the first hint of dawn was showing along the eastern horizon. The air was cold, he could feel frost forming on his mustache as the dancing flames started to warm the air around the fire. They all knew they were still nearly three days behind Red

Eagle and his band of renegades. They also believed since the four warriors they left behind were now missing, Red Eagle would know he was being followed.

As Zach enjoyed the warmth of the fire, he knew as they got closer to the renegade band of Sahpeech Ute warriors they wouldn't be able to have a fire to give away their position. For now, they had a lot of country to cover before freeing Red Eagle's captives.

The others weren't far behind Zach, getting to the warmth of the fire. As Zach threaded strips of venison on the sticks they used for the same purpose the night before he wondered about Jimbo, he had been gone for hours. This was not his normal morning hunt and although he wasn't worried, he knew the big dog could survive on his own, he still wondered if he had found something.

The stars were fading fast as the light of the new day spread across the early morning sky. They were saddling up when movement caught Zach's eye. Coming up the canyon behind them was Jimbo, but what surprised them all, Thunder, the spotted stallion was right behind him.

Thunder whinnied, and Ol' Red let out a bray that echoed through the canyon. Ol' Red shook the saddle free of his back as Zach had not connected the cinch and trotted out to greet his friends. First Jimbo, he stopped and touched noses with the big dog, then he and Thunder greeted one another with their usual head nods.

Zach stood there and watched his dog, mule, and the spotted stallion. Thunder had found them once again. He wondered what power the horse had that he could find them over a hundred miles away, and why he would have left the big meadow and the herd of mares that he had claimed for his own. These were questions he knew he would never get answers to, so he would just continue to be mystified by the horse he had set free after taking him from the Cheyenne medicine man White Snake. It seemed no matter where he went, the spotted stallion followed, and he had no idea why.

Everyone else was just as surprised to see Thunder as Zach was. Buffalo Heart explained the history of the horse to Coyote Talker and he just shook his head in disbelief. But there was no doubt the horse was here, he was right before them, and he was one of the most magnificent stallions Coyote Talker had ever seen. He found it hard to believe Grizzly Killer wasn't riding such a magnificent horse instead of the ugly, scarred, long eared mule.

The sun was still an hour from rising as they started out on the trail again. Jimbo headed out in the lead and Thunder, running free, went on ahead of even the big dog. They saw the horse for only a brief moment as he crossed a barren hill a mile in front of them sometime around midday. But other than that, the stallion had stayed out of sight.

Now with the trail so easy to follow they made much better time, and when Ely finally called a stop for the day, Zach figured they had covered more than twice the distance they had in the last couple of days.

About midafternoon, they had turned south, through hills covered with oak brush. He could see far ahead to the south, where the trail was leading them into a long wide valley. There was a high towering mountain peak to the west, but to the east the high mountains looked to go on forever. Running Wolf told them this was the valley of the Sahpeech, the Tule People and he expected they would find the village somewhere along the river that wound its way through the valley.

For the first time since they had been chasing Red Eagle, Ely could tell they were actually getting closer. He believed they had made up a half day on the renegade slavers, but the horses were exhausted. They had to stop and let them rest, eat, and drink or they would end up afoot and never would catch Red Eagle and free his captives.

As they sat around the fire they had built in between two hills so the light could not be seen from any distance, Ely said, "If we have a few more days like today, we is gonna catch up to this here Red Eagle. You know we is gonna be outnumbered, you give any thought about what we is gonna do when we catch 'em, Grizzly Killer?"

Zach was staring into the flames and looked up at Ely, then shifted his gaze to Coyote Talker, and said, "There are too many of them for a straight on attack. I figure once we do catch up we will need to use ambush and hit-and-run tactics until their numbers are down to where we can handle them. The most important thing is for all of us to stay alive. I don't plan on trading any of our lives for theirs."

His blue eyes and penetrating stare never left the dark eyes of Coyote Talker. The young Bannock warrior knew he was talking directly to him. And for the first time in his life, he understood his emotions, if he could not control them, he could get these men killed. Men whom he had come to respect, if not like. Coyote Talker made a solemn vow to himself that he would not let that happen.

Chapter 11

Grizzly on the Trail

Zach, as usual, was the first to rise the next morning. Just after Jimbo had left on his morning hunt. Zach had noticed that Thunder had never come back to Ol' Red and their other horses before they called it a night and climbed under their buffalo robes.

Before building a fire, he climbed to the top of the hill to their south and studied the dark expanse of the valley before them. He was looking for the flickering light of a fire. A fire may mean the Sahpeech village or a hunting camp. He wanted to know if they would be riding into any danger that may lie ahead. It was dark for as far as he could see. He walked to the west just a little ways and down off the hill to where the horses were picketed. Ol' Red was there, standing guard over the horses. It had been years since Zach had hobbled him or tied him in any way. He smiled and walked up to his big red mule. Ol' Red nuzzled his hand, saying good morning. Those that had spent much time around the man called Grizzly Killer, knew his bond with the big mule was as strong as it was with the great medicine dog. Zach patted the side of Ol' Red's neck and ran his hand over the scars left by the killer grizzly years ago and whispered, "Get 'em ready big feller, we have another long hard day in front of us." Ol' Red nodded his head like he had understood every word.

Zach heard movement back at the fire and turned to see flames starting to grow. Coyote Talker had got the fire started and as Zach walked back to him, he said, "I still did not leave my robes before you Grizzly Killer, do you not ever sleep?" Zach smiled, and answered, "Ya, I sleep alright, I have always been an early riser. Mornings are my favorite time of the day. I love to watch the stars fade with the coming of dawn, as I wonder what each new day will bring." Coyote Talker, like so many men that had met Zach Connors in the past, believed there were no others like him. That he was truly a special man.

As Buffalo Heart joined them, he asked, "Did Thunder ever come back?" Zach shook his head and said, "Ain't seen him, if he did, he left again." Coyote Talker asked, "What could he be doing?" Zach shook his head and Buffalo Heart said, "I gave up long ago trying to figure out that horse. He doesn't do anything or act like any other horse I ever saw." Zach smiled and a slight chuckled escaped his lips as he said, "That's for sure!"

The stars were not bright this morning, and they looked distant. As they faded with the coming light, Zach could see why. There were high wispy clouds, not thick enough to hide them, but it made them look far away. They were only a couple of miles from their campsite when those clouds started to turn pink with the coming sun. A couple of minutes later they turned a brilliant flame red, and that color extended over the entire eastern half of the sky.

The glowing red orange sky turned the already yellow orange leaves of the oak brush an iridescent orange and it looked as though they were riding through the land of a child's fairy tale.

Ely watched, the glowing red sky. The horizon looked as if it were burning, and asked, "I wonder if that is what the flames of hell is like?" Zach looked up at the horizon and said, "That is a beautiful sunrise, Ely. I don't figure there is anything pretty about the flames of hell."

The glow lasted only minutes and was gone with the rising sun. As the sun shot its warming rays across the long valley before them, a south wind started up blowing right into their faces. Zach wondered if that wind was blowing in another winter storm.

The trail was easy enough to follow. It did not take Ely's tracking skills to follow Red Eagle, his renegades, and their captives any longer. Ely had been out in front of everyone except Jimbo for the last several days. It was a position he was comfortable with as he usually led the way when it was just him, Grub, and Benny. Over the last few days, he had watched Jimbo closely. He had learned to read the actions and movement of the great medicine dog. This morning he was convinced there was something in the air that had Jimbo concerned.

Ely watched as the big dog reduced his lead on the rest of them. He was sure there was something ahead of them and called for Zach to come up to the lead. Zach urged Ol' Red a little faster and a moment later rode up alongside Ely. After hearing Ely's concerns, Zach rode on ahead. It took only minutes, and he too knew there was something ahead of them. Not wanting to ride into an ambush, he held his hand up to stop everyone. He had them split up and ride off the trail through the thick oak brush for the next few miles, staying off the easy to follow trail.

Zach stepped off Ol' Red and handed his reins to Buffalo Heart. Buffalo Heart would lead the big mule while Zach, staying with Jimbo, would carefully move ahead on foot. Everyone was out of sight and Zach waited holding Jimbo back with a hand signal until he was sure the others were well away from the trail and before pointing ahead telling Jimbo to go, and he then followed his dog.

Jimbo stayed close, no more than twenty-five yards from Zach. They had only gone a hundred yards when Jimbo stopped and the hairs started to raise down the center of his back. Zach had wished many times what many Indians believed was true, but no more so than right now. He wished he knew just what Jimbo knew, but he didn't. He knew there was danger just ahead, but he had no idea what that danger might be.

He knew it could be Sahpeech hunters, or more of Red Eagles Renegades, it could be a bear or mountain lion or even just a porcupine, or badger in the trail. Zach now stepped off the trail. He checked the powder in the pan of his rifle and the horse pistol he had tucked under his belt. Then carefully placing each silent step, he moved forward.

Jimbo was now less than ten yards in front of Zach and Zach could hear the faint rumble coming from deep in his chest. Zach strained to see or hear anything through the thick brush ahead. But whatever was there must only be a scent on the breeze, for he could not hear or see anything.

He took a few more steps when suddenly a bush nearly exploded only a few feet in front of them. At first all he could see were the leaves violently shaken off the oak. But less than a blink of his eye later, there was a silvertip grizzly charging right at Jimbo. The big dog's reaction was like that of a snake striking as he jumped out of the way of the grizzlies' deadly claws. Zach's reaction was pure instinct. He shouldered his rifle and pulled the trigger as the bear went after his dog. The .54 caliber lead ball hit the bear just behind his ribs. The bear stopped his chase of Jimbo, biting at the pain in his side. Zach knew his shot had missed the vitals, and he had no time to reload.

Zach knew the bear was hurt, but he knew a wounded bear is more dangerous than a healthy one. The bear went down on his side, but for only a moment, before letting out a roar and coming at Zach. The sight of his Pa lying under the huge bear in the trail flashed before his eyes. Just before he felt the horse pistol discharge in his right hand. He didn't even realize he had pulled the pistol from his belt. The bear hesitated but only for a moment, but that gave Zach enough time to jump behind a large oak bush.

He drew his knife and Cherokee tomahawk from his belt. The picture of his wives and children flashed before him, as he saw movement through the brush. He knew he had but a brief moment before the big bear reached him. He heard Jimbo attack. The attack was swift and vicious. But a moment later he saw Jimbo thrown through the air as the bear shook him off his back. Jimbo landed with a yelp but was not deterred. He attacked again, this time keeping the bear occupied but staying out of range of the deadly claws.

Jimbo had given Zach a few moments, and he reloaded his rifle. He had never reloaded a rifle as fast as he did right then. He put in extra powder but being in such a hurry he wondered if he had put in too much. He didn't have time for second guessing. He had to stop the enraged bear. Zach knew he already had two of the heavy lead balls in him, but he didn't believe either of them would be fatal.

Zach stepped to the edge of the oak, his rifle already at his shoulder just as Jimbo came at the grizzly again. Zach fired from less than ten yards away. The rifle violently slammed back into Zach's shoulder. He had used a little too much powder. A huge plume of blue gray smoke shot out from the barrel right behind the deadly lead ball, obscuring the bear for a brief moment.

The .54 caliber ball entered the bear's left shoulder, shattering the shoulder joint. He went down on his side once again. Jimbo took advantage and attacked from behind, keeping the now severely wound grizzly occupied again as Zach reloaded.

Just as Zach pulled the ramrod after seating the lead ball, he heard another rifle and then another as Benny and Ely both fired. The bear raised his head one more time and Zach fired again. This time the extra charge of powder drove the ball through the grizzly's ribs and into his lung. The bear was dying as the three men reloaded once again. The silver tip grizzly laid his massive head on the ground and took his last breath.

Jimbo was still standing near the bear, his teeth bared and the soft rumbling growl still coming from deep in his chest. Zach could see blood on his dog's shoulder but didn't know if it was his or the bears. He looked up at Ely and Benny and slowly approached the big bruin and said, "Sure glad you two showed up when you did." Ely nodded, amazed that Zach had fought off the bear for as long as he had. He then asked, "Grizzly Killer, you figure this here grizz is what Jimbo was a smelling?" Zach nodded, "Ya, I figure it was. Jimbo never has thought much of the big beasts."

"Smart dog." Ely replied.

Benny hadn't said a word. This was only the second grizzly he had ever seen. This one wasn't as big as the one that had terrorized the Shoshone village of Charging Bull, but it was by far the second biggest bear he had ever seen. Benny slowly walked around the big bruin as Ely said, "I don't figure we can use all this meat, but if Running Wolf is right and there is a Ute village up ahead, I am sure they can use it. Benny let's get to work while Zach gets the others, we'll load the meat up on them there extra horses. If there ain't a village ahead we can always dump what we can't use in a day or two."

The hair down the center of Jimbo's back had finally laid down. The growling had stopped and his lips were no longer curled. He stayed with Ely and Benny, still standing guard over the bear as Zach left the small clearing to get Running Wolf, Buffalo Heart and Coyote Talker. Ely looked at the big dog and said, "You ain't got to worry about this feller no more, Jimbo. He is dead enough we is gonna get 'em skinned." Jimbo's tail wagged, but he didn't take his eyes off of the dead bruin.

Zach didn't have to go far, at hearing the shots, his partners and Coyote Talker were not all that far behind where Ely and Benny had been. As the four men walked into the clearing Zach had told them what happened. Coyote Talker approached the dead Grizzly very reverently. Like Benny, this was only the second grizzly he had ever seen. Unlike the huge killer bear that Benny had helped kill in Charging Bull's village, this bear was even bigger than the first one Coyote Talker had seen.

The Bannock warrior looked with even more respect and asked, "You killed this great white bear by yourself"? Zach shook his head saying, "no, not by myself, Jimbo, Ely, and Benny all helped." Benny said, "Don't let him kid you Coyote Talker, the bear was down and dying before Ely and me ever fired." Coyote Talker was in awe of Grizzly Killer and his powerful medicine. Although he had grown to respect Zach in the last several days, killing this grizzly with just him and his dog made him the most powerful man Coyote Talker had ever seen.

Coyote Talker didn't say anything as he stood back

and watched these men skin the silver tipped hide from the carcass. Finally he told them of the only other Grizzly he had ever seen, "The bear killed three of their hunters and hurt two others before finally being killed by eighteen others. Even with eighteen of us, we shot every arrow we had into that bear." He looked at Zach's rifle and asked, "Do all guns have that big of medicine." This time it was Ely that looked up and said, "It depends who's a shooting 'em, how deadly they is Coyote Talker. In the hands of Grizzly Killer any rifle has mighty powerful medicine, 'cause that man is that good of a shot."

Zach just shook his head, a bit embarrassed by the praise, and turned to the south and said to no one in particular, "Wonder how long we are gonna be in all this oak brush. It sure makes it hard to see ahead." Running Wolf stepped up alongside his partner as said, "I don't remember this thick brush Grizzly Killer, but I was young when we came through here. I don't believe it will go on much farther or I think I would remember it."

Zach nodded and turned back to see how the skinning and butchering of the grizzly was coming. Like Ely, Zach knew a village always needed meat. Maybe this bear would provide some good will with the people of the village and they could find out something more about Red Eagle and his renegades.

Running Wolf was right, the thick oak became scarce in only a few more miles, and they made better time once they were out in the open valley. The Wind was still gusting into their faces, but it wasn't a hard wind and to Zach it didn't feel like the precursor to a storm. But this time of year, he knew a storm could move in at any time.

Since the last storm the weather had stayed clear, although well below freezing at night the afternoons were comfortably warm. With the wind coming from the south, this day was even a little warmer than the ones before.

Ely had taken charge of the butchering of the bear and loading the meat onto the horses and had stayed with Benny and Buffalo Heart leading the pack horses. Zach took Ely's place at the front of the column. The trail was very easy to follow. It reminded Zach of years before when he had followed the trail of the men that had killed Henry Clayson and several of his men some years before. Although this trail wasn't quite that easy they all knew any one of them could follow it at a full run.

Coyote Talker was worried about his brother, was Brave Fox hurt? Were they feeding their captives? He wanted to move faster, but he knew like all the others knew, they were moving as fast as they could and still keep their horses fresh, but this was taking much longer than any of them had thought it would.

Chapter 12

Four Bears

Early that morning Star awakened from a nightmare. The little girl had seen a great grizzly coming after her Pa. She climbed out from under her warm robe and wiped tears from her eyes, then went over and climbed under the robe with Sun Flower and her mother. Sun Flower put her arms around the five-year-old snuggling her close and whispered, "What is it, little one." Star whispered back, "I had a bad dream Momma Sun Flower."

Shining Star then rolled over and kissed her daughter on the forehead and asked, "What was the dream about Star."

"Papa," Star replied, "A big white bear was after Papa." Zach's wives looked at one another. Both knew that there could be much more to Star's dreams than just a child's nightmare. Sun Flower then asked, "What happened in the dream?" Star shook her head and said, "I don't know, I woke up."

"Tell us what you saw before you woke," Shining Star said, with more than a little concern in her voice.

"Papa got off Ol' Red, I think he knew something was ahead of him when suddenly the big silver looking bear was charging right at him and I woke up." Once again Shining Star's and Sun Flower's eyes met. They were both very worried. Since Shining Star was closest to the small fire they used for warmth in the center of their teepee, she rolled out from under the robe. She turned and tucked the robe in snuggly around Star as Sun Flower still held her close. They could both see goose bumps on the bare skin of Shining Star as she slipped the doe skin dress over her head and then started to rekindle the fire.

Within minutes the inside of the teepee was warm, and Star had gone back to sleep in Sun Flowers' arms. Sun Flower started to move, but Shining Star shook her head and whispered, "No Sun Flower, let Star sleep awhile longer. Maybe we will find out if it was just a nightmare or if our husband is alright." Sun Flower did not move again, she just closed her eyes and tried to dream of Grizzly Killer, but her mind didn't work the way Star's or Raven Wings did. Oh, she could see Grizzly Killer alright in her mind. But what she saw was all from memories, very good memories from the nearly ten summers they had been together.

*****

Zach studied the land in front of them as they rode along. Although similar to the valley Running Wolf had called Yambow, with creeks running from the mountains to the east forming the Sahpeech River, the Sahpeech valley was much longer. Zach could not see where the valley ended and believed he could see nearly fifty miles.

As he stared south down the length of the valley, he wondered where Thunder was. Where had the spotted stallion gone? Was he following Red Eagle and his renegades like they were, and if so, how did he know to do so?

By midafternoon they were following the Sahpeech River south through the long broad valley. They jumped several groups of deer, but the further south they traveled the sign of game became scarce. Then Coyote Talker saw several sets of horse tracks heading to the northeast and called out to Ely to come over to them. Everyone stopped as Ely studied the tracks. It took him only moments before he said, "these here tracks ain't the same ones we is a following. No sir, I figure they must be a village up ahead and this here is a hunting party heading for that canyon up yonder. Must be, this here area is hunted out, ain't seen much sign the last few miles." Running Wolf asked, "How long ago do you think the hunters passed by?"

"Maybe yesterday, don't figure these here tracks is any older than that." Running Wolf nodded as Ely asked, "How much longer you figure before we find this here village?"

Running Wolf looked ahead, he could see the valley was making a gradual turn to the west. Hard as he tried, he could not remember what lay ahead of them. He could remember going to the Sahpeech village that one time, but he could not remember where it was. Even if he could, he knew that villages moved all the time. It was spring when he was here with his father as a youngster and now being fall the village could be anywhere. He finally just shook his head and said, "Just don't know Ely, I was only through here once and I was young. I just can't remember."

Ely could see it troubled Running Wolf and as he walked back toward the others he said, "Running Wolf, you sure did better than most getting us this far. I figure we just gotta follow these here tracks 'til we's catch up. We is a gaining on 'em, but we's still got us a ways to go. We best put a few more miles in 'fore that there sun goes to bed for the night."

The tracks continued to follow the river through the valley of the Sahpeech Utes. The river had now spread out into a wide marshland covered with tulles. They followed the tracks around the marsh and covered several more miles before sundown. Zach, still in the lead, started looking for a place to camp for the night when he noticed a smoke haze two or three miles in front of them.

Zach was sure there was a village ahead. But the tracks of Red Eagle left the river and turned directly south. He and Running Wolf once again left the others, while they made camp on the bank of the river, Zach and Running Wolf rode on down the river toward what they were sure was a village. They were still a half mile out when they saw both teepees and wickiups among the willows and cottonwoods ahead.

This wasn't a large village, not more than fifteen or so lodges. As the two of them were seen, shouts of alarm could be heard through the lodges. Women and children ran into the willows to hide, and a half dozen warriors appeared to block the entry into the village.

Running Wolf rode ahead of Zach. He was leading two of the horses loaded down with meat from the grizzly. One of the men said, just loud enough for Running Wolf to hear, "He is Ute." The six warriors seemed to relax just a little but did not welcome Running Wolf either.

Running Wolf stopped just out of the range of their arrows and held up his hand in the sign for friend, and shouted, "I am Running Wolf of the Uintah Utes, my friend is the great white warrior Grizzly Killer, we are friends, may we come in and talk?" Running Wolf could see his partner's reputation had reached these men. It seemed the name Grizzly Killer was known regardless of how far they traveled.

The older of the Sahpeech warriors raised his hand and motioned them forward. Running Wolf waited for Zach to reach him, then Zach dismounted and they walked toward the six warriors. Zach noticed movement in the willows to his left and figured they were being watched closely by other unseen warriors. Neither Zach nor Running Wolf were carrying their rifles, they were tucked safely into the scabbards tied to their saddles.

As Running Wolf led the two horses carrying the meat of the grizzly forward, Zach could tell at least one of the warriors recognized either one or both of the horses. He stayed quiet, but the look on his face put Zach on full alert.

Running Wolf stopped only a few feet in front of the older warrior and once again said, "I am Running Wolf, I visited your village many summers ago with my father. Grizzly Killer is my partner. We have been following Red Eagle south for many suns. He has taken captives that are friends of ours."

At the mention of Red Eagle, Zach could see disdain written on the face of the old man and a couple of the others. His hopes were high these men would help them learn where Red Eagle might be going.

The old warrior said, "I am Four Bears, Chief of the Sahpeech, you are welcome into our village. Running Wolf thanked the chief and stepped forward, handing the reins of the two horses laden with meat to the man next to the chief. As he did, he said, "Grizzly Killer killed a great grizzly on the trail this morning. It is much more meat than we can use. Please take the meat and the horses that carry it as gifts."

Four Bears smiled and nodded, and the warrior led the

two horses away. The chief led them into the village to a fire set in front of the chief's own teepee. They sat down around the fire and an older squaw brought out the chief's well used pipe. Running Wolf pulled a twist of tobacco from his possibles bag and handed it to Four Bears.

After the formality of passing the pipe around the fire was over, the warrior that Zach believed recognized the horses said, "Running Wolf, I am Brave Hunter and one of the horses carrying the meat belongs to my brother, Swift Arrow." Running Wolf nodded, which seemed to surprise them all, and said, "That very well could be true. Three suns ago we believe Red Eagle knew we were following him and left four warriors to watch their back trail. Grizzly Killer and two of our friends fought the four warriors, one of them was killed and the others hurt. We took their horses so they could not reach Red Eagle to warn him."

Zach then spoke for the first time, as he said, "Brave Hunter, I am sorry about your brother, I do not know the names of the four warriors. I left three of them alive, but one of the three was severely wounded in the fight. The other two badly hurt, but I believe they will live. We left them afoot." Zach could see anger building in the face of Brave Hunter, but the chief had welcomed them into the village and Zach did not believe they were in danger, at least not at this time.

Four Bears said, "Red Eagle has been cast out of our village. He has not been here in more than four moons. When he left, several young men followed him, believing he would lead them to victorious battles." Running Wolf then said, "They went on a raid to gather slaves, when they took the younger brother of a friend of ours, we started tracking them. They followed the river until it turned to the west and then turned south. Our friends are now camped where their trail left the river. We came to your village seeking information and to give you the meat from the great bear. We did not want it to be wasted."

Four Bears nodded and asked, "What do you wish to know, Running Wolf."

"With it being so late in the fall, is there some place Red Eagle will go, or do you believe he will go all the way to trade the slaves to the Spanish," Running Wolf asked.

Zach could see Brave Hunter was appalled that his chief was willing to help them against his own warriors. But to Four Bears, Red Eagle and the men that follow him were no longer Sahpeech. He no longer had any reason to protect them in any way. He believed Running Wolf and Grizzly Killer were honorable men. They had not tried to hide what happened to the warriors they fought. They had brought them meat and horses, and he would help them if he could. Although, he would not put any of his warriors in danger doing so.

Four Bears said, "Since Red Eagle and his followers have been cast out, I do not believe they have anyplace to spend the winter, although it is possible for them to be welcomed into a Piute village to the south. I believe they will follow an old trail of the Spanish and try to reach the Spanish lands before all the mountain passes are closed with snow."

Disgusted at what his chief had just done, Brave Hunter stood and stomped away from the fire, Zach could see a couple of the other warriors there had similar sentiments as Brave Hunter as he stomped away.

Four Bears said, "I will try to calm Brave Hunter, though I tried to do the same with Swift Arrow. Red Eagle is a very dangerous man, and too many of our young warriors believe he will lead them to great victories. They do not realize those victories put our whole village in danger of attacks by other tribes, or villages. Red Eagle knows, but he does not care." Zach asked, "How many of your young warriors followed him?" Four Bears held up the fingers of one hand and said, "Five." Running Wolf then said, "He has recruited many more, we are following at least twelve plus about 8 captives."

Four Bears could see the disdain on several of his warriors not only for Running Wolf and Grizzly Killer but for himself as well. Not everyone had agreed with his decision to cast Red Eagle from their village. Even though they all knew why Four Bears had done it and had reluctantly supported his decision. They still felt Red Eagle and his followers were Sahpeech and what Four Bears had just done, was done against his own people.

Four Bears looked at Running Wolf and then Grizzly Killer saying, "We thank you for the meat of the bear, but I believe it is now time for you to go." Zach and Running Wolf stood they could see the chief was going to have his hands full with several disgruntled warriors. Neither Zach nor Running Wolf felt really safe here now and was glad to mount up and ride out.

Jimbo met them just outside the village. He had followed but stayed out of sight. Zach smiled as they set a fast lope back to the others, knowing Jimbo was always there to protect him, whether from man or beast.

They arrived back to where the others had stopped to camp. There was a welcoming fire burning and bear meat dripping fat into the flames. As they told the others of their talk with Four Bears and how he had not hesitated to answer their question, they also told of Brave Hunter and some of the others. They decided they better ride into the night, putting more distance between them and Brave Hunter and any of the others that may wish to fight to stop or slow them.

Even Jimbo got a big piece of fatty bear meat before

they saddled up and followed the valley south through the darkness for a few more miles.

As dawn spread light across the valley, they could see they were not far from the river and rode over to it to let the horses drink their fill. This was a different river, this one larger, and it was flowing north. Although neither Zach nor Running Wolf saw where the Sahpeech River flowed into this one, they were sure it did, and that is where the Sahpeech village sat.

Chapter 13

Red Mounds of Salt

They stood guard throughout the night, not really sure what to expect from Brave Hunter. Coyotes sang their high-pitched chorus from the hills on both sides of the valley. As usual, Zach took the last watch of the night. There was just a faint line of light along the eastern horizon as he got their fire started.

Although the night had been uneventful, Zach kept thinking about Brave Hunter, he wondered which of the Sahpeech he had left behind, was his brother one of them, or was he the one that died. He wasn't sure, but he figured Brave Hunter was upset enough he may try to stop them from catching Red Eagle and whoever else he may talk into coming after them.

The weather was still holding, and with a trail so easy to follow he believed they could cover more than fifty miles today, making it hard for Brave Hunter to catch them and closing the distance between them and Red Eagle. As they roasted more of the bear on sticks over the fire for their breakfast, Zach told the others of his concerns, then asked Ely how far he figured Red Eagle was ahead of them.

Ely stared into the flames for a few minutes then looked across the fire at Zach and said, "Ain't sure, but my best guess is a day and a half. Problem be, they picked up their pace too. I don't figure we is a gaining more than two or three hours a day on 'em."

That was the answer Zach was expecting. It wasn't what he hoped to hear, but it was what he thought as well. Buffalo Heart asked, "Grizzly Killer, you think me and Benny should stay back and if Brave Hunter is following, we could sure discourage him." Zach thought for a minute but it was Running Wolf that answered, "No Buffalo Heart, I think we have enough bad blood with the Sahpeech and if it led to more fighting or death, it may not be to our advantage." Everyone around the fire understood Running Wolf's meaning. If they killed one of the warriors from the village, they may have the whole band of Sahpeech Utes to fight.

Ely added, "We best not waste no time. We got us some renegades to catch and maybe some more to outrun. We best get mounted up and put some miles behind us."

Ely set an easy lope, knowing they could cover more than ten miles each hour as long as the horses could maintain it. Jimbo ran out in front, it amazed him how Jimbo never seemed to tire. He could run all day with the horses and then stand guard at night. Ely thought back to the pups of Jimbo and Luna. The two that he and Grub had given to the boys in Charging Bulls village before leaving. He smiled and wondered if they were as great as their father. Then he wondered if Jimbo would be as great as he was, without Grizzly Killer.

Their horses were all strong mountain horses, and he

believed they could stay at the gentle lope all day long if the ground permitted it.

An hour to the south of where the Sahpeech River ran into the larger river, Ely stopped. Red Eagle and his men had taken two deer along the riverbank. They then crossed the river, and as Ely followed, they all wondered what this sudden change of direction meant.

The trail led to three barren knolls about a mile and a half west of the river. The knolls had no vegetation on them and were streaked with red. They could see, as they followed the tracks to the knolls, that someone had been digging in the side of the center knoll. The tracks led to where the deer had been butchered on the reddish brown dirt. They all looked at the scene curiously. It was Coyote Taker that slid off his horse and touched the red soil. He brought a hand full up to his nose and sniffed, then slowly touch his tongue to it. A broad smile formed on his face and he handed some of it to Ely. Ely did the same then turned to the others and said, "Why, this here is a mountain of salt. Red Eagle and his bunch, brought the deer they took over here to salt 'em down. We best do the same, get the rest of that there bear down here and let's get it salted 'fore we move on."

It took only minutes for them to have their meat heavily salted, as well as the heavy hide of the grizzly. They also had what food pouches they had emptied filled with the reddish salt. Their stop was brief, Zach was sure Red Eagle's stop at the salt mounds was much longer.

The trail crossed back over to the east side of the river and thirty minutes later they came to another creek running into the river from a very large canyon cutting through the mountains to the east. The mountains to the southwest were lined with dark red cliffs that led south to even higher, more formidable mountains that Zach figured were forty or fifty miles away. Directly south of them were a series of barren, steep pointed gray hills. They reminded Zach of the badlands just northeast of their home on Blacks Fork.

That made him think of home, he wondered what his children and wives were doing right then, he missed them all. Jimbo came running back to them and barked twice. He was normally very quiet and his barking got Zach's attention. What had his dog found this time?

The trail led up the creek in this large canyon and only a couple of miles ahead Jimbo led them to another of Red Eagles camp sites. Ely held up his hand to stop the others so they wouldn't disturb any of the tracks as he then dismounted and slowly covered every inch of the ground.

He found a cattail leaf that had to come from crossing the river and smiled again, believing the young Bannock warrior was leaving a trail to follow. Though he smiled, he wished the youngster would not take that risk now the trail was so plain without it. The leaf did make Coyote Talker feel better knowing his younger brother was still alright.

Ely found where he believed a girl had been held down and raped. The way her body imprint was left in the dry dirt, he figured several of the braves had taken their turns with her. They rode on, following Red Eagle's trail up the canyon. They passed through an area of red rock and cliffs along the north side, but to the south the hills were slate gray dirt.

Juniper and pinion now covered the hills. Even though they couldn't make as good of time as they did out in the valley, Ely believed they were still catching up. Eight or ten miles up the canyon, the trail turned to the south once again into another broad shallow canyon. The trail followed a smaller creek as they rode higher into the mountains.

Zach nor any of these men had ever been in this country

before. And once again Ely marveled at how this land of the Utes was all mountains. They had traveled for what he figured was more than two hundred miles and had never been out of the mountains. Mountains were in every direction for as far as he could see.

A high dominate peak had been to the east of them as they rode south through the valley of the larger river. Now, as they rode east up this canyon that peak was to the northeast. It reminded them all, of a woman's breast. With dark pines below leading up to the white cliffs that formed the nipple. Ely chuckled as he told the others it reminded him of a plump woman he had met in Saint Louis years ago by the name of Molly, "Yep," he said, "That there is just like Molly's Nipple." The others chuckled along with him and at him, for he kept turning in the saddle looking back at the peak, and each time he did, he would chuckle again.

By late in the afternoon they had climbed high onto the mountains. The Pinion and juniper forest had changed to thick oak brush, and maple. The oak and maple in these western mountains weren't like the oak and maple trees back east. Although the leaves were the same, these were more like brush than trees. Gooseberries, chokecherry, currents, and service berries grew thick along the creek, making their journey up the creek nearly impossible in places. In those places Red Eagle had led his men and captives off the creek and up onto the hillsides. Ely did the same. Some places they had to go nearly a half mile from the creek to find a passable route.

They reached a ridge somewhat barren of trees and brush just as the sun was setting. They had climbed even higher. They were now out of the thick impassable oak brush and were now into aspen and pine. It had been a long, hard day on the horses. Even Ol' Red was exhausted. The only one of them that acted as if he could keep going was Jimbo. The big dog never seemed to tire, but as soon as they stopped, he curled up and was fast asleep before the horses were even picketed.

They set camp in a stand of aspen just below the ridge top. As the sun set in the west, Zach walked to the crest only a hundred yards above them. The land dropped off abruptly to the east and the creek they had been following dropped off to the west. They were high in the mountains now, and the views were spectacular. The huge stands of aspen were a brilliant yellow, with stands of dark green pine scattered throughout. They had seen many herds of deer and a few elk, and one herd of mountain sheep throughout the day, but hunting wasn't necessary as they still had plenty of the now salted grizzly meat.

The temperature fell abruptly as the last of the sun's rays dropped below the western mountains. Zach looked at the extensive land in all directions and wondered where the spotted stallion was and what he was doing. He had no idea that Thunder was high on a ridge only thirty miles south of them, watching Red Eagle and his warriors picket their own horses.

Thunder had caught up with Red Eagle earlier that day and had followed them through a long wide high mountain valley that ran for miles nearly straight south. They had skirted ancient lava flows with great broken boulders, showing the volcanic action that had formed these mountains in a time long before the first man walked on the earth.

A small crystal-clear creek ran the length of the mile-wide valley with mostly open meadows in the center with occasional stands of aspen or pine. The high mountains to the east and west were covered with thick stands of aspen and dense pine forests.

*****

Luna had been restless throughout the evening, Grub had noticed even the horses in the big meadow and their own mounts in the pole corral next to the dugout were restless. He figured something was in the air that was bothering them all. As they ate a rich mutton stew, he warned them all he figured something was out there that neither Luna nor the horses liked.

He never put down his rifle and had it leaning against his knee as he ate. Growling Bear had grown to respect Grub and was now worried for their safety. He turned to go for his bow and quiver of arrows and was once again shocked that Little Dove was right there handing him his weapons. He smiled at her, nodding his thanks. It was the first time she had seen anything but anger in his eyes as he looked at her. No words were spoken as she smiled back. She hoped that meant he was starting to forgive her for the pain he still felt almost constantly in his head.

As they ate, Luna walked in circles around camp. She would stop and check on the children with every pass she made. As the evening star shone bright in the western sky and the last of the light faded from the big meadow, the women put the children to bed. Not knowing what was out there, they wanted them safely inside the buffalo hide lodges. Gray Wolf and Star both protested going to the robes so early, but they were obedient and did as their mother's wished.

Luna crossed the river but didn't go out into the big meadow. She raised her head to the star filled sky and howled a long mournful howl. Grub, Growling Bear and all six women were silently watching the white wolf. She howled just the one time then laid down watching to the south.

None of them knew what was wrong. Raven Wing tried as she had each night staring into the fire, to connect with her husband or the others, but to avail. Little Star had not seen or heard anything in her mind since Thunder had left the big meadow.

Luna jumped to her feet as if she had heard something. That made Grub get his rifle and Growling Bear his bow ready for action. Sun Flower hurried to their teepee and got her rifle as well. They had no idea that what Luna was hearing, was taking place nearly two hundred miles to the south.

The white wolf stared south across the big meadow, waiting for Jimbo or Thunder to answer her.

*****

They were sitting around their fire eating roasted bear meat once again. Jimbo, lying by Zach's side, raised his head so abruptly they all knew he had heard something out in the darkness that none of them had heard. Zach watched his dog as he instinctively checked the powder in the pan of his rifle and re-snapped the frizzen in place.

Jimbo stood and trotted to the north side of their camp area, right at the outside edge of the light from their fire and raised his head, howling into the night sky.

Thirty miles to the south, Thunder was prancing back and forth in a meadow a half mile above the camp of Red Eagle. The spotted stallion could smell the twenty horses they had tied to two separate picket lines.

Jimbo started circling the camp, staying just at the outside edge of the light from their fire. The cold night air settled in on this high mountain camp and even with the fire they all got their sleeping robes to wrap around their shoulders.

Zach stood, holding the buffalo robe tightly around him, and walked over to his dog. Jimbo stopped circling the camp and Zach rubbed his ears asking, "What is big feller, what has you so nervous tonight?"

Zach walked back to the fire and Running Wolf asked, "Do you think something is out there we need to be worried about?" Zach shook his head, "No, Jimbo would let me know if there is danger near. I don't know what has him bothered." Ely then stated, "It's the unknown that can put a feller under. We best set a double guard tonight." They all nodded their agreement.

They all believed they were getting close to Red Eagle and his renegades. Zach looked up to where the sky disappeared behind the horizon to the south and wonder what awaited them over that distant ridge.

Chapter 14

Stolen in the Night

Red Eagle walked to the edge of their camp. He looked to the north and wondered what had happened to Swift Arrow and the others. He knew whatever had happened could not be good. They'd had more than enough time to catch up. He knew they had been traveling at a fast pace, but his four warriors should have caught up to them long before now.

A lone wolf howled just above them, and the horses reacted by stomping the ground and pulling against their pickets. A chill ran down Red Eagle's back. He wasn't sure if it was from the cold or something unseen that he felt was out there. He stared out into the darkness, all off his senses tuned to hearing or seeing something, but nothing was there.

He turned and looked back at their camp. His warriors were all huddled around the fire, their captives tied to trees in the cold night air. They had taken two women, two girls under ten summers and a boy about the same age. They had one girl he figured was about 14 summers old. His men had been taking turns with the women, and wanted the younger girl, but he had forbidden anyone to touch her. She would bring the highest price if untouched, on the big Rancheros of the Spanish. The last captive, the boy about the same age as the girl, would also bring a good price. He would make a strong slave to work in the fields.

He walked back to the fire. As he did, he saw the boy and girl were shivering, and knew they must remain alive and healthy to make the long trip to the lands of the Spanish worthwhile. He walked over to the girl and untied her from the tree. Tears formed in her eyes as she believed her fate was now that of her aunt and older cousin. The two older women had been used every night by the cruel warriors.

They were Western Shoshone and had been gathering roots along the river, running into the great lake of salt when Red Eagle and his warriors rode down on them. The young girls and one boy of about eight were already captives when Red Eagle had taken the three of them. Red Eagle roughly pulled her over to the tree where Brave Fox was tied and retied her there, then went over and took a small robe from one of their packs and put it around the two teenagers, knowing they would be warmer together. The younger children he didn't seem to care about. They had cried each night, and he knew they would not be worth much. He considered leaving them, as they were all tired of listening to their cries. The boy had been beaten several times to make him stop, but it had only made it worse.

Tonight was the most intense cold they had faced yet, and the crying of the three youngest captive raked the nerves of these ruthless renegades. One of the braves walked over to them and took the older of the two girls to his robes. She fought and screamed at the pain as he raped her. Then suddenly all was quiet except for the whimpering of the other two children. A little while later Brave Fox watched as he dragged the body of the little girl out into the darkness, discarding her as if she was nothing. Brave Fox felt tears drip from Willow's face onto his arm as she knew the child was dead. She feared for all their lives, knowing these men could kill them at any time.

Neither Brave Fox nor any of the captives could understand the Ute tongue of their captors. They had not been allowed to speak to one another. Brave Fox whispered to the girl that had been thrust upon him, "I am Brave Fox." She looked into his eyes and he could see she understood him. She glanced over at the others, afraid to make a sound before whispering back, "I am Willow." Brave Fox smiled, she was Shoshone and spoke his language. He did not feel so alone any longer.

He could feel her body shivering from both the cold and fear. She cuddled closer to him for his warmth, but with their hands tied around the tree, neither could position the small elk robe Red Eagle had thrown over them.

The two older women, Willow's aunt and cousin had already been taken to the sleeping robes of two of the renegades. Brave Fox and Willow could hear the men on top of them as the nightly raping continued. Willow did not understand why she had not been taken to their robes like the others. Whatever the reason she was grateful at least for that. Neither Willow nor Brave Fox knew what their fate would be, neither had any idea where these men were taking them.

They had camped alongside a small river, two or three miles below the large lake. As a child, Red Eagle had spent many summers at the lake with his Sahpeech village. The game was plentiful and the creek running into the lake from the west was always full of fish. This was along an old Spanish trail that he had been told led to the great waters that lived below the setting sun. He planned on following this trail to the Spanish settlements where he would trade his captives to a wealthy Spanish Ranchero for horses and the supplies they needed for the winter.

Red Eagle was normally a restless man. Tonight even more so than usual. He paced around the fire, his men staying out of his way. He stared out into the darkness, he could feel something was there and then he couldn't. Finally he went to the robe where Willow's cousin, Sage Blossom was lying with Broken Tongue. He kicked Broken Tongue from her and grabbed her by her long black hair and roughly dragged her naked body to his own robes.

Again, Brave Fox felt tears from Willow, as she softly whispered, "Sage Blossom was going to be married in seven suns."

Sage Blossom, as with Broken Tongue and all the others that had had their way with her since she had been taken, laid there motionless. She felt nothing but disgust as they had sweated and rutted on top of her. Red Eagle was more brutal, yelling at her in a language she did not understand. She did not know he wanted her to move and be active as he raped her. He slapped her hard, she could taste blood in her mouth, he bit her breasts so hard she thought they were bleeding as well.

Totally unsatisfied, he got off her and dragged her completely naked back to the tree where she had been tied and tied her there again. This time she was naked, no robe and no dress in the freezing night air.

All of Red Eagle's warriors could see he was in a very foul mood and were giving him a wide berth. He walked out to where their horses were picketed and stared out into the darkness again. He did not know why he was in such a foul mood. Something was wrong, but he did not know what. He had been nervous ever since he sent Swift Arrow and his friends to watch their back trail and now they had not returned he wondered who or what was out there. He walked back to the fire seeing the shivering woman he had beaten and left naked feeling nothing for her. He did not care whether she lived or died. She had not satisfied him, and he did not care if she froze during the night. As he looked around at the captives, most of his men had already gone to their robes.

He felt nothing for these weak and helpless women and children, no sympathy at all. He thought about killing them all, then thought about taking the teenage girl and see if she would satisfy him. He looked at Willow and Brave Fox huddled together and decided he would take the young woman. Just then a horse squealed at the picket line and then another. He heard the pounding of hooves as their horses ran into the darkness.

Thunder had come down from the ridge as darkness fell and had slowly approached the picketed horses, letting them get used to his smell. Being a stallion, the mares and geldings did not seem to mind his presence as none of the warriors' horses were stallions.

Standing alongside the other horses, Thunder gnawed through the rawhide picket ropes. After the rope hit the ground, he reared up and squealed, sending the twelve horses, on that line, into a panicked run. He stayed behind them, herding them back to the north. He ran the twelve horses for more than a dozen miles back to the north. Then let them settle and graze along the creek. Thunder stood watch over them the rest of the night. But all were satisfied to be free and grazing on the plentiful dry grass.

Red Eagle was furious. He believed one of his men had not secured the picket properly. His own horse was gone, no one ever saw Thunder, neither Red Eagle, nor his men had any idea their horses were stolen by another horse.

One of his warriors showed him the rawhide rope had been gnawed through. They all believed one of their own horses had done it. Red Eagle totally forgot about the young Shoshone girl. The next morning, he led seven of his warriors on their eight remaining mounts to find and round up their horses.

They followed the tracks for miles and hadn't seen even one of their escaped horses. They all knew if the horses had simply gotten loose they would not have run this far. Yet there were still only tracks to follow, tracks that were following their back trail, heading back farther to the north.

*****

Not long after full darkness, Jimbo settled down. He stopped pacing around camp and curled up at the bottom of Zach's buffalo robe just as he usually did. Zach knew something had happened, but he had no idea what that something was.

Zach watched the stars overhead. The air was crystal clear, the stars looked close enough to touch. He wondered what Sun Flower and Shining Star were doing. Just then, a shooting star streaked across the sky and he wondered if his wives had seen it too. He thought about their belief that a shooting star was a warrior following the great white trail in the sky to the land and life that lay beyond this world.

Though Zach didn't really believe in that or many of the other superstitions of his wives' people, he didn't discount them either. At the very least he felt it was a comforting story, a way their loved ones continue their journey past this mortal life.

Jimbo, with another sudden move, raised his head and this time he was staring straight south. Zach whispered, "What is it Jimbo, what is out there?" A whine escaped the big dog's throat and without any warning he was on his paws and running south. Within three silent bounds he was out of sight in the darkness.

Running Wolf was standing the first guard for the night. He saw the great medicine dog leave. Although the fire had died down, there was still enough light to see Jimbo leave and Zach with his head up watching him.

He walked over to his partner wondering where Zach had sent the big dog, and asked, "You think something is out there Grizzly Killer, you send Jimbo to have a look?" All the others were sitting up, wondering what was happening. Zach shook his head and said, "Wasn't me, Jimbo just up and took off by himself. He raised his head like he had heard something again, then just took off heading south."

Although tired, none of them could lay back down and sleep. They all believed Jimbo had heard something and they built up the fire, plumped up their sleeping robes to look like they were sleeping and each disappeared into the darkness. They would wait, out of sight for what Jimbo had heard to come in, or the big dog returned to let them know it was clear.

They kept the fire burning throughout the night, while staying back in the shadows away from the flames and heat they all spent a long, miserably cold night. As the first hint of dawn started to spread along the eastern horizon, they all came to the fire for its warmth.

Jimbo had not returned. There had been no sign the great medicine dog was near. Zach did not know where he had gone, but somehow he knew the dog was many miles from them. Ely looked up the steep ridge to the south. He turned to Zach and asked, "Where you figure that there dog a yours took off to, Grizzly Killer?" Everyone was watching Zach, either expecting an answer or hoping for one. Zach shook his head, "Wish I knew, but I ain't got any idea. Something tells me that we won't see him for a while, whatever he is doing, I figure he is miles from here." Ely commented, to no one in particular, "I wonder what kind of hell is waitin' over that yonder horizon?"

A lone wolf howled from a long way off. It was a haunting mournful howl that made a shiver run through all of them. After standing there in silence for a couple of more minutes, Zach said, "We best move on. Something tells me we are getting close to Red Eagle, we can't let up now. Jimbo will find us no matter where he went." Running Wolf added, "We best stay alert, if they are waiting for us up there, we better be ready."

*****

Jimbo ran to the south for nearly an hour, the steep high mountain didn't slow him at all. He had traversed steep side hills and dense timber. He had gone around, over, and under hundreds of fallen trees. He stopped and looked back to the north. He wanted his master to be behind him, but he knew he was alone.

The big dog did not know where he was going, but he had sensed, if not heard, Thunder needed help. He had never been in this country before. He had no idea what lie in front of him, He only sensed one of his family needed help, and it was his job to help.

It was still several hours before dawn as he made his way up and over the top of a very high ridge. A high mountain peak rose up out of the darkness just a little way to the south, and another to the northwest. But from where he stood, both looked like small rises on the ridge where he was standing.

Another whine escaped his throat as he looked down off the ridge to where he had left Zach, Running Wolf, and other members of his family. But they were together, Thunder was alone. Jimbo started down into the high mountain valley not knowing Thunder, and his herd of stolen Sahpeech horses were less than five miles in front of him.

Jimbo stopped, as he was coming around a stand of pines less than a mile from the top of the ridge. The scent of a bear filled his senses. He turned to the trees and a large black bear bounded away. Every fiber in his body wanted to chase. Just out of habit, Jimbo looked behind him to see what Zach wanted him to do. But Zach wasn't there, and the dog knew he would not be there this night.

He stopped only long enough that he could no longer hear or sense the bear, and then moved on, angling down the ridge to the south.

A bright three-quarters moon lit the wide meadows before him. He could feel he was getting close to Thunder. He slowed to a walk, staying along the tree line along the east side of the valley until he saw them, a dozen horse grazing peacefully in center of the valley. Just like their own horses in the big meadow back home.

There, a quarter mile south of the grazing horses, was Thunder, prancing back and forth across the open meadows keeping the other horses from going back.

Chapter 15

The Long Pond

As the sun made its way over the ridge separating Blacks Fork and Smiths Fork, Luna was still laying on the edge of the big meadow, just across the river. She had paced around the teepees many times through the night but always returned to the same spot, looking south.

Grub and Growling Bear had gone out into the big meadow to check the horses and Growling Bear's buckskin stud had run right up to him. Grub smiled, knowing this Bannock warrior must really love and care for his horse. If not, the horse would not show him that kind of affection.

Raven Wing had dreamed throughout the night, confusing and conflicting dreams. As they made biscuits, Raven Wing told the others of her dreams. She had seen their husbands camped in a place she had never seen before. A beautiful mountain where the aspen leaves were brilliant yellow, and the trails were covered with the yellow leaves. She had seen a young man and woman together, shivering from the cold. Then Thunder was running with a dozen horses she had not seen before, and Jimbo was some place by himself. The dream was confusing and did not tell a story. She told them, "I do not know what it all means."

The children were all eating a bowl of mush, made with the coarse ground wheat from Turley's Mill in Arroyo Hondo north of Taos. Jack and Little Moon where playing more than eating when Star set her bowl down and walked over to Shining Star, who was frying the heavy biscuits in an iron skillet and said, "Papa and Uncle Running Wolf, and Uncle Buffalo Heart, and Grandfather Ely and Uncle Benny are fine Mama. Even Growling Bear's friend is fine. They are getting close to the men they are chasing."

The little girl's words concerned them all. Shining Star moved the heavy frying pan from the coals and turned to Star and asked, "Who is Papa chasing," Star looked at her mother and then at Raven Wing and said, like they should already know, "The warriors that took the girls and boys."

Grub and Growling Bear were just coming back into camp. Grub knew immediately the way they were huddled around Grizzly Killer's little girl. She had seen something. Suddenly Raven Wing started to understand her own dream. The girl and boy must be captives, and their husbands were going to free them.

When Grub and Growling Bear reached the fire, she told them what she thought their husbands were doing. They were now all concerned, their husbands, and Grubs partners were not just looking for lost boys, they were going to rescue captured ones from some unknown warriors.

Raven Wing stopped talking as she was telling them what she had seen once again. Sun Flower watched her sister as Raven Wing stared into the flames of the fire. Grub was about to say something, but Sun Flower raised her hand for silence. A moment later, Raven Wing looked up with a very concerned look, as she said, "They are Ute, they are chasing Ute warriors."

Everyone but Growling Bear was stunned by hearing this. He had never been around Utes before. To him it meant nothing. Shining Star said, "Slavers, they must be chasing slavers." Growling Bear then asked, "Are you saying, Brave Fox, Little Bull, and Grey Deer have been taken as slaves?" It was Raven Wing that answered, "I saw only one young warrior, huddled with a girl against a tree. I do not know if there are other captives, and I do not know where they are." Once again Shining Star spoke, "Taos, they trade slaves to the Spanish for horses, guns, iron knives and other things they can only get from the Spanish."

Grub then spoke, "Then there is gonna be a fight." Shining Star nodded, and said, "No warrior will give up their slaves without one." Growling Bear then said, "I must find them, I must go and help." Grub put his hand on Growling Bear shoulder, and said, "I know just how you feel, but there just ain't no way to ever find 'em, but even if there was, they asked us to stay behind and protect their families, and believe me Grizzly Killer figures that is more important than fighting by his side."

*****

Red Eagle was still ten miles from his grazing horses as Jimbo came out of the stand of aspen and headed right for Thunder. The spotted stallion stopped pacing and watched Jimbo coming to him. Thunder nickered and threw his head up and down, then trotted forward as Jimbo got there. They touched noses, greeting one another, then Thunder left him standing there and herded his dozen stolen horses further north. Jimbo stood there and watched them go. A couple of them did not want to leave the plush grass they were grazing on but did not challenge Thunder as he push them ahead.

Jimbo sensed danger was coming. He instinctively looked to the south, then back to the north, where he knew Zach would be following his trail. He sat down, where Thunder had been, and watched as the stallion pushed the horses out of sight. He was torn whether to wait for Zach and Ol' Red, or head south to meet an unknown danger. His instinct to protect was strong, he headed south to where his instincts drove him. He would face whatever danger was there, knowing Zach and the others would be coming this way.

He ran for another five miles to the south, through meadows of tall grass along the crystal-clear waters of the creek. He bounded across the ancient lava flows, not taking the time to go around them as the horses had to do. For nearly seven miles he ran along the creek, when suddenly the scent of strange men and horses caught his attention. He stopped, testing the air with his nose. The breeze was almost imperceptible, but what there was, was blowing the scent of these strangers up the creek to him. He sensed danger, much stronger now, and the hair down the center of his back started to rise. The soft low rumble of a growl started deep in his chest, and with all off his senses on alert he jumped the creek to the other side and started back to the south. This time he was moving at a very deliberate walk.

Five minutes later he saw the riders coming at him. He dropped down in the grass. A herd of a dozen deer scattered from along the creek as the riders approached, but Jimbo's eyes were focused on only the riders. He knew his job was too slow these riders down. Until Zach and the others caught up with him.

He waited, motionless as they got closer, hidden in the tall dry grass he was on the opposite side of the creek from the riders, They were coming at an easy lope, thinking only about recovering their escaped horses. The warrior that had raped and killed the little girl was riding along next to Red Eagle, only closer to the creek. He was the closest to where Jimbo lay motionless in the grass.

Every muscle in the big dog was tense. He inched closer to the creek bank as they got closer. His instincts alone told these were the men he had been following. He moved his paws back and forth, making sure he had good traction. At five yards he attacked. He cleared the creek in one bound and with one more jump he was in the air. The attack was so swift the horses did not have time to react before the two hundred pound dog, with a loud, vicious growl went for the throat of that closest warrior.

The sudden attack of the two hundred pound dog sent all of their horses into a panic. The warrior raised his arm against the attack and Jimbo's powerful jaws clamped down, tearing muscle and breaking bone. His weight threw the warrior off his horse and into Red Eagle, who went off the far side of his horse as well. Jimbo didn't stop, there he bit another horse on the hamstring and which sent it into a bucking fit, throwing its rider as well. Although the other riders stayed mounted, their horses were in a panicked run, away from the vicious attack.

Red Eagle had landed hard, breaking his bow and scattering the arrows from his quiver. The thrown warrior was gasping for air, having the wind knocked from his lungs when he hit the ground. Jimbo, with a few barks to keep them going, herded the three loose horses to the north, following Thunder's trail.

Disgusted, Red Eagle threw his broken bow to the

ground and watched his horse and the other two, running hard to the north, trying to stay in front of the big dog. He watched until they were out of sight. Then turned to his severely wounded friend. He could see at once the warrior's arm was ruined. It would be a very long time before he would be able to use the arm, if he ever could.

Jimbo pushed the three horses, following Thunder and the other horses for another six or seven miles to where the trail led down into a rugged canyon. They had slipped and slid down a very steep slope, to a large shelf, across it and down another steep step to a wide flat clearing. A herd of elk scattered through the aspen at the far end of the clearing as Jimbo pushed the horses into the sage and grass covered meadow. Thunder trotted out of the aspens on the west side. He had found a long pond in the trees. It was ten to twenty yards wide and nearly a hundred yards long. It was a place with plenty of grass nearby and water with natural barriers to hold the horses.

The three horses running from Jimbo ran across the flat to Thunder and into the trees. Nervously stopping only when they reached the other dozen horses. Thunder reared up and whinnied, throwing his head up and down as Jimbo barked once, then turned and started back out of the canyon.

*****

Zach let Ely take the lead as they followed the trail up the steep ridge to the south. He could see Coyote Talker was frustrated. It was taking much too long to catch Red Eagle and free his brother. He knew the quick-tempered young warrior was worried about his younger brother and felt responsible for him. After he had lost control in the canyon of the old Spanish trail and they had tied him down, he had been much more reasonable and had his emotions better under control. At least from the outside, Zach thought.

They climbed higher up the steep ridge, through large stands of golden aspen and skirting thick pine where the deadfall was so thick the horses couldn't get through. The canyon to the east dropped off to the north. It was steep, very deep, and over a mile across. A barren peak lay to the south, Zach knew it was well above the timberline.

They crossed a particularly steep side hill and Ely pointed to a track and shouted back to Zach as he kept riding, "Looks like that big dog of yours come this way. Ain't no wolf with a paw that big."

It was nearly midday when they crested the very top of the pass. From there they could see this high mountain pass dropped off to a wide and mostly open valley that ran for miles to the south.

Zach called up for Ely to stop, and they rode up to the oldest of them all. Ely looked at the troubled look on Zach's face and asked, "What is it Grizzly Killer?" Zach stared at the trail ahead. Then finally shook his head, and said, "Don't know if it's anything, but something just don't feel right. I figure this is a good spot to noon. Give the horses a break after that climb. Me and Ol' Red will ride on ahead just to make sure we ain't riding into an ambush of some kind."

He then turned to Running Wolf and asked, "You feel like coming along Running Wolf?" With big smile his partner said, "Thought you wasn't going to ask." Buffalo Heart and Benny both volunteered to go along but Zach said, "I figure two of us can stay hidden but four would be twice as hard. No, let your horses rest, Running Wolf and I won't be more than a couple of hours. Just want to make sure it's clear for the next few miles."

*****

Red Eagle didn't know whether to continue after their horses or not. He had never experienced anything like what had just happened to them. He could tell the large gray dog was indeed a dog, maybe with some wolf in him, but why would a dog drive their horses away? Was it that dog that chewed through their picket rope and chased away their horses in the night?

What he did know, was they were down to just five horses, and they could not get their captives to Nuevo Mexico with only five mounts. Should they try to recover their horses or move south to the Piute village of Broken Lance? What did they have to trade Broken Lance for more horses? All they had were their captives. No, he decided, they would have to steal the horses they needed from the Piute Chief.

Red Eagle looked at the wounded warrior. He was angry he had gotten wounded and even angrier that he had made him lose his own mount. With disgust he said, "We will not wait for you." He then stopped short and looked back at where the big gray dog and horses had disappeared out of sight. He was quiet for a minute then said, "A dog would not attack us and drive the horses off on his own. No, someone is back there, someone has been following us. We will find a place in the pines and wait to ambush them. They will have horses and supplies that we will take."

Chapter 16

Ambushed

Zach and Running Wolf rode on ahead. Neither had any idea what lay before them. Zach knew Jimbo and Thunder were out there somewhere, but he had no idea where either of them had gone.

He had a feeling there was danger close at hand. He couldn't really explain what he felt, even to himself, so he didn't try. He just reacted to that feeling the only way he knew how, with caution. If nothing was there, he may feel a little foolish, but that was better than he or any of his friends going under.

They stayed just inside the tree line along the eastern side of the high mountain valley. As they looked to the west, they could see for many, many miles, all the way across the broad valley of the river they had followed south from the Sahpeech village. They could see the dark red cliffs on the face of the mountains on the west side of that huge valley. Looking down across it looked like this high ridge they were on was the top of the world.

Zach had felt like that many times as he rode the ridges in the Uintah Mountains above Blacks Fork. He was starting to understand Ely's belief that this land of the Utes was all mountains. He was sure they had traveled more than two hundred miles and had never been out of the mountains yet, and there were mountains for as far as he could see in every direction.

The stand of pines they were in ended, and before riding into the open, he stopped to study the land before them. Running Wolf didn't question Zach's feelings. Too many times in the nearly ten years they had been partners, Grizzly Killer had been right. Running Wolf believed deeply if Zach had a feeling that something was out there, there was something out there.

Before moving on, Zach thought about Jimbo once again. He wasn't really angry with the dog for leaving, but he sure wished he was with them now. He trusted Jimbo's senses and nose to find danger much more than he did his own feelings.

The tree line turned to the east, but the tracks that Red Eagle and his warriors had left a little over a day ago led straight down through the center of the valley. Zach would not follow the tracks, he pointed to the east along the tree line. They rode on, staying out of sight just inside the edge of the timber.

Out in the center of the valley, there was a stand of pines. Zach could see the path of a tiny little creek running from the peak to the east to that stand of pines. There were willows and a few colorful aspen growing along its course before it disappeared into the pines. To the northwest, another deep canyon cut its way out of the mountains to the vast valley below.

They continued in the trees until they reached the tiny

creek. This time of year, it wasn't more than a trickle of water coming out of a few small seeps on the western slope of the peak just above them. Zach had been watching that stand of pines intently. There was something about that place he didn't like. It looked like any other stand of pines on the mountains. But all of his senses told him something was there and danger was close at hand.

He had faced a grizzly in the trail just days ago, so he was well aware danger could take many forms in this unforgiving wilderness. He thought he should avoid that stand of pines, but he had to know. He wasn't going to lead the others through this valley without knowing where the feeling of danger was coming from.

He stepped off Ol' Red and Running Wolf slid off his pinto gelding. They left their mounts a mile east of the pines and slowly started down the trickle of water on foot.

As they got closer all of their senses were tuned into what lay ahead of them. Zach noticed he could not hear the birds, squirrels, and chipmunks that they had been hearing all morning. He believed something was in the timber ahead, but right now he had no idea what it was.

A bear, a cougar, something even more dangerous, a warrior. He knew any of those could be there. He wished his dog was with them once again. He slowly knelt down and checked the powder in the pan of his rifle. Running Wolf did the same.

The willows had become quite thick, and neither of them could see more than a few yards ahead. They watched and listened for any movement or sound before them. Zach took another step, carefully placing his moccasin covered foot so as not to make a sound but as he did, a pair of pine hens burst into the air, shattering the silence and letting anyone close by know something was in those willows.

A moment later an arrow streaked from seemingly thin

air and found its mark in Running Wolf's left arm. He hit the ground and Zach dove off to the side. Neither of them had seen where the arrow had come from, only the general direction. The wound was painful, but not serious. Unable to move without giving away their position, Zach watched his partner break the arrow shaft off, leaving the sharp chipped stone point and two inches of the shaft in his upper arm.

Concerned, but knowing he could do nothing to help Running Wolf right then, and staying on the ground, he crawled silently, inching away from the creek.

Running Wolf, with his teeth clenched together from the pain, removed his elk hide jacket. Each time the leather hit the arrow shaft, another lightning bolt of pain shot through his arm. He was pale by the time he got the jacket off, and felt blood dripping off his elbow, but knew he didn't have time to dress the wound right then. He laid the jacket over a willow branch then just as Zach had done, slowly and silently moved just a few yards away. There he waited, sure the warrior that shot that arrow would come forward to take his scalp.

Zach was working his way closer to the pines, staying along the outside edge of the willows. He had not heard any sound since the sound of the arrow striking Running Wolf or seen any movement. Zach figured it had been ten or fifteen minutes since the arrow struck Running Wolf, but it seemed like that many hours. When suddenly the thundering boom of his partner's rifle shattered the stillness. The smoke had not had time to clear above the willows when a vicious growl and muffled scream came from inside the pines less than seventy-five yards from Zach.

Zach recognized the sound of Jimbo's attack instantly. He believed there were at least two warriors that would not be leaving this stand of pines and wondered how many more Red Eagle had left to ambush them. He had no doubt that was what had happened. He had no way of knowing that between his dog and the spotted stallion, Red Eagle was now down to only five horses. With a dozen men and eight captives, they would not be moving very fast any time soon.

Less than a minute after all was quiet once again, Jimbo silently appeared at Zach's side. Blood was smeared across his face and chest. Zach couldn't help but form a smile, he was so glad to see his big dog.

Zach moved his hand in a half circle and brought it back to his chest, then closed his fist and moved it toward the ground. Jimbo didn't hesitate, and he ran off, skirting the willows and pines. The hand signal had told Jimbo to circle half-way around the pines and then work his way through them and kill any enemy he found.

Less than five minutes passed by and another vicious growl shattered the midday calm within the pines. Only a couple of minutes after that, Zach heard horses running hard to the south.

Zach didn't move, he waited for Jimbo to let him know all was clear. When Jimbo came running through the willows wagging his tail. He knew the remaining warriors had left. He rushed to Running Wolf, worried about how bad his partner, friend, and brother-in-law was hurt. He almost stumbled over the dead Ute warrior Running Wolf had shot. Hesitating only a moment, he saw the ball from Running Wolf rifle had struck the warrior in the center of his chest.

When Zach reached him a moment later, Running Wolf was tying a long piece of tanned antelope hide they carried for just that purpose, around the arrow wound. Zach stopped him and said, "We best get that thing out of your arm pard, then wrap it up right."

Zach could see by the amount of blood on the ground the wound had bled a lot. Running Wolf was pale, and he was worried about him losing more blood when the arrow point came out. With Running Wolf already sitting on the ground, Zach took the soft antelope bandage strip and tied it as tight as he could just above the arrow, then asked, "Is it stuck into bone?" Running Wolf nodded, saying, "Feels like it, it is painful." Zach just nodded his agreement.

Zach took his partner's arm and looked into his eyes. He remembered just like it was yesterday, setting Running Wolf's broken leg all those years ago. He remembered Running Wolf's stoic strength, how he never made a sound even though the pain had been tremendous. Zach cut off the blood-soaked sleeve of his buckskin shirt, then rested his arm on his own knee. He asked, "You want a stick to bite down on?" Running Wolf took a deep breath and shook his head.

Zach took a firm grip on the broken wooden shaft and said, "Try to relax, I'll count to three." Running Wolf closed his eye and Zach felt the muscles in his arm relax. Without a count or any warning, he pulled the broken arrow from the wound. Blood oozed from the inch-long hole as Running Wolf jumped from the shock and pain. Zach wrapped the wound tightly, so tight it was stopping the blood flow to his hand. They both knew they could loosen it as soon as the bleeding stopped.

Jimbo had been watching. When they were finished, he came up and licked Running Wolf's face. Running Wolf forced a smile and asked, "Where have you been Jimbo?" Jimbo tilted his head to the side just as Zach said, "We have a problem." He then held up the arrow head. The last half inch of the stone tip was missing. Running Wolf did not need to be told. He knew the tip of the stone point was stuck into the bone of his left arm. He could feel it under the bandage but said, "It will have to stay in there until we get back to Raven Wing." Zach looked at the bandaged wound, then into his partner's eyes, and asked, "You sure? It might get feverish and be mighty painful." Running Wolf hesitated for a moment before answering, "We don't have time, we are close to them now, I will wait here while you ride back and get the others."

Zach thought for only a moment then said, "I can have the tip of arrow-head out of there before Jimbo gets back here with the guys." Before Running Wolf could respond, Zach turned and told Jimbo, "Get Buffalo Heart big feller." Jimbo was already taking ten yards bounds, running to the north by the time Zach turned back to his partner.

He and Running Wolf both knew what had to be done. As bad as Running Wolf dreaded it, he knew the wound would fester and he would likely become feverish if the stone tip wasn't removed. It still might, even if Zach got it all out. He wished his wife was there, he knew her healing plants would keep the wound from getting angry and hot.

Zach opened up his possibles bag and removed a small stick with sinew rolled up around it and a large leather sewing needle. Along with all the strips of soft tanned antelope hide they carried for bandages. Running Wolf had watched wounds get sewn together on Zach several times and on others as well, but he had never experienced just how unpleasant pushing a needle through a fresh wound could be.

Running Wolf was already leaning against an aspen and had the wounded arm resting on his knee. Zach tied a tourniquet about three inches above the wound and took a couple of twists of the stick, then asked, "You figure you can keep this tight enough to slow up the bleeding?" Running Wolf nodded. He too remembered the day he had met his partner. As painful as that day had been, it had completely changed his life and the life of his sister. He remembered how hard it had been to show no pain as Grizzly Killer set his broken leg. It was partly his own pride and partly fear of this unknown white man that had made him strong enough to endure without making a sound. Today was different. He knew he did not need to prove his bravery to his partner. The only fear he felt right then was for the pain he knew he was going to feel.

Zach could see the uncertainty in his eyes and said, "You know it has to come out of there, Running Wolf." As Running Wolf nodded Zach said, "I'll be as careful as I can."

"Just get it over with as quick as you can, we're going to have to ride as soon as the others get here," he responded.

Running Wolf laid his head back against the tree and closed his eyes. He pictured Raven Wing coming toward him, but the image was shattered and his eyes opened wide as the tip of Zach's knife found the tip of the arrow head firmly lodged in the bone. He could see blood on Zach's hand and tightened the tourniquet even more. He clinched his teeth together as hard as he could and wished he would have taken the stick Zach offered to put between them. The pain was nearly unbearable when suddenly the stone tip broke free of the bone. He wasn't sure whether he heard or just felt the pop as the arrow-head broke free, but the awful pressure was gone.

Once Zach had the bloody point in his fingers, he examined it closely making sure another piece had not broken off. He then took the sinew and needle and put five stitches in the now jagged cut. As Running Wolf released some pressure from the tourniquet that was now nearly as painful as the extraction had been, blood started to seep from around each stitch. Zach wrapped his widest bandage strip around the closed wound and tied it tight. That stopped the oozing blood.

Running Wolf tried to flex the muscles in his arm, but the pain stopped him. He then made a fist, but once again the pain in his arm stopped him from tightening his knuckles.

They had left their water pouches on their saddles, and Zach knew Running Wolf must drink a lot of water over the next several days to help his body replace the blood he had lost. "Running Wolf, lay back and relax while I go up and fetch Ol' Red and your pinto," Zach told him. Running Wolf just nodded Zach could see in his eyes he did not feel like doing anything else.

Zach knew it would not take Jimbo long to reach Buffalo Heart, Ely, and the others. He figured they were only about five miles from them. It was Coyote Talker that first saw the big dog running toward them along the tree line. He called to the others and Jimbo stopped and backed twice, then ran right to Buffalo Heart. Buffalo Heart saw the blood that was just starting to dry on his chin and face. Now concerned, they were all rushing to get mounted up and find out if Zach and Running Wolf were alright.

Buffalo Heart now was out in front of all of them, trying to keep up with Jimbo. The powerful long-legged dog had no trouble staying out in front of the horses. They were nearly two miles in the open as Jimbo led them to the stand of pines that stood at the head of the large canyon dropping off to the northwest.

While still a half mile out Zach stepped from the willows on the eastern edge of the pines. As they rode up, he could see the worried look on all off their faces. It wasn't until then he realized Jimbo's face was still covered with blood, he said, loud enough for all of them to hear, "We are alright. Running Wolf took an arrow in his right arm and has lost a lot of blood, but he will be fine. They have about a half hour lead on us now."

Just then Running Wolf came out behind Zach and Buffalo Heart jumped down and rushed to his partner. He remembered well the Cheyenne arrow that had killed Red Hawk. He didn't believe he could stand losing another close friend.

Zach said, "Don't know how many of them rode out, but several did. Running Wolf killed one, and I think you will find two more that Jimbo killed in the pines. I never did see anyone."

Benny and Coyote Talker rode into the pines, and a few minutes later they were back. Coyote Talker had taken the two scalps. Benny said, "One of them had a fresh bandage on his arm, looks like he had tangled with a wolf or something in the night." They all looked at Jimbo and Benny just nodded and added, "Or a Jimbo."

Chapter 17

Hell on the Horizon

Raven Wing had been quiet all morning, she had a feeling her husband was in danger. She had not had another dream, it was just something she felt deep inside, and she was concerned. They could all tell something was bothering her. She was quiet again today, and Sun Flower noticed she did not eat any of the mutton that had been roasting all morning when the rest of them ate at midday.

Luna had taken up her vigilance at the spot just across the stream that she seemed to prefer, starring south as she had been doing for a couple of days now.

Raven Wing was standing between the fire and river, looking out across the big meadow, when Luna yelped and jumped to her feet. Raven Wing watched their white wolf and said, "What is it girl, did a bee sting you." But she didn't believe that, she believed something had just happened to Running Wolf.

Luna bounded across the stream to her side and as she

put her hand on the wolf's head to rub her ears, she saw her husband through a cloudy haze. He was on the ground, leaning against a tree, and there was blood everywhere. Her knees buckled, and she went to the ground beside Luna. The wolf licked her face and whined. Sun Flower was the first to get to her, although the others, even Growling Bear, were right behind her. Raven Wing looked up and Sun Flower saw the tears streaking down her checks.

It took several minutes for Raven Wing to compose herself and tell them what had happened. Star ran and hugged her, and as she did the little girl whispered, "Uncle Running Wolf will be alright. Papa and Jimbo helped him."

*****

They could all see Running Wolf was pale and a bit unstable on his feet, even though he insisted he was fine. Ely walked into the pines to study the tracks and see how many warriors had been there.

He wasn't gone long and when he came back, he had a puzzled look on the face. He shook his head and said, "Ain't but five horses rode out a here, and each one of 'em had a rider. You can plainly see where the five of 'em mounted up. So where's these dead ones horses? And, I figure they was a waiting to ambush us, not just watching their back trail, or there wouldn't have been so many of 'em. I figure you two surprised the hell out of 'em, by not following their tracks."

Zach thought for a minute, then asked no one in particular, "Where are the other horses?" None of them believed they would have stayed behind on foot. He looked at Jimbo and asked, "You know anything about this big feller?" Jimbo looked up at him and wagged his tail. Zach had no way of knowing, but he figured Jimbo knew more about it than the rest of them.

Buffalo Heart slid Running Wolf's rifle into its scabbard on the side of the saddle, then helped Running Wolf up. He was light-headed from the loss of blood and his left arm was nearly useless, but he was determined to go on while the trail was this fresh.

Coyote Talker offered to take the scalp of the warrior Running Wolf had killed for him and didn't understand when Running Wolf said, "If you want the scalp Coyote Talker, it is yours, I do not want it."

Coyote Talker had nearly given up trying to understand these men and wondered. *Why would Running Wolf not want the scalp of an enemy he killed in battle?* He took the scalp. He wanted these scalps for his brother, and to show White Crow, Yellow Horse, and Growling Bear they had taken their revenge on the warriors that had taken Brave Fox.

As they started out from that stand of pines Zach hesitated as he looked to the distant southern horizon, they all knew something was on his mind. Ely quietly asked, "What is it Pard, what you seeing out there." Zach shook his head and said, "Nothing really, just hoping we don't find the hell on that horizon I am afraid we're going to." Ely got a grim look on his face as he looked south and slowly nodded his agreement.

As they rode south from the stand of pines. Buffalo Heart rode on one side of Running Wolf and as Benny headed for the other, Coyote Talker beat him there. Although still not understanding the reasons these men were helping him. The young Bannock warrior had gained a great respect for them all. Now, Running Wolf, a Ute, had killed one of his own people and been wounded to help save his brother, whom he had never met. He would always be grateful, and he would do everything he could to ensure Running Wolf stayed safe.

Running Wolf insisted he was alright, but Benny and Coyote Talker both stayed close enough to catch him if he lost his balance.

It wasn't long before Ely stopped and held up his hand for the others to stay back. They all watched as Ely studied the ground before them. Five minutes later he burst out laughing right out loud. He motioned the others to come up to him and as they did. He said, "You sure was right Grizzly Killer, that there dog of yours knows more about them there missing horses than you think. He stole 'em, right while they was riding 'em. Lookie here, you can see where Jimbo attacked 'em. Looks like their horses scattered and three of 'em bastards, hit the ground. Then, after chewing one of them there warriors up pretty bad, that there big dog herded the three horses off to the north. What I can't figure out is there is another dozen or so tracks going north and it looks like Jimbo was leading these three horses along that same trail." Zach got down and studied the ground as Ely spoke and pointed. He saw the blood where Jimbo had attacked one of them. Just the size of Jimbo's track told them it was him but a missing toe on his right front paw from fighting a badger when he was young removed any doubt anyone might have.

Ely looked to the north. Where were those tracks going? Did they have more warriors now behind them? Ely looked at the tracks going north and the ones going south side by side, and said, "Don't figure them there horses heading back to the north had riders on their backs. They is a running different from the ones with riders going south. Seems like a strange place to keep horses but maybe they be a village up ahead and somebody spooked some of their horses."

At that Running Wolf said, "I don't think so Ely, it is too late in the year for a village to be up this high. Maybe a party of hunters, but not a village." Ely nodded his agreement, then said, "We best be mighty alert going forward, 'til we know what we is up against." At that, everyone nodded.

They rode south, still curious about the tracks going north. Now the tracks were trampled over with the eight horses running north over the track of Thunder's stolen horses and now five running back south. Ely had finally given up trying to figure out what had happened. He knew now they must all concentrate on what lay ahead.

They passed more ancient lava flows, and the valley started to narrow, and head down through a small canyon. There it ran into another stream, this one larger. It turned to the east, heading down yet another canyon, but the tracks lead up stream. They rode past a steep pointed knoll several hundred feet high just west of the stream and found where Red Eagle and his men had camped.

Ely was a hundred yards in front of the rest, Buffalo Heart still worried about Running Wolf, had not left his side and neither had Coyote Talker. They all watched Ely stop when he reached the top of a sage and grass covered rise and standup in his saddle. A moment later he sat back down and waved the others to him. Red Eagle and his warriors had camped here. Zach, nor any of them moved as Ely stepped off his horse and studied the ground to learn whatever the tracks might tell him.

As he looked around, he found where the horses had been picketed, and where many of them had broken the picket and ran back to the north. Now Ely was methodical as he studied the tracks. What would have spooked the horses? He found the piece of the rawhide rope still tied around one end of a tree. He could plainly see the rope had been gnawed through. He stopped and looked at Jimbo, but he didn't believe the horse would have stayed calm enough with the big dog that close to them. Then he found the fresh tracks leading to the south. These tracks were only an hour or two old.

Ely had no idea what had happened, but he now knew most of the warriors they were chasing and all of their captives were on foot. The only horses they had were the five that had left the ambush site of Running Wolf and Zach.

He walked out around one more time, making sure he didn't miss anything when he stopped. Zach and others were still watching him, Coyote Talker still hoped that one day he would be able to read tracks as good as this old white trapper. Zach watched close and Ely knelt down and reverently picked up the naked body of a little girl. There was blood between her legs, and dark bruises around her neck where she had been strangled.

Zach could see both anger and sadness on Ely's face. Zach jumped off Ol' Red and ran to him. This was an innocent child that had been brutalized by these men. Zach offered to take her from Ely but with a shaky voice, Ely said, "I got her Grizzly Killer, just get a grave dug."

The volcanic rock right there made scrapping out a suitable grave impossible. Not knowing what lie ahead, they rode back nearly a mile before finding a place to bury the child. They all knew the type of men they were chasing, but this brutality upset them all.

Coyote Talker watched Grizzly Killer's eyes change from warm blue to an ice-cold gray. The determination to make these men pay for this unforgiveable act now showed on his dark tanned brow. A chill ran down the back of Coyote Talker and he was mighty glad, this blue-eyed trapper wasn't after him.

After the girl was buried, they moved on. Two or three more miles and they saw a large lake spread out before them. It looked to be nearly round, with tall dry grasses on the south, west, and north, but on the east the pine-covered ridge dropped right to the water's edge.

They studied the shore-line carefully around the lake and after seeing no sign of Red Eagle or his renegades they moved on, following the tracks around the west side of the lake. The tracks were now of only five horses and well over a dozen men, women, and children on foot. They all knew they would catch these renegades soon.

A ridge came off the high, flat-topped mountain on the west. It came out into the valley and from where they were riding, it looked to be what had formed the south shore of the lake. As they rode around that ridge, they were all shocked at the view before them. A very large lake filled the entire valley. It looked to be a mile wide, and Zach figured at least five or six miles to the far southern end. Timber came to the water's edge on both the east and west sides. They could see now the first lake and this big lake were connected along the eastern shoreline.

Although he had never been here, Running Wolf and heard stories of a large lake, high in the mountains, and far to the south of his home, where both Ute and Piute villages would come to fish in the summers. He wondered if this was that lake, he had heard it called Fish Lake.

They stopped and dismounted. This was a spectacularly beautiful place. Some of the aspen along the west side of the lake had dropped their leaves, but there were still large stands of golden aspen standing out among the dark green pines.

With the timber reaching the lake shore along this western side where the trail was leading them, they could not see into the trees for any sign that Red Eagle may be somewhere along the lake. Ely led his horse back to the others and said, "Don't figure we best move forward like we been doing. This here be a mighty fine place to camp or set up another ambush. Wouldn't take many warriors to block our path forward, with the lake on one side and the mountain on the other. No sir, I figure we best check this here lake shore out mighty careful. Don't want nobody else catching one of them there arrows."

Coyote Talker and Buffalo Heart helped Running Wolf from the saddle. He was exhausted, and after setting down he laid back and closed his eyes. Coyote Talker then went forward and said, "Grizzly Killer, I would like to go forward to check the shoreline ahead." Zach looked at him, Coyote Talker knew none of them really trusted him to keep a level head if they found the enemy or his brother. He looked down at the ground, ashamed of his actions of a few days ago.

Zach didn't say anything, acting as if he hadn't even heard him. He turned to Ely and asked, "You figure we ought to do like before, and sneak through the timber on foot." Ely looked ahead for a moment and nodded, "Ya, I figure that is the only way we is gonna know for sure if it's safe to go on." Zach nodded and turned back to the others and said, "Buffalo Heart," at hearing that name, Coyote Talker's body went tense. He knew Grizzly Killer didn't trust him to stay calm and rational, and now he wanted Buffalo Heart to go with him. He was doing his best to control his disappointment and anger, but his whole body was starting to shake when Grizzly Killer continued, "Buffalo Heart, you stay with Running Wolf, and get him drinking as much water as he can hold. Ely, will take a perch up the hill a little higher and keep a close watch in all directions, I still ain't sure what those tracks going back to the north means." Ely nodded as Zach continued, "I'll take

Benny and Coyote Talker and go have us a look ahead."

Coyote Talker jerked his head up, surprised at Grizzly Killer's words and that any of these men trusted him after the way he had acted just a few days before. He swore to himself that he would not let them down again.

Just as Zach, Benny, and Coyote Talker were leaving, Ely put his hand on Coyote Talkers shoulder and leaned forward and quietly said, "Remember son, trust and respect ain't gifts, they must be earned." He then smiled and nodded at the volatile young warrior and started up the hill to find a place where he could see in all directions.

Chapter 18

A Long Way Home

Raven Wing held on to her niece for a couple of minutes longer, even though neither of them spoke. She had heard Star's words, but she could not get the vision of her husband with blood all over him from her mind. As she finally released Star, Gray Wolf ran to her. He too had tears in his eyes. He had never seen his mother that upset before, and it scared him. She held him as tight as she had Star, rocking back and forth on her knees. Sun Flower knelt in front of her and as their eyes met, Sun Flower could see the fear her sister felt.

Sun Flower was more worried now. She had never seen fear in the eyes of her older sister before. Not even when the Cheyenne had taken the two of them, Raven Wing never showed any fear. Even though Sun Flower knew the fear was for Running Wolf, she knew their husbands were together, and that meant they were all in danger.

Raven Wing released Gray Wolf and through tear-swollen eyes looked at Sun Flower and said, "I need to go to my husband, he needs me, but I do not know where he is".

Raven Wing's words and actions had all of the women upset. Even Grub and Growling Bear now believed their friends were facing a very real threat. After a couple of minutes of silence Grub, acting as jovial as he could, said, "Well now girls, I been in these here mountains as long as some of you has been alive, and I ain't never seen nobody as good of a fighter as Grizzly Killer, or nobody as good at smelling trouble as Ely. No Siree, them there boys is gonna be just fine, you all will see, every one of 'em is gonna come riding back here in a few more days."

Grub's optimism and jovial attitude put a smile on most of their faces. In Raven Wing's mind, she could still see her husband on the ground, hurt, and bleeding. Although she had heard Grub's words and knew they were true, she could not shake the feeling that she needed to be at Running Wolf's side, and she wasn't. She did not even know where he was, and that upset her even more.

Although Growling Bear's head still ached much of the time, and Raven Wing's bitter tea was welcome each time she prepared it, his vision had cleared and it had been a couple of days since he'd had a dizzy spell. The back of his head was still mighty tender, and he believed it would be for a long time yet.

Spending the time he had with these women, and Grub had changed his way of thinking a lot. He no longer felt any resentment toward Little Dove, he understood why she had hit him. He admired these women. They were not afraid to fight to protect one another, or their families. They believed very deeply in the powers of their medicine woman and the little girl with the sky-blue eyes. He believed it was Raven Wing and her medicine that had saved him. Yes, he knew these were extraordinary women and believed their husbands must be as well to keep these exceptional women as loyal to them as they were.

Growling Bear knew he could not stay here, his own village needed meat, White Crow's was only one of four hunting parties that had left their Bannock village on the banks of the great river the white men call the Snake. He knew they were many days of hard travel from home. And even if White Crow and the others freed the boys, it would take many days for them to return. They had already been gone for too many suns. Growling Bear felt he had to leave and return home. He felt a grave responsibility, not only to bring in the meat the village desperately needed, but to let them know what had happened. He had no way of knowing White Crow, Yellow Horse, Gray Deer a Little Bull were already well north of the great lake of salt and another day would find them back to their homes. They had found game along the river they had followed, and each of them was leading a pack horse laden with meat.

Growling Bear was quiet throughout the afternoon as he contemplated making the trip home by himself. He knew his friends would come here for him before they go back to their village on the Snake River, and he was torn as to what to do.

The next morning, he waited until Raven Wing was up and moving. He wanted to know if she'd had another dream. If she knew what the status of White Crow, Yellow Horse, and Coyote Talker were. She said nothing as they ate their biscuits and coffee. When they finished, Growling Bear told them he was leaving and the reasons why. Each of them understood and slowly nodded. But in the short time he had been there he had become a friend, and they hated to see him travel that far alone.

Raven Wing prepared enough of the ground up willow and aspen bark for him to make tea for the next few days and gave him a tin cup to brew it in. The others prepared a food pouch, with dried mutton, elk, deer, and pemmican, enough for at least a week. Grub went out and brought in his horse and helped him put his simple blanket saddle on it.

When he was ready to leave, he turned to Raven Wing and smiled and then to Little Dove. He stepped toward her and said, "You are the bravest woman I have ever met, Little Dove, you did not think of yourself, when I grabbed Raven Wing, you only thought of protecting your friends."

He then turned and mounted up, Little Dove handed him his bow that he put over his back. He then headed across the big meadow. It was a long and dangerous trip, and he knew he must stay alert every foot of the way, and it was a long way home.

*****

Ely found a large rock only a long rifle shot above where Buffalo Heart was caring for Running Wolf. Even though Running Wolf was still insisting he was fine, he felt weak and was glad for the break. There was a flat area along the north side of this ridge where they could camp tonight, Buffalo Heart led the horses while Running Wolf slowly followed along. Even though the walk was only a hundred yards, Running Wolf was exhausted when he sat down on the blanket of Aspen leaves.

Ely sat at the base of the rock so his silhouette could not be seen. From there he had a great view of the big lake to the south and their back trail looking back to the north. He watched Zach, Jimbo, Benny, and Coyote Talker disappear into the trees only a few hundred yards to the south. He didn't believe he would see them again until they returned. He knew they were on a very dangerous scout, but Grizzly Killer was the most capable warrior he had ever met. He wished he could be more help, but all he could see along the lake shore for many miles was a mixture of aspen and pine.

As he watched, the beauty of this area brought a smile to his beard covered face. The blue sky was dotted with white puffy clouds, the lake a deep, dark blue, telling of the depth of its crystal-clear water. The mountains were covered with dark green timber and large stands of golden aspen. Ely looked again at where Zach and the others had gone and thought, *"This here is too purty of a place for a bunch of killing."*

Zach had been gone for about thirty minutes and Ely figured the sun would be down in just a couple of hours. He wondered if he would see them again before dark.

Zach knew they couldn't check out the shoreline all the way to the south end of the lake before dark. The lake was just too big, but he hoped they could get half-way there. He knew if Red Eagle and his renegades had really lost all but five of their horses, their first priority would be to get others. Where would he find other horses? He then thought, *"The closest horses to Red Eagle were their own."* A sudden panic shot through him and he instinctively looked behind him but all he could see was timber. He wondered. *Should I run back and help Buffalo Heart and Ely protect our horses and have Benny and Coyote Talker continue checking the area ahead?*

He raised his hand to his lips and chattered like a squirrel, two other squirrels answered back, and a few moments later Benny and Coyote Talker appeared from the timber above him. Zach told them his concern.

All three men were torn between going forward, for they all knew they were getting close, but protecting their own mounts was every bit as important.

Coyote Talker was especially torn. He knew this was the closest he had been to his brother since they had started this search for him. But he knew Grizzly Killer was right, theirs were probably the only horses for days around, and Red Eagle needed horses.

Even though dark was still close to three hours away, the sun had already dropped behind this high flat-topped ridge to the west. It was Benny that said, "If they try to steal our horses, it won't be until after dark. Let's go on for another mile or so, if we don't find where they're camped by then, we'll high tail it back to the others." Zach looked at Coyote Talker and asked, "That sound good to you?" Shocked that Grizzly Killer had asked his opinion, he hesitated and looked both Zach and Benny in the eyes. The longer he was around these white men he could not understand why so many of his own people, even in his own village, were so against them. Grizzly Killer, Benny, and Ely were strong honorable men that he was proud to be riding with, then said, "We could go on, but, if they get our horses, my brother will be lost forever. I think we must protect the horses, before moving on." Benny nodded, and they turned and started to jog back to where they had left the others.

Just before Zach, Benny, and Coyote Talker returned, Buffalo Heart mounted up and rode to the part of the lake that was north of them to fill their water pouches. As much water as Running Wolf had been drinking, he didn't believe the water they had would last.

Ely watched him ride to the water's edge, carefully studying the grass brush and willows before him. Other than a doe with two fawn running from the willows, all was clear. Without the sun shining on the ground, the air was cooling rapidly. When Buffalo Heart got back with the water Running Wolf had started to shiver. The wound in his arm wasn't all that bad, but the amount of blood he lost before they got the bleeding under control was. He was weak and dizzy and as hard as he was trying to resist the cool air, he could not. He felt cold, a cold that seeped deep inside. He needed a fire, Buffalo Heart knew that, but did they dare build one while they were as close as they believed they were to the enemy.

The light was fading fast and when Ely could no longer see the tree line, he made his way down to Buffalo Heart and Running Wolf. Only moments before Ely got there, Zach, Benny, and Coyote Talker returned.

Buffalo Heart had laid Running Wolf's sleeping robe on the ground and then covered him with his own and Grizzly Killers robes. Trying to warm him enough to stop him from shivering. Zach looked at Ely as he knelt down and put his hand on Running Wolf's face. Then looked up at the older trapper and said, "We must have a fire Ely, I sure ain't Raven Wing but I can boil up aspen, and willow bark and it may help him, find us a spot where a fire won't be seen." As Ely disappeared into the now dark aspen forest, he looked at the others and said, "We need some willow branches, but make sure you take them from where they won't be noticed." Coyote Talker and Benny both headed for the lake shore that was only a quarter mile to their north.

Zach had enough aspen bark stripped when Coyote Talker and Benny returned. Jimbo was lying on the buffalo robes next to Running Wolf, keeping them warm, at least on one side. They had just started to strip the bark from the willow branches was when Ely voice came from the dark trees, "I figure I found our spot boys, but it might be a might tough for Running Wolf. There is a big rock outcropping just a quarter mile up the ridge and once we is down in between them there rocks, we can have as big a fire as you want, nobody will see it unless they is right on top of it."

Running Wolf didn't feel like moving, but he knew he must. He felt much worse now than he had all day. He couldn't get warm, even with the extra robes and Jimbo he was still shivering uncontrollably. Zach helped him to his feet, and a wave of dizziness come on strong, his knees buckled. If not for Zach he would have hit the ground.

Zach and Buffalo Heart lifted him up onto Ol' Red and Zach climbed on behind him, the rest just led their horses following Ely through the darkness. It was nearly a half mile to the outcropping of rocks Ely had found. Zach did his best to keep Running Wolf covered with his sleeping robe. As they rode along, Zach looked into the star filled sky and silently prayed. He asked for help in caring for Running Wolf, and for safely returning the captives to their homes. He asked for protection for all off these men in the battle he knew was coming. Ely's voice brought him out of the trance like state he was in, "We is here boys, but it is a tight squeeze to get in there. The horses ain't gonna fit. We is gonna to have to take turns guarding 'em 'til morning"

Before Zach even tried to move, Benny, Buffalo Heart, and Coyote Talker was there to help Running Wolf down. Ely had already disappeared between the rocks, and they all got a whiff of smoke as they helped Running Wolf squeeze through the narrow entrance.

Coyote Talker and Benny set up a picket rope for the horses as the others got Running Wolf situated by the rapidly growing flames of the fire Ely had started. These rocks were like a grotto. After squeezing through the narrow opening it opened up into an area nearly a dozen feet across. The jagged volcanic rocks towered nearly twenty feet above them, and they could see stars in the sky overhead.

Soon the heat from the fire reflecting off the rock walls had raised the temperature inside the grotto enough they were all comfortable. Zach boiled the aspen and willow bark until the liquid was dark brown. He had watched Raven Wing do this many times, but she already had the barks dry and ground into a powder. Zach nor any of the rest of them knew whether the tea would help.

Zach had done the same thing, years before. When he and Running Wolf first met and he had set Running Wolf's broken leg. His partner had developed a fever then, and Zach had boiled aspen bark that seemed to help. Even without the bitterness the bark left in the water, just drinking the hot liquid, and the warmth of the air in the grotto, helped him warm up enough to stop shivering. Not long after that, he was asleep.

They stood watch over the horses in pairs throughout the night. Even though they were well hidden, they were taking no chances.

As always, Zach was on the last watch of the night. Although usually alone, tonight Coyote Talker was with him. The stars were just starting to fade above the ridge on the east side of the lake when Zach sent Jimbo out to scout the area. Coyote Talker watched Zach move his hand in a large circle over his head, and the dog was out of sight in three or four long bounds.

Coyote Talker watched in amazement, although he had been with Grizzly Killer and the great medicine dog now for many suns. He still had no idea how the dog knew what Zach wanted him to do. Quietly, Zach told him the story of finding Jimbo as an abandoned pup after his fight with Shoshone warriors. How Jimbo and Ol' Red had been his only companions through the long, cold winter. He told how he had worked with Jimbo every day, all day for most of that winter. He told Coyote Talker that he knew right off that Jimbo was a special animal. Now after eight years, almost everyone knew just how special Jimbo really was. Coyote Talker nodded his agreement and smiled and said, "It is more than just the dog that is special, my friend." Zach smiled at the compliment, and said, "Coyote Talker, we are all special in our own ways."

Coyote Talker smiled back, but thought as he did, *That may be true, but there isn't anybody else that would have done what you and your friends have done for strangers.*

They could hear the others moving inside the grotto and smell the smoke as they built up the fire. It was light enough to see the edge of the lake when Zach said, "Coyote Talker go inside and eat more bear meat, I will be in as soon as Jimbo gets back."

The others had all eaten, and they still had not seen Zach. Ely pushed his way out of this open topped cavern just in time to see Zach heading southeast toward the spot he had watched from until dark.

Now concerned, he told the others to douse the fire. Soon they all were outside by the horses. Running Wolf was with them. They had put his arm in a sling, and his color was much better and the fever was gone this morning. Buffalo Heart turned to him and said, "You and me best stay with the horses, Running Wolf. Least until we know what Grizzly Killer is looking at." A simple nod from Running Wolf and Buffalo Heart could see the fierce determination in his partner's dark eyes. Buffalo Heart smiled, he had seen that look many times, and he knew now Running Wolf was going to be fine.

Chapter 19

Like a Ghost

Not a lot had changed in Grizzly Killer's small village, other than Growling Bear was no longer there. However, there was a difference, all the women were quiet. Even Grub's perennial smile and jovial attitude was subdued.

They no longer had a guest to care for, and the daily routine, just one day after he had left, somehow seemed trivial and a bit monotonous. Neither Raven Wing nor Star had any more visions or insight into what was happening with the men so far away. Every time Raven Wing closed her eyes, she could see Running Wolf covered with blood and she had remained exceptionally quiet and worried.

Grub left to go hunting about mid-morning. He could feel the tension and worry among the women and needed to be alone for a while.

Like everyone else, Two Flowers could feel the tension in the air. She watched her husband. He was quiet and not like his normal self. She knew he missed his partners. Ely had been his family for longer than the rest of them had been alive and he was worried about him. Now, it seems, without Growling Bear here, everyone had time to dwell on the unknown. Where were their husbands, partners, and friends? How bad was Running Wolf hurt? And the most disturbing question for most of them, was Running Wolf the only one hurt?

Try as she might, Raven Wing had not had another dream or vision about her husband. Except for the scene that kept flashing before her, of him hurt and bleeding. She believed he needed her, and she was not there to help him, and for her, that was the worst of all possible feelings.

They were sitting around the fire, working on warm winter moccasins and leggings, when a distant shot echoed down the canyon. It was Little Dove that said, "Sounds like we will have fresh meat for supper tonight." That brought a brief smile to all of their faces, but it didn't change the solemn mood they were in.

They had been expecting the men to be gone three or four suns and it had been over ten, and none of them believed they would be back anytime soon. It was now the middle of naa-mea', the rutting moon. The whistles and grunts of the bull elk were no longer heard coming from the canyon and ridges. More of the bright yellow aspen leaves were falling to the ground each day, leaving most of the aspen just bare skeletons of their former selves. Their white trunks and black knots standing in stark contrast to the dark green of the pine, fir, and spruce all around them. They were ready for winter. They had finished making the pemmican. Grinding the dried buffalo meat, pine nuts, berries, and acorns together and stuffing it all into buffalo gut casings. Then pouring in the hot buffalo grease binding it all together. The dugout was full of dried and smoked meat, buffalo, elk, and mountain sheep. Deer and antelope were usually eaten fresh, and right now they hoped Grub's shot would bring in fresh venison.

Fresh meat was always welcome, their dried and smoked meat must sustain them through the long cold winter, after the game migrated out of the high country. Another moon and fresh meat would no longer be available until the weather broke next spring, and the game returned to their summer range.

*****

Zach was concerned as he headed to the ridge top. If all was clear Jimbo should have been back by now. As he approached the massive rock where Ely sat until dark the night before, he dropped down to his belly and crawled the last few feet. He then carefully parted the branches of a sage to see the big lake and its shoreline that was at least a mile away.

At first sight there was no movement. The distance was great, but Zach was patient. The others who were just behind him stopped well below the crest of the hill waiting for Zach to move or give them some instructions. Even though he could see no movement, he believed something was out there. If not, his dog would already be back.

Then, only a couple of hundred yards from the water's edge, there was movement. He couldn't tell whether it was man or animal at that distance, but something was moving. He backed off the crest of the ridge and then told the others he had seen movement, but it is too far away to tell what it is. Benny and Coyote Talker both said, "we will stay behind the ridge and find out what is there." Ely asked, "Any sign of that there big dog?" Zach shook his head then added, "No, but he's found something, or he would be back by now." Ely nodded and said, "We best be for finding out what. I don't cotton to the idea of letting them find us." He then watched Benny and Coyote Talker jogging straight east, well below the line of sight from anyone on the south side of the ridge.

They were a little over a half mile from Zach and Ely, nearly to where the ridge tapered down to the lake, when they stopped and dropped down into the grass and sage. They inched their way to where they could see through the brush, only to find a dozen deer browsing on the brush just above the shore-line. Even though Coyote Talker was disappointed, he stayed there to make sure nothing else was there.

Only minutes later his patience was rewarded when he saw one of the deer kick into the air. All the others ran toward the willows that were still over a half mile from them. But the one that had kicked was hurt and ran only a hundred yards before giving up and lying down. Even though neither of them had seen anything, they both knew there were hunters there, and the doe had been shot with at least one arrow, if not more.

There was no way they could get closer without being seen, so they just watched. They didn't want to let their enemy know they were close or how many of them there were. They eased back to where they were once again behind the hill and jogged back up to Zach and Ely. When they told those two what had happened. Ely said, "It be a might strange they take the time to hunt, knowing we are this close to 'em."

Zach was quiet for a moment, then said, "Maybe the hunters are just that, innocent hunters that have nothing to do with the captives." That made them all pause. If other hunters are in the area, then Red Eagle has another way to get at least a few horses.

Zach then said, "We're just guessing again boys, we have to know who is out there and what they are doing." As they were all nodding and thinking about how to go about finding out, Jimbo silently appeared next to Zach. The hair was standing up down the center of his back. As Zach reached for him, he shook his head and ran forward a few feet. Zach turned to the others and said, "He found something he wants to show us. Guess we better follow." Benny asked, "What about those hunters."

"Well," Ely said, "If they is just hunters, let 'em be. If they is part of this bunch we's after, we'll meet up with 'em 'fore long."

Coyote Talker looked back down the ridge. He believed those hunters were his best chance of finding out where his brother was. But he knew these men he was with would not tolerate him going off by himself, he had been tied up before to prove that. As bad as he hated to he nodded and the four of them followed Jimbo south through the timber.

*****

Red Eagle had been furious that they had been surprised like they had while they waited to ambush whoever was following. He was now down to just seven warriors and only five horses. They had no food and must take time to hunt. The only place he thought they could get enough horses to get their slaves to the land of the Spanish was from Broken Lance's Piute village. But he did not know how far south Broken Lance would have moved for the winter.

The following morning, he took the two women, both had survived the brutal treatment and cold nights, to trade with Broken Lance. He took three of the five horses, leaving all seven warriors with the two teenagers and the two remaining children captives. The two remaining horses they could use for hunting.

Red Eagle wasn't worried about the men following, even though they were wise enough not to follow the trail he and his men had left, there wasn't enough of them to matter, and he had seen one of them take an arrow. Even though he had lost three men, he didn't believe there were enough men behind them to dare attack his warriors.

Only two hours after Red Eagle had left their camp on the western shore of the big lake. Brave Hunter and four more young warriors from their Sahpeech village rode in from the south. Brave Hunter and these others were so upset by the news Zach and Running Wolf had brought with them into their village, they had rode out the next morning. Brave Hunter had believed he knew the trail Red Eagle would follow and thought he could catch them by following the river further south and going around the high flat top mountain to the west and meet them along the old Spanish trail at the lake.

Brave Hunter's plan had worked. He met them at the lake, but Red Eagle had gone looking for the village of Broken Lance. They were welcomed by the others, most of whom were friends of the five newcomers.

Brave Fox and Willow were still tied to the same tree. The younger children whom Brave Fox thought to be about ten summers were tied to another tree only a few feet from him and Willow. None of them had dared talk, they had seen how brutal their captors were. The two younger children had stopped crying most of the time. Brave Fox believed they were too tired to continue. Both of them were bruised and hurt from being slapped often and hard to get them to stop.

Brave Fox's wrists were both bloody from his fight with the rawhide they had tied him with. Even Willow's wrists were raw and ready to start bleeding. They were hungry, they hadn't had anything to eat in nearly three days. Even Red Eagle's warriors were hungry he had not let them take the time to hunt along the way.

Two of them were out hunting this morning, and they all hoped they would bring in some meat. A porcupine made the mistake of waddling along the creek, in only minutes after he was seen, he was roasting over the fire. The fat dripping into the flames and the aroma of the roasting meat made the two children start to cry again, while Brave Fox and Willow's belly's growled with hunger.

Brave Hunter confirmed to those in camp they were being followed. He told them it was the white man, Grizzly Killer and his Ute partner, Running Wolf. The warriors were all silent. Every one of them had heard of this great white warrior. From the stories they had heard, he was not just another warrior. His medicine was stronger than that of any other man. Brave Hunter could see what looked to him like fear on some of their faces. He told them all that Grizzly Killer is just a man like every other man. He told them of sitting around the fire with him and that he could be defeated just like anyone else.

Brave Hunter's words were heard, but words did not change the fact that they were already missing seven warriors and most of their horses, and none of them had even seen Grizzly Killer yet. None of them were afraid of a warrior, they could kill any warrior, but the question many of them had, was Grizzly Killer just another warrior or was he an evil spirit in the form of a man sent to kill them.

*****

Jimbo loped through the thick timber like a ghost floating on air as Zach and the others jogged along trying to keep up. Zach figured they were at the middle of the lake, well above the water, when Jimbo stopped, waiting for them at a creek. As they stopped, the smell of smoke was in the air and they knew they were close to a camp. What they didn't know was this a camp of hunters or was it Red Eagle and his renegades.

Jimbo dropped to his belly and very quietly Zach told the others to wait for him here. He looked at Coyote Talker and could see the anxiety in his eyes. Zach nodded at him and he smiled and quietly approached. Zach got close and whispered, "For now Coyote Talker, we will only watch. We will do nothing to get any of the captives, or ourselves hurt. Do you understand that?" Coyote Talker took a deep breath and nodded.

They silently crept forward on hands and knees, following Jimbo along the creek. Moving as slowly as they were moving it took over a half hour before they heard the first voices. Coyote Talker looked puzzled and Zach whispered, "Ute." Another hundred yards and although they could not see into the camp yet, Zach could hear them talking. He was motionless and listened as they talked about guarding the camp and the horses they had left. He smiled as he heard two of them saying it was a spirit dog that had attacked and killed two of them. No dog was that big or could kill that fast. No, they believed Red Eagle had angered the spirits, and they had sent the dog after them.

Zach leaned toward Coyote Talker to whisper what he had heard, but before he whispered anything, the sound of a footstep was heard. Zach stopped and listened. Someone was walking toward them. He quietly rolled into the icy water of the creek and Coyote Talker followed. He rolled over Zach and down into the water that felt as though it should already be ice.

Zach hugged the bank, but still only partially hidden by the tall dry grass along the creek bank, Coyote Talker did the same. A few moments in the icy water seemed like an eternity. Only a moment later he watched a Ute warrior bend down and drink from the creek only twenty feet below them. The warrior then stood, studied the forest all around, then stepped through the creek and disappeared out of sight.

Zach waited another couple of minutes before moving. The icy water had made it hard to even breathe. His muscles ached from the cold. He now knew where Red Eagle was camped, but he knew he and Coyote Talker must get to a fire or they would both be in serious trouble.

Chapter 20

A Warm Fire

Both Zach and Coyote Talker were shivering uncontrol-
lably by the time they crawled back up to Ely and Benny.
A wind had started up and clouds had covered the sun.
They knew they must get far enough away from Red
Eagle's camp for a fire, or both of their lives could be at
risk from the cold.

This wasn't the first time for any of these men to be wet
and dangerously cold. After all, trapping beaver meant
wading in bone chilling water much of the time. But with
a dangerous enemy so close, a fire wasn't an option.

Once again Jimbo led them back to the north, they
knew the faster Zach and Coyote Talker ran the more heat
their own bodies would produce, but their muscles were
too cold. Even as big and powerful as Zach was, he could
not get his legs to work right, and he was doing better
than Coyote Talker who had fallen three times in the first
quarter mile. Benny and Ely got on each side of him and

partially carried his nearly frozen body. The further Zach ran, the better his legs were working, his working muscles forcing more blood to his legs.

They jogged a little over halfway back to the ridge before stopping in a particularly dense stand of pines. There Ely said, "Benny, Coyote Talker ain't gonna make it no further, go back and get some robes, we got to risk a fire."

As Benny ran on ahead, Ely scrapped the pines away from an area and built a small fire. He used the very dry dead twigs and branches from the base of the pines. Once the fire was going he helped Coyote Talker, who was still shivering uncontrollably, lay down alongside the fire while Zach sat cross legged leaning over it. Neither of them could remember a warm fire feeling as good. As the two of them tried to soak up the heat from the hand sized fire, Ely continuously fed the small dry branches to the flames.

Ely had seen men freeze to death before. He knew once a man's body got so cold, their heart would just stop. He was worried about Coyote Talker. His lips and his finger-nails were turning blue. He took his own coat off and laid it over the young man, and added more twigs, letting the fire grow as high as he dared.

The sky was growing dark as heavy clouds rolled over the lake from the west. Even though the thick pines were protecting them from the gusting wind, there was still enough of a breeze reaching their wet buckskins to make the cold even more intense.

With shaking hands, Zach pulled his jacket and buck-skin shirt off. Coyote Talker could not make his hands and arms work together, so Ely roughly pulled the buckskins over his head. Their wet bare skin even felt colder now, but they all knew their skin would dry much quicker without the wet leather touching it.

Zach had Jimbo lay down alongside Coyote Talker's

back. It took Benny over an hour to return, and to their surprise, Buffalo Heart and Running Wolf was with him. They had brought four buffalo sleeping robes. Coyote Talker and Zach were still shivering, but they were warming up and Ely believed they were out of danger now. Even though they were still mighty cold.

They quickly wrapped the robes around the two men and while Ely stayed with them, the other three set up a watch out in the forest a couple of hundred yards from the fire.

Running Wolf still felt weak, but he had fought that weakness as they ran back to Zach and the others. His partner needed help, and as long as he could do it, he was going to help.

Once they had the robes, Zach stripped naked and then Ely helped Coyote Talker do the same. Then Ely hung the wet buckskins on some branches over the fire, as the two nearly frozen men huddled next to the warm flames.

A bright flash of lightning lit the darkening forest, and only a moment later thunder shook the trees all around them. Although midday, in the forest it looked to be late evening. And before their buckskins had dried, there were snowflakes being whipped through the trees.

After the amount of blood Running Wolf had lost, the cold wind and snow had him shivering as he watched out into the dark forest. He needed the warmth of the fire nearly as bad as Zach and Coyote Talker had. Jimbo had gone out to him and the big dog leaning against him helped a lot. He was surprised when only an hour later, Zach, with a robe wrapped around his shoulders, appeared behind him and said, "Go up to the fire Running Wolf, get warmed up, we'll be heading back to camp soon."

"Did you find them?" Running Wolf asked. Zach nodded and said, "Ya, they are there alright. But they're watching mighty close, we'll have to wait 'til dark. Couldn't see 'em, just listened. Brave Hunter and some of his friends from the Sahpeech village have joined them. Don't know how many we're up against."

Not long after that, Zach cupped his hand to his mouth and made the chattering sound of a squirrel and within minutes they all met at the fire. Coyote Talker was dressed but still shaking and Zach knew the faster he got moving the better he would feel.

They headed out following Jimbo jogging through the forest once again, Ely stayed behind long enough to smother the fire and hide it under rocks and logs. He didn't leave until he was satisfied no one would ever know they had been there.

By the time they got back to the grotto, there was already an inch of snow on the ground. The clouds and snow had the far side of the lake hidden, and even from a mile away they could see the white-capped waves crashing into the western shore.

Even though some snow was falling inside the grotto, the high rocks were protecting it from most of the storm. They got a fire going inside and within a half hour the temperature inside was much warmer than on the other side of the narrow entrance.

While Zach and Coyote Talker finished drying their buckskins, Benny and Buffalo Heart brought in enough firewood to last them until the next day.

*****

Shining Star stood on the bank of the river, looking out across the big meadow. The cold fall wind hitting her in the face. She could tell a storm was coming. The wind brought the smell of snow with it.

The other women were getting the camp prepared for the storm they all knew was coming. Grub walked up beside Shining Star and put his hand on her shoulder and said, "They are fine, Shining Star. They all been in storms before." She smiled up at him and nodded. But knowing that didn't make her want her husband home any less. By late afternoon the dark clouds had obscured the high peaks south of them. They had firewood gathered and stored for their inside fires, and a large venison roast was on a green willow spit over the fire in Zach's big teepee.

They had two coffee pots on the coals on the edge of the fire, and Sun Flower was making a pan full of biscuits to go with the roast. As the wind shifted with the storm, Shining Star stepped out and adjusted the smoke flap of their teepee to better draw the smoke from inside. Sleet had started to pelt the southwest side of the teepee, and she was wet and cold when she stepped back inside.

Star said, "Mama, you almost as wet as papa." They all stopped and looked at Star, wondering what the little girl had seen. Still shivering, Shining Star knelt down and asked, "What did you see Star?" Star looked up with her bright blue eyes and shook her head saying, "Nothing Mama, I just know papa is wet and cold."

Raven Wing knew how clear Star's visions had been in the past, and to a lesser degree her own. She was puzzled now. Why had neither of them had been able to see where the men were and what they were doing? She prayed every day and every night, but still did not know if their husbands were alright. She was tired. She had slept very little, for every time she closed her eyes the vision of Running Wolf lying there covered with blood filled her mind.

They ate in relative silence, all worried and wondering about the men that they believed were still far away.

Luna pushed her way out through the teepee flap and stood facing south with the sleet blowing right into her face. She knew Running Wolf was hurt and weak, she was his spirit helper. She longed to go to him to help him, but she knew her duty was with the children. She howled a long mournful howl into the face of the storm. She was calling out to Jimbo. She knew he was with them and he would protect them at any cost.

She pushed her way back inside and curled up in front of the entrance. She would stay there protecting her pack, just as she knew Jimbo would be protecting his.

*****

The Ute renegades were tired of the trail and they were miserable, the storm, cold and now the snow was starting to pile up. Most of them wanted the warmth of a teepee and a woman. They had been all for the idea of trading slaves to the Spanish, but now they were being chased and they didn't know by how many. They did know Grizzly Killer was one of the men behind them, and most of them did not want to face him in battle.

They were beginning to wonder if the price of these slaves would be worth the trouble of getting them to the Spanish this late in the year. The problem was, where could they go? Four Bears would not welcome them into their own village, and the Piute, Broken Lance may trade with them but none of them believed they would be welcome to stay there. They were on foot, not even able to get away from the great white warrior. They all hoped Red Eagle was right. There wasn't enough men with Grizzly Killer to attack them. Now with Brave Hunter and the others with them, their force was even stronger, and that made them feel a little better.

Brave Hunter knew the slaves were the only thing of value they had to trade for supplies they would need for the winter. He knew if they died they would have nothing. He took a heavy robe and warm roasted deer to the children, who ate the meat in a hurry. He then went to Willow and cut the rawhide she was bound with. He pulled her to her feet and led her over to their fire and handed her a warm slice of the roast. He then threw a slice of the meat to Brave Fox. With his hands still tied around the tree. He had to eat it like a dog off the ground, but it was the first food they'd had in days and he knew it may keep him alive.

The renegades laughed as they watched him eat it, right then he was glad he could not understand what they were saying.

There were two inches of snow by the time all daylight was gone. The two children were huddled together under the robe and with food in their bellies they had gone right to sleep. Willow kept looking back at Brave Fox, she wanted to go back to help keep him warm. Brave Hunter didn't seem as cruel as Red Eagle, but she still had no idea what he was going to do with them. She didn't know if he would let her help her new friend. She pointed at him then Brave Hunter told one of the others to cover him so he would not freeze. But signed to Willow to stay where she was.

He set a two-man guard on the horses after learning what had happened to the rest of them. None of the original renegades seemed to mind Brave Hunter taking charge. They were followers, not leaders. It was much easier for them to be told, than to make decisions on their own. A couple even wondered if Red Eagle would even come back for them. He had the two women and horses and they doubted they would ever see him again. They were glad Brave Hunter, and the others had come. The glorious raids that Red Eagle had promised had turned in to nothing but a run for their lives.

*****

Zach and the others sat in relative comfort inside the warm grotto like outcropping. They had spent the afternoon discussing what they should do to free Brave Fox and the other captives. The storm along with darkness, they felt would be the perfect cover to get in close enough to free them. They still did not know how many of the enemy they would be facing or how fiercely they would fight to keep their captives.

Ely reminded them about the snow, saying, "I figure we can get in under the cover of night, especially with this here storm, but everywhere we go is gonna leave tracks, both a going and a coming, we is gonna be mighty easy to track." Zach nodded, then said, "Unless the snow covers up our tracks by morning, I don't think they will come after us in the night, especially if we can throw a real fright into them." Coyote Talker asked, "How can we do that."

Zach's eyes turned from sky-blue to ice-gray once again. His friends had all seen that look before. Many times in the past Zach's enemies had outnumbered him. He used their own superstitions and fears to even the odds. He looked at Coyote Talker and said, "I don't think they have more than a half dozen horses among them. They are not gonna take any chances of losing them. They will have at least two guards on them, maybe more. If we can sneak in and take out those guards, we should be able to quietly take the captives. Then I'll leave a surprise for them in the trail that will make them pretty nervous about following us."

Coyote Talker still looked puzzled and asked, "What would make them not want to follow?" It was Buffalo Heart that answered, "Their friends scalped heads on a pole in the trail, usually makes them not want to follow." Zach saw a shiver run through Coyote Talker and said no more. As he looked at the now cold eyes of Grizzly Killer he was mighty glad he was on his side. He had never seen anyone he would hate to have as an enemy as much as Grizzly Killer.

Chapter 21

Into the Raging Storm

Darkness fell rapidly as the storm raged on. The wind howled through the trees on the ridge above the grotto. The fire had warmed the rocks on the inside, and both Zach and Coyote Talker was once again warm and dry. Zach could still feel a little moisture in his moccasins, but he didn't believe they would cause any real discomfort.

They stayed together as they pushed south, through the dark night into the raging storm. Zach followed, Jimbo leading the way. The thick timber was welcome when they reached it, for it blocked most of the wind and driving snow from hitting them in their faces. They reached the creek and Zach figured he would rather fight a dozen men before hiding in that cold water again.

The forest was so dark, they were feeling their way toward the lake. Zach, Running Wolf, and Coyote Talker were on the north side and Ely, Benny, and Buffalo Heart were on the south. They had all tried to get Running Wolf to stay behind, but he would not, even though his arm would not support his rifle and he couldn't pull back his bow. He carried his knife in his right hand and his toma-hawk was tucked under his belt. He believed he could get the captives away while the others were fighting a battle.

An all-out battle is something Zach wanted to avoid. He knew the chances of one of them getting hurt or even killed was too great, and he hoped to avoid that. He had even said a silent prayer as they trekked through the dark forest. He was hoping to sneak the captives out rather than have to fight an unknown number of warriors to free them.

They were following the creek down from the west and the wind was gusting from the south, blowing the smoke away from them. Zach hadn't smelled the fire until they were very close. He froze as another wind gust made the fire flare up enough that he could see figures wrapped in their bed robes around the fire. Then someone walked in from the south side of their camp with another arm full of wood and built the fire up once again.

As the flames grew with the added wood, he saw figures bundled at the base of two aspen trees out away from the fire, and he knew that would be the captives. But which one of them was Brave Fox, there was no way to tell. He knew if they chose wrong and any of the captives were startled enough to cry out, it would mean a battle. One in which the outcome was far from certain.

The guard had come from the north with the wood, so Zach figured that is where he would find the horses and other guards if there were more. He huddled with Coyote Talker and Running Wolf, telling them to crawl on their bellies as silently as they could and cut the captives loose. But make sure they do not move or make a sound. They knew there were children among them, they had seen their tracks. Right then, Zach's greatest fear was the children crying out.

He told them to give him time enough to find the guards and kill them. He knew very well their timing would be only a guess. He told Running Wolf to let the others know the plans and to have their rifles ready. Two silent steps and he and Jimbo faded into the pitch-black night.

How Zach wished he had Jimbo's night vision, and sense of smell. He was carefully feeling the ground with his moccasin'd feet, making sure he didn't step on a stick or twig that would break. Jimbo stayed close, leading the way until Zach felt him stop. Although not able to see the horses or the guards, he could hear the horses munching on a little dry grass the warriors had pulled up for them.

Zach knelt down. He could feel the hair on Jimbo's back was standing up. Then, just to his left, one of the guards made a slight cough. He didn't believe he could be more than five feet away. He was motionless, waiting for another sound, wondering if Coyote Talker would give him the time he needed.

Zach didn't want to make another move until he was certain there were no other guards, or if there was, in knowing where they were. Killing a man without making a sound was a very difficult thing to do, and it was many times harder in the pitch blackness of a storm filled night.

He waited, hoping the guard would take more wood to the fire, and hoping Coyote Talker did not get inpatient. Finally, the guard moved. He walked toward the horses, softly speaking to them. Zach still could not see him, but he felt his presence only an arm's length away. Zach was thankful for the wind. It had to be blowing his and Jimbo's scent away from the horses. A particularly strong gust made the fire flare up, and in that moment Zach could see the warrior. He was facing the horses and away from Zach. With his Cherokee tomahawk firmly in hand, he swung the deadly blade, planting it solidly in the back of the warrior's head. He took a swift step forward and caught the warrior before he fell, gently lowering him to the ground.

Zach didn't move for several moments, listening for any other sound that may be near. If another guard was there watching the horses, he was being mighty quiet, for even Jimbo's hair had laid back down.

Coyote Talker and Running Wolf had both moved up to the aspens where Brave Fox and the children were tied. Neither had made a sound. With full stomachs, the young boy and girl were sound asleep and Running Wolf had already cut the rawhide that was holding them to the tree.

Coyote Talker carefully cut the rawhide holding his younger brother's hands. Then gently reached out and touched his arm. Brave Fox jumped, he had gone to sleep but was so tired, he thought his mind was playing tricks on him. He had watched Brave Hunter take Willow to his robes. Only by the light of the fire he knew she was being raped and he could do nothing about. He saw his brother's face there next to the tree trunk but thought he must be dreaming. Then he felt the touch and jumped, but only slightly. He saw Coyote Talker move his hand for silence. It was only then he realized his hands were free.

They both heard another struggle on the far side of the fire as Willow fought to keep Brave Hunter from raping her again. She kicked her knee hard into his groin. He doubled over in pain as the naked young girl struggled out from under his robe and ran toward Brave Fox. The shock of the snow and cold air didn't deter her, she would rather freeze than let him take her again. She was crying and afraid. Her bare feet slipped in the snow and she fell hard but continued to struggle toward Brave Fox. She was on her hands and knees when Brave Hunter caught her. He was naked as well. Brave Fox surprised them all. Before Coyote

Talker could stop him, he was on his feet. Brave Hunter was bent over dragging the naked girl back to his robes when the young captive kicked him in the face. It sent him over backwards into the fire as his bare skin touched the coals that the gusting wind had fanned into a glowing red. He screamed and all the warriors were suddenly up.

The flash of burning powder and hot lead flashed in the night and three of the warriors were blown off their feet as Buffalo Heart, Benny, and Ely all fired. A moment later Ely's pistol spat lead and flame and another warrior was down.

Running Wolf yelled for Buffalo Heart, and before the stunned Ute warriors knew what was happening, the two frightened children were being carried out into the darkness. Brave Fox threw the robe that had been over him, around Willow and was running through the darkness east along the creek.

The other guard had been on the far side of the horses and came running to the fire with an arrow ready to shoot, only to meet the powerful jaws of the great medicine dog. Jimbo's teeth buried deep in his thigh, tearing muscle and sending the stunned warrior to the ground.

Zach did not have time to set up the guard's head on a spike, but he had cut the head off. He rolled it toward the fire, where some of his friends could see it, then he fired his own rifle. In the dark and confusion he didn't know if his shot had hit his intended victim.

Coyote Hunter got three arrows away, but in the dark and confusion, did not know if any of them hit their target either. In under a minute the camp was quiet once again, except for the howling wind, and Brave Hunters cursing moans. The back of his head and shoulders were severely burned. But that was nothing to the burning hatred he felt for Grizzly Killer and his partner that was a Ute traitor, or the boy that had kicked him in the face.

Jimbo, Ely, and Zach ran only a couple of hundred yards then stopped to discourage any pursuit, but none came. The Sahpeech had had enough for the night, but Zach did not believe this fight was over yet. He believed these were the type of men that would seek revenge. As he and Ely turned to continue up the creek, Ely said, "Ya know this ain't over don't ya." Zach just nodded and continued, even though Ely could not see him in the darkness.

Both children were crying uncontrollably, and Willow had slipped and fell several times as they ran through the cold dark forest. They stopped for a few moments to catch their breath not far from where they'd had the fire earlier in the day. Willow's bare feet were half frozen and bleeding by then. The Elk robe she was trying to hold around herself did not cover her legs at all. Buffalo Heart took off his fox lined coat and put it on her and they wrapped her feet with pieces of the robe.

Willow and Brave Fox both jumped with surprise and fright as Jimbo ran up to them. Coyote Talker smiled at the two of them and said, "That's Jimbo, the great medicine dog of Grizzly Killer. He is a friend."

Benny took the young boy from Running Wolf, and Buffalo Heart kept the girl as they continued to their rocky grotto. The fire inside was still glowing coals as they squeezed through the narrow opening. It took only a moment, after adding wood, for the flames to light the inside and the rock walls had still retained some heat they had soaked up from the fire earlier. Inside the small grotto was much warmer than it was on the outside.

The children were so frightened neither could stop crying. Once again strange men had taken them. While Zach, Benny, Buffalo Heart, and Coyote Talker went back out into the dark and climbed back up the ridge to watch their back trail, Ely sat down by the fire with them. Brave Fox and Willow both wondered who these men were, but the children were only afraid.

Their world had been turned upside down as they were brutally taken from their mothers. They had lost track of how many suns had passed, since they had been bound, beaten, starved, and forced to ride with those strange warriors. Now it had happened again, only this time they were not bound, and these men were speaking in a way they could understand.

Ely picked up the little girl and set her on his knee. He could see the fear in her eyes and smiled the best he could. He wished Grub was here, Grub was the happy-go-lucky one. Grub always had the ability to make people feel better. Ely just smiled, and asked, speaking nearly perfect Shoshone, and in as gentle and friendly voice as he could muster, "What is your name, little one?" The girl's dark, bloodshot eyes looked up at his. Her bottom lip stopped quivering, but she did not speak. Ely, still smiling, said, "My name is Ely," the corners of her mouth started to turn up into a smile and she said, "That is a funny name." Ely chuckled and nodded and said, "I suppose it is." He gently took her hand and looked at the raw skin around her wrist from the rawhide bindings. He slipped his shooting pouch over his head and brought out a small pouch of bear grease from inside of it. He was so gentle with her she didn't pull away as he put a little of the soothing grease, he used to grease his round lead balls before shooting, around her wrists.

Brave Fox and Willow were silent as they watched the grizzled old mountain man gently care for the children. The boy wasn't quite as shy as the girl and told Ely he was, Little Robe. He laid them both on his buffalo robe next to the fire and covered them. Then turned his attention to

Willow. She was a pretty young girl, but she was bruised, cut, and had just been brutally raped. She was silent as Ely carefully removed the elk robe they had cut and wrapped around her feet. The warmth of the fire felt good to her very cold and painful feet. He gently smeared bear grease on both of her feet, then went out to his saddle and brought in his extra pair of moccasins. He always carried when trapping. After wading in the icy waters setting his traps, he always had a dry pair to change in to.

When he was finished, she smiled. Her dirty face was streaked with tears, but her pretty dark eyes sparkled in the light of the fire, as she said, "I am Willow."

After warming the cold moccasins over the fire, he gently slid them over her feet. She closed her eyes for a moment and Ely could see it was a great relief to her. He then looked at Brave Fox and said, "Little Bull and Gray Deer are fine. They went back to your village with White Crow and Yellow Horse."

Ely could see the shock on Brave Fox's face. And he continued, "White Crow and your brother came into our village looking for the three of you, we have been tracking you ever since."

"Who are you," Brave Fox asked. Ely smiled and again said, "I am Ely, the others that helped are Grizzly Killer, Buffalo Heart, Benny, and Running Wolf." Just then Running Wolf came back inside carrying more bear meat. Ely said, "This here is Running Wolf. He caught an arrow a couple of days ago. Willow started to get up to help Running Wolf put the meat over the fire, but bent over in pain, from both her feet and from where she had been raped. She felt a trickle of blood running down her leg. Although Buffalo Hearts' coat was warm and covered her to below her hips, her legs were completely bare. Ely turned to Running Wolf and said, "We got to figure out some leggings for her before we head out in the morning. Those there bare legs of hers will freeze, even wrapped around a horse."

Ely then handed Willow the small pouch of bear grease and said, "I figure he would rather have you hold his hands than me to smear that there grease on them sore looking wrists." He then winked and turned back to Running Wolf and said, "Don't let that there ol' bear burn, I'm gonna go up and spell Coyote Talker, I am all warm now and I'm sure he wants to be with his brother." Running Wolf smiled and nodded.

The storm raged on through the night, and by morning there was a foot of snow on the ground. The men each got just a couple hours of sleep as they watched through the night. The gusting wind blew right in their faces most of the night.

As daylight spread across the wide gray waters of the lake, the clouds were still low and dark covering the ridge tops, but the wind had calmed. There had been no sign they had been followed. They had kept the fire burning through the night, and inside the grotto it was warm and mostly dry.

As Ely sat by the fire watching over the children all night, he didn't realize he had dozed off. He opened his eyes and saw Grizzly Killer standing just outside the opening of the Grotto. A quick glance around told him that Benny and Buffalo Heart were still out watching, he was sure they were on top of the ridge. He pushed through the narrow opening and walked to a tree to relieve himself and as he was standing with his back to Zach, Zach said, "I don't much care to have them renegades following us like we been following them, Ely. Now we have the children, I don't figure we can stay ahead of them any better than they stayed ahead of us."

Ely finished and slowly turned around. "You do have a point, Grizzly Killer. You didn't hear everything that Brave Fox told us last night. He says, Red Eagle took two women captives and headed out someplace, going south. That left them with only two horses. Something chewed through their picket rope and run most of their horses off. Then when they went to find them, they lost even more horses and three more men. That is all they had until Brave Hunter and four others rode in."

Zach thought about that for a minute then said, "Thunder, I bet that's where that spotted stallion is. He stole their horses for himself." Ely burst out laughing and asked, "You really figure that horse is that smart?"

"I wouldn't put anything past that stallion, he has surprised me too many times."

Ely stared out across the white expanse to the large round bay that made up the north end of the lake, then asked, "How many of them there devils you figure is still there?" Zach shook his head, "Don't know Ely, it was too dark and too much confusion. I figure we did some real damage, but we still may be outnumbered." Ely nodded, then said, "We got a mighty long trail in front of us and you are right, I don't much cotton to the idea of having to looking over my shoulder all the way home."

Chapter 22

Ambushed

Everyone except Grub and Two Feathers had stayed in Zach's large teepee as the storm rolled through the Uintah Mountains. Grub and Two Feathers went to their own lodge once the storm's fury reached Blacks Fork.

As with Zach and the others two hundred miles to the south, the dark clouds hung low, covering the mountain tops long before darkness and the snow started to fall.

Raven Wing had not slept as the first light of dawn filtered through the heavy gray clouds. She felt something had happened with their husbands and had sat at the fire, keeping the small flames going through the night. She prayed, hoping the smoke from the bundle of sweet sage she was holding at the fire, would carry her prayers to the Great Spirit above.

Sun Flower had watched her sister through much of the night. So had most of the others. It had been too many suns since the men had left, they were all worried. Raven Wing had dark circles under her eyes from the lack of sleep. Sun Flower sat up when she heard Grub and Two Flowers getting the outside fire started. Quietly, they all got up, careful not to wake the still sleeping children. They slowly filed out into the world that had been transformed overnight by a blanket of snow. The dancing yellow flames of the growing fire felt very good to them all. Within minutes they had two coffee pots full of water on the edge of the fire and Shining Star was roasting a tin cup full of coffee beans.

Raven Wing had stayed inside. Finally giving up on knowing where their husbands were and what they were doing. She laid down and fell into a restless sleep. She saw a tall rock formation and men squeezing between two tall rocks, then saw water running over the top of Grizzly Killer. She saw a severed head rolling toward a fire and a warrior falling into the same fire. The dream was in bits and pieces. She could not see any of their faces, and she had no idea who was there or what was happening. Finally, a gunshot echoed in the night and she sat up startled. Had Grub fired his rifle or was it part of the dream, she didn't know. Beads of sweat covered her brow. The dream was nothing but confusion, but she believed their husbands were going through hell on some distant horizon.

This was not the vision she had prayed for, this was a nightmare that she could not understand. She wiped her brow, then saw the blue eyes of Star smiling up at her. Luna licked her face and Star grave her a hug and whispered, "Uncle Running Wolf and Papa are all right, Aunt Raven Wing." She wished she had the optimism of her blue-eyed niece, but the only clear vision she'd had since the men left was of Running Wolf hurt and bleeding.

Not wanting to fall back asleep she got up and joined the others that were all bundled up against the cold and drinking hot coffee around the outside fire.

*****

After the attack, none of the remaining warriors would follow the attackers into the dark forest. Most of Brave Hunters hair was burned off and the burns on his head and shoulders were painful, but the burns would not stop him from getting his revenge. Three of the twelve had been killed, and two wounded, one severely where the huge dog had ripped the muscle apart in his leg. The other with an arrow in his butt. It was painful, but like Brave Hunter the wound would not stop him. All seven of their horses were still on the picket line. Brave Hunter sent four of the warriors out at first light, looking for tracks in the snow. Since they had come from the north, they all believed the attackers would leave the same way.

At first light, Iron Knife and Crooked Snake rode along the lake shore to the north. To make sure they didn't miss them, Tall Bull and Two Fists rode the shoreline south. When they reached the end of the lake, they were to turn to the west and ride to the trees. They were sure they would find the tracks in the fresh snow. If they rode all the way to where the mountain became too steep for the horses, the tracks had to be there.

Iron Knife's brother, Long Arrow, had been guarding the horses. He vowed revenge for his brother's brutal death, even if it took the rest of his life or into the next.

Before the riders returned, Roars Like Thunder was delirious with fever. The big dog's teeth had torn through his leg so severely it had ripped the muscle from the bone. They did what they could to stop the bleeding, but they all knew he was not going to live long.

They were down to just seven warriors, but they still believed they outnumbered their attackers. Now the attackers were burdened with the children, they believed they would be easy to catch.

There would be tracks in the fresh snow, there had to be. There was no place for them to hide around the lake, and no one could have braved the violent storm to ride all night. Now they had the captives, they believed Grizzly Killer and the men with him would get as far away as they could.

*****

The only tracks Zach and the others had left in the newly fallen snow were from the rocks that formed the grotto to the top of the ridge seventy-five yards above them, and that trail was hidden by thick aspens. The horses were picketed in the trees just outside the opening to the grotto. Ely figured they would be out looking at first light, but he was confident they were well concealed. As the children woke up well after daylight, they ate ravenously. For the first time in many days they were warm and being treated well and were given all they wanted to eat.

The little girl after they had eaten their fill of roast bear and slices of pemmican, climbed up on Ely's lap and whispered so no one else could hear her, "I am Red Fawn, Grandfather." Ely smiled from ear to ear and hugged her. Then turned to the other men and said, "She called me Grandfather." Running Wolf thought he saw a tear in Ely's eyes as he continued, "Ain't never been called that before."

None of them wanted these Ute renegades behind them. Ely said, "If we can sneak in on them one more time, I don't figure they will be much in the mood to tangle with us again." They all nodded their agreement. Zach asked, to no one in particular, "If you had been surprised in the night once, would you let it happen again?" They all shook their heads then Ely said, "You figure they will be a waiting for us tonight?"

"I don't figure they will, but what if they are?" Zach replied.

All was quiet around the fire. Willow was sitting with the children. Jimbo was curled up in front of them. Brave Fox was next to Coyote Talker as they discussed what they should do. Before anything else was said, Benny pushed into the grotto and said, forgetting that Coyote Talker couldn't understand, he spoke English, "There's two riders out looking for tracks." Without even thinking about it, Ely started kicking the fire apart and said, "We don't need 'em seeing or smelling our smoke, least 'til we know what we is doing."

Zach saw the puzzled and concerned look on Coyote Talker and Brave Fox's face. Then repeated what Benny had said in Shoshone. Coyote Talker stood and said, "We should make sure they do not make it back to their camp."

Ely commented, "If we do that, they will know for sure we ain't left this here area. Right now they is just trying to find out which way we went." Coyote Talker nodded he understood, then Running Wolf said, "But Ely, there would be two less of them to fight, and they are going to find out mighty quick we didn't leave." Ely thought for a moment, and as a grin crossed his rugged beard covered face, he said, "You do make a good point, Running Wolf."

There was a moment of silence, then Zach asked, "What is the very last thing they would expect us to do." Running Wolf didn't even hesitate when he said, "Attack them again." Ely laughed at that until he saw the look on Zach's face. He then said, "We don't even know how many of 'em we is up against." Zach turned to Brave Fox and Willow and asked, "How many was in their camp?" Brave Fox said twelve before you attacked. Willow nodded her agreement. "There ain't more than eight of them left if that many. I saw at least four of them down." Zach said.

Benny added, "If we take out these two, at least we will be down to even odds. Brave Fox then said, a little louder than he intended to, "I can fight, and I want to get even with them more than all the rest of you. That makes our odds about even." Benny looked at him and said, "Nobody is doubting your courage Brave Fox, and if you need to fight, you can use my bow and arrows," But right now we don't need numbers, we need quiet and surprise. If you will go up and keep a lookout with Buffalo Heart, me and Coyote Talker will go see if we can make a couple polecats disappear."

They could all see that Benny asking him to stand guard made him feel like a warrior. And although he was young, Benny was right, not one of them doubted his courage. He proved that when he kicked Brave Hunter off Willow last night.

They all knew any tracks they left in the snow could be seen from a long way off. So any time they left the grotto they must stay inside the tree line. Benny left his rifle and took his bow, putting his quiver of arrows over his back. Coyote Talker did the same, and they headed north, staying in the trees and nearly a mile west of where Iron Knife and Crooked Snake were riding along the lake shore. They were moving as fast as they could trying to get far enough in front of the two mounted riders that they could set up an ambush.

Although in the forest the snow wasn't as deep as it was out in the open, it was still tiring as the two of them pushed through. They jogged non-stop for nearly two miles, then stopped long enough to see where the renegade warriors were.

Benny figured they were a mile ahead now but the valley below them, all the way to the north end of the big round bay at the north end of the lake was open. There was no way they could cross in front of them without being seen.

They pushed on, running now as fast as they could for another mile. Now they were less than a quarter mile from the steep sided knoll that rose up in the center of the valley. Coming into this area they had followed the creek that ran from the lake along the east side of the knoll. They believed these riders would follow that creek. They just didn't know how far they would ride before turning back to report to the others.

They broke out into the open, running straight toward the timber covered knoll. They couldn't see the riders from where they were, and Benny just hoped the riders continued along the creek. They were now committed to their plan. Both of them knew their tracks in the fresh snow would lead anyone right back to their small rocky sanctuary. They must kill these two riders and get back to the others. If the little grotto in the outcropping of rocks was found it would mean a battle in which not only their friends, but the children could be killed.

They moved through the timber around the south end of the knoll until they were less than a hundred yards from the creek. From there they could see the riders were less than a quarter mile from them. They moved through the timber, staying even with the creek and then at the closest point, about twenty-five yards, they headed for the willows along the creek. Knowing their tracks would be seen but hoping they would think it was an animal coming from the timber to the creek for water. That is, until they were close enough that it would not matter.

The willows were thick enough to hide the two of them, and they waited as the two Sahpeech renegades got closer. Iron Knife was in the lead and stopped just out of range of Benny's arrow. Although very fluent in Shoshone he knew very little of the Ute language. Although he could hear them talking, he didn't know they were discussing turning back. Crooked Snake believed they had gone far enough, he was convinced their attackers had left the valley in the night. He didn't want, with just two of them, to get any further from the other warriors. He wanted to find their tracks, but he didn't want to find them, at least not with just the two of them.

Iron Knife understood Crooked Snake's concern, but he kept seeing the severed head of his brother laying by the fire. He wanted to find the man that did that and make him suffer a very slow and painful death. He finally talked Crooked Snake into riding on, continuing to the north end of the knoll. They would then ride back along the west side of the knoll. From there they could plainly see any tracks.

They continued on and had not ridden more than forty yards when suddenly Iron Knife felt a sudden, piercing pain in his neck. The pain was so bad he fell off the side of his horse. Crooked Snake saw the arrow enter the side of Iron Knife's neck, but before he could react he saw an arrow coming at him. Time seemed to stop as he watched the arrow coming straight for him. The arrow seemed to be moving extremely slowly, but he was moving even slower. Then, in less than the blink of an eye it was too late. He felt a terrible blow in the center of his chest. He knew he was falling off the back of his horse, but he never felt himself hit the ground. The world disappeared as Coyote Talker's arrow penetrated his heart.

Iron Knife hit the ground hard, gasping for air. He could feel his blood spurting out through his fingers as he reached for his neck. Then the dark clouds overhead became nothing but a blur and the light started to fade. He heard a voice but could not understand the strange words, then the voice became distant and slowly faded into silence. The terrible pain was gone and the world around him faded away as he drifted off into the unknown.

Coyote Talker burst out of the willows, so excited he spooked the two horses, Benny ran out to cut them off. His waving arms stopped them, and his gentle voice helped calm them down. He approached Iron Knife's gray mare, speaking softly. Once he got hold of her reins, he stroked her neck. Her nostrils were flared with the scent of a stranger, but his calming voice and gentle touch let her know she was safe.

He mounted the gray mare and rode the fifty yards to where Crooked Snake's dark dun was nervously standing. Again, his voice seemed to calm the gelding, and he leaned out and got his reins, leading him back to where Coyote Talker was taking the scalp of Crooked Snake. Benny said, "We must get back to the others Coyote Talker, lets go." Coyote Talker responded, "Are you not going to take the scalp you earned?" Benny shook his head, as he said, "I do not take scalps, the man is dead, that is enough."

"But what about the scalp dance to celebrate our victory?"

Benny shook his head. Knowing it meant a lot to the Bannock warrior he said, "Coyote Talker, you take the scalp for me. When we are safely away from danger, I will join you and your brother in your scalp dance."

Coyote Talker didn't take but a few moments, as he savagely cut the scalp from the dead Sahpeech warrior. He tucked both of the scalps under his belt, then mounted the dun and they started back toward Zach and the others following the same tracks they had made getting there.

Coyote Talker looked at Benny as they rode back, thinking these white men are truly strange men. They were as fierce of warriors as he had ever seen, but he would never understand them.

Chapter 23

Tracks in the Snow

Raven Wing was still upset from the nightmare. She believed their husbands had been in a battle or were going to be. She felt uneasy, she believed Running Wolf was already wounded, and she could not see the outcome of the battle. She did not know if the severed head was that of an enemy or one of their own.

She kept the nightmare to herself, she did not want to upset her sister and her closest friends. But Sun Flower knew her sister too well. She could see Raven Wing was even more troubled now than she had been during the long sleepless night.

When Raven Wing left the lodge, Star closed her eyes again, and went right to sleep. Luna checked on the sleeping children, sniffing the hair of each one, then pushed her way through the flap. She stood on the riverbank looking across the big meadow. Then started pacing up and down the bank.

It was Morning Song, Buffalo Heart's young wife that said, "Luna is restless this morning." She then looked at Raven Wing and continued, "Nearly as restless as you are, Raven Wing." The others were all watching their Shaman, and Raven Wing knew they all believed she knew more than she did. A tear formed in her eye and she told them of the nightmare.

She told them. "I do not know why the Great Spirit is keeping the fate of our husbands from me. I do not know if my dream is real or just a nightmare from my troubled mind." Just then Star started to cry and both Shining Star and Sun Flower rushed inside to her. Through tears and crying she said, "There are mean warriors trying to hurt Papa." They all heard the little girl's words, and now the women, and even the normally happy-go-lucky Grub, were worried.

He wished he was with Ely. This was the longest he could ever remember being away from him since they had left their father's farms, twenty-five years before. He looked around at the worried, sad faces of the women. He took a deep breath, forced a smile on his face and said, "Now ladies, you all gots to remember them husbands of yours ain't just ordinary men. No sir, they be the best warriors and mountain men that has ever walked in these here Rocky Mountains. And, don't you be forgetting the great medicine dog, why together there ain't no warriors is gonna put those men under. No sir, no warriors at all."

Even though they all knew Grub was just trying to make them feel better, it had worked. His words helped. Even Raven Wing walked over and hugged him, then looked up into his gray eyes and thanked him. Grub always had a way of making them all feel better, and this morning more than ever she appreciated that.

*****

Brave Fox and Buffalo Heart were still watching from their spot on the ridge top when Benny and Coyote Talker returned riding the two horses. Zach was standing next to Ol' Red and the horses when he first spotted the two of them coming through the trees. Not being able to tell who was riding the horses for the trees, he checked the prime in the pan of his rifle and quietly said, "Ely, Running Wolf, we might have trouble." It was only a moment later that Zach saw the familiar wolf hide hat of Benny just as Ely squeezed out between the rocks.

Benny and Coyote Talker was still fifty yards out when Running Wolf's pinto caught the scent of the strange horses and whinnied. The gray Benny was on nickered back as Benny patted her neck to keep her quiet. They were all worried about how far the sound would carry. They knew it would not be heard all the way to Red Eagle's camp. But were other warriors in the forest much closer looking for them? None of them knew the answer to that.

Buffalo Heart left Brave Eagle on the ridge when he heard the horses and ran back down to make sure they didn't need help. Zach's sky-blue eyes had turned as dark as the clouds overhead as he stared down the ridge to the lake. Coyote Talker noticed his knuckles were white, he was gripping his rifle so tightly. Without saying anything, he pointed, so the rest of them would look at Zach. When Zach turned back to face them he said, "It ain't just a hunch any more, they are looking for us, and I am tired, of this, it is time to end it and get back home."

"What you got in mind?" Ely asked.

"They ain't gonna be expecting another attack like last night, especially first thing this morning. I say we hit them again, just like we did last night. If we can take out even two or three more of them I don't believe the others will follow." It was Running Wolf that said, "Not unless they get help from the Piute village Four Bears was saying, might give them sanctuary for the winter." They all thought about that for a few moments, and Zach said, "Then we will just have to be violent enough no one will want to follow."

All but Coyote Talker and Brave Fox had seen Grizzly Killer's violent wrath before. They knew what Zach meant. Ely was by far the oldest of these men, and he had seen violent warriors from the Blackfeet, the Sioux, Cheyenne, and Crow leave mutilated bodies to frighten their enemies. He knew, even better than the others, that no one in the mountains was better at sending that kind of a message than Grizzly Killer. There was no doubt in his mind that before this day was over, if any of these Sahpeech Utes survived, they would never want to tangle with Grizzly Killer again.

They all knew to attack in the daylight was going to be dangerous. Even getting close enough to fire their rifles would be mighty dangerous. They all believed the warriors that survived last nights attack would never expect another attack. That fact alone, they believed, would give them the advantage they needed.

*****

In the Sahpeech camp, Brave Hunter had smeared bear grease on his painful burns. Each time he moved his arms, the burns across his shoulders pulled and hurt. He wanted revenge, his anger was fueled, not only by his own wounds and his dead companions, but by the fact his own Chief, Four Bears had helped Grizzly Killer and the Ute traitor, Running Wolf.

Brave Hunter wanted to see Running Wolf dead even more than Grizzly Killer. Running Wolf was Ute, maybe from a different band, but still a Ute. The way Brave Hunter saw it, he was betraying his own people.

Brave Hunter had sent Laughing Fox up the creek looking for any sign as to where their attackers had run in the dark forest. But the wind and snow had covered any sign of them. Then Laughing Fox saw a broken twig. He knew the wind might have broken it. But somehow. he knew he had found the direction their attackers had fled, if not the actual trail. He closed his eyes as though it was dark and moved another twenty feet forward. Yes, he was sure he had found their trail. He turned to go back and tell the others.

While Laughing Fox was out in the forest looking for sign. Tall Bull and Two Fists rode back into camp from the south. Brave Hunter was not surprised when they reported seeing no sign at all. He believed they would be running north.

He was ready to have everyone mount up and ride to the north. Not believing they could have much of a lead because of the storm when Laughing Fox came back. For Brave Hunter, Laughing Fox's words told him what he wanted to hear, Grizzly Killer and Running Wolf were heading north along with whoever else was with them. Within minutes they were mounted up and riding north, believing they would run into Iron Knife and Crooked Snake along the trail.

*****

Jimbo led the way as they climbed higher to the west, finding even denser forest than they had the night before. They were making sure they could not be seen as they approached the Sahpeech camp.

With silent hand signals, Zach kept Jimbo close. The dog stayed only a few yards in front of Zach as they made their way toward the creek. They were over an hour getting into position on both sides of the creek. Since it was daylight, they kept their movements slow and deliberate, making sure they would not be seen or heard.

*****

Running Wolf stayed in the grotto with Willow and the children. The men had all sacrificed pieces of their sleeping robes, and she and Running Wolf were sewing together leggings to cover her exposed legs. The heavy green hide of the grizzly was salted down with the reddish salt they carried with them, and they would use it for sleeping if needed.

Running Wolf was surprised at the resiliency of the children. After two weeks of being cold, bound, and beaten, this morning they were playing. Climbing up the jagged rock walls of the grotto and laughing at each other as they would fall.

Willow hadn't taken Buffalo Hearts coat off even for a moment. He had been glad he had brought an extra wool blanket. He was using it like a poncho, like he had seen the Spanish wearing when they were in Nuevo Mexico earlier in the year.

An hour passed in the Grotto and nearly another. Running Wolf was surprised he had not heard gun shots. He didn't think the distant was too great for the sound to reach his ears, but he wasn't sure. He went out and climbed to the top of the ridge to their lookout point and saw six warriors spread out along the lake shore riding north. Had Grizzly Killer, and the others missed them?

Troubling thoughts crossed his mind, *"Had there been a battle that he could not hear? Had Grizzly Killer and the others been ambushed and killed? Were these warriors leaving to go back to their Sahpeech village? Or were they just following the tracks that would lead them back to the children and to him?"*

Running Wolf did not know the answers to any of these questions, but the children and Willow were his responsibility now. He knew he must protect them. He knew with the children he couldn't outrun the Sahpeech. He also knew where-ever he tried to hide, Brave Hunter and his warriors could track them in the fresh snow.

In his mind, Running Wolf could see no way out of this deadly situation. But he vowed he would not go down without a fight. He pushed his way back into the grotto and told Willow and the children he had to leave for a little while. He warned them to stay inside the grotto no matter what they heard.

He picked up a black coal from the fire and used it to put three black stripes on his cheeks and one across his forehead. Willow and the children knew he was preparing for battle and the three of them huddled in the back of the grotto. They were now afraid.

Running Wolf pushed back out and mounted his pinto. He stayed on the trail that Benny and Coyote Talker had made through the trees going north. He rode as fast as he could for three miles until the trail turned to the east and led out of the trees into the open. He could plainly see the tracks as they led across the open and into the timber on the knoll. He backtracked a quarter of a mile and tied the pinto in a thicket where he knew he couldn't be seen. He then hid down behind two dead fallen pines. He did his best to ignore the pain in his injured arm, but the arm was weak, he knew he could not support the weight of his rifle and keep it steady, so he laid it over the log and let the downed tree support the heavy barrel. He was sure his first shot would eliminate one of the enemy, he just wasn't sure what would happen after that.

While he waited for what he believed would likely be his last battle. He thought of Raven Wing and Gray Wolf, he prayed to the Great Spirit for help in the coming fight, but he knew he was one man against six. He longed to be with his wife once more. But he was a warrior, and if he must give his life to protect the children that were now his responsibility, he would do so. He thought of Willow, Red Fawn, and Little Robe back in the grotto, and wondered what would become of them if this was indeed his last battle.

A pair of crows flew high overhead, the raspy calls shattering the quiet of the forest. Movement caught his eye, and he watched a weasel run the length of another fallen tree only twenty yards from him. The black tip of his tail was the only part of the deadly little hunter that stood out. His pure white fur blended nearly perfectly with the snow. He thought, *This is a good place to die.* He prayed again, if this was indeed the day of his death, he ask the Great Spirit to make his journey to the other side a good one.

He wondered how long it would take the six Sahpeech warriors to reach him. He took six of the .50 caliber lead balls from his shooting pouch and set them on the log he was hiding behind. He pulled the ram rod from its keepers under the barrel and set it beside him and set his powder horn next to it. He didn't worry about patch cloth. If he had to load that fast he would not have time to use patches.

He took his bow and set it beside him, leaving his quiver full of arrows over his shoulder. He was ready to meet the enemy. Even if he didn't survive the coming battle, he hoped he could do enough damage that the children would stay safe. But could they survive alone? With Willow, he believed they could.

He didn't know the fate of Grizzly Killer and the others, he knew it was possible they were alright. But he knew he must try to keep the enemy warriors away from the children, and he knew no other way than to discourage these Sahpeech renegades other than by an ambush.

Chapter 24

First Kill

Zach had led the way along the creek as they crept toward
the Sahpeech warrior's camp. He kept Jimbo right at his
side. It had taken much longer than he had expected to get
into position.

One hundred yards out, they spread out even more.
They would form a semi-circle and with the lake at their
back, the warriors would have no place to run when they
fired upon them. None of them had expected the camp to
be empty. As they all stood up out of the cold wet snow,
Zach shouted, "Running Wolf!" As one, they turned and
ran back toward the grotto. Zach shouted to Jimbo, "Find
Running Wolf!" The big dog was out of sight of them in
only a few bounds.

They weren't concerned about leaving a trail back to the
grotto. There only concern was getting back to Running
Wolf before the Sahpeech found him. Each of them knew
they would follow the tracks from the two dead warriors

right back to Running Wolf and the Children.

Jimbo's sudden appearance in the grotto frightened the children and even gave Willow a scare. He was inside the tiny rocky fortress for only a moment, then following the familiar scent he bounded off again to the north.

*****

From his hiding position, Running Wolf couldn't see the tracks leading across the quarter mile of open meadows to where the tracks once again disappeared into the timber of the knoll. He couldn't see more than seventy or eighty yards through the timber. He believed he would hear them coming before he saw them. As he waited, he prepared his mind for the upcoming battle and his probable death. He tried to keep Raven Wing and little Gray Wolf out of his thoughts. He knew he could not let those thoughts distract him from what had to be done. But he was not successful. His wife and little boy were foremost in his mind.

A wood-pecker was pounding on the dead tree not far above him and a squirrel chattered a warning to others in the forest that a weasel was on the hunt. Then all around him was quiet. He concentrated on nothing but the tracks in the snow. He felt a presence was close and was startled that Jimbo was only a foot away. He had not heard the dog approach. He took a deep breath and tried to slow his rapidly beating heart. Jimbo had startled him, but even so, he had never been so glad to see the great medicine dog.

Running Wolf was relieved, he didn't know, but he hoped Jimbo's presence meant his partners were alright. If they were, were they on the way to him? With that thought now in his mind, he wondered who would reach him first, his partners or these Sahpeech renegades.

*****

Zach was a hundred yards in front of the others, ignoring the burning pain in his legs from the nearly three-mile run. He pushed up over the ridge and then down to the rock outcropping that formed the grotto.

He could see the relief on the children's face when they saw it was him, but he startled them by nearly shouting, "Where is Running Wolf." Willow said, "he left a while ago, he told us to stay here and he rode out."

Zach was in a near panic. He knew his wounded partner couldn't take on the Sahpeech by himself. Ely was just starting to squeeze through the open when Zach yelled, "get mounted up, Running Wolf's gone out to stop them."

None of them took the time to saddle their horses, they all mounted up bare back. Ol' Red could sense the urgency in Zach and was loping along the tracks Jimbo and Running Wolf's pinto had left without even the slightest prompt from Zach.

Zach turned and shouted back, "Ely, somebody needs to stay back and look out for the children." Ely stopped, he knew Grizzly Killer was right. If the battle turned against them, it would be up to him to get the children to safety.

He watched his friends ride away. That was one of the hardest things he could ever remember doing. He knew they would need his rifle, but the children he believed would perish, or worse, be condemned to life as a slave, if none of them returned.

Ol' Red wasn't as fast as a horse, but this wasn't a race out in the open. This was running through snow covered timber. Over down logs and around trees. The horses could not keep up with the sure-footed mule as he carried Zach north to find his partner.

*****

Brave Hunter was the first to see the dead bodies lying in the snow, now stained red with their blood. They approached with caution, not sure if another ambush might be waiting for them in the willows.

They were all quiet when they saw the scalped, and stiff bodies of Iron Knife and Crooked Snake lying in the blood-stained snow. Brave Hunter, although quiet like the rest, burned inside, his need to revenge his fallen friends was even stronger now.

Laughing Fox slipped off his mount and studied the tracks in the snow. He could see where the ambush had been set up and where the two warriors that had killed Iron Knife and Crooked Snake had come on foot but left on the two horses. He told them all, "We follow these tracks and we can avenge these deaths." None of these men were even thinking about the captives. Right now, their only thought was of revenge.

They stayed out of range of arrows as they rode around the south end of the knoll. They could see the trail in the fresh snow leading from the knoll to the thick timber a quarter mile to the west. They rode across the open meadows to within a hundred yards of the timber, but none of them wanted to follow the trail into the thick trees.

They dismounted and ground picketed their horses. They spread out and approached the trees from a hundred-yard wide front.

*****

Jimbo whined softly, then stood and ran back along the trail to meet Zach. Zach stopped when he saw his dog. As he dismounted, Benny, Buffalo Heart, Coyote Talker, and Brave Fox all rode up behind him. Zach turned to the others and whispered, "I think we best leave the horses here." Jimbo led them the two hundred yards to where Running Wolf was waiting. He breathed a deep sigh of relief as he saw Zach and all the others except Ely following.

He was about to ask Zach about Ely, but Zach was first, "What did you figure on doing out here by yourself, and with only one good arm?" Not wanting to admit that he'd had thoughts of all of them going under Running Wolf said, "I was just going to slow them down until you got here."

Jimbo growled, and they all watched the hair stand up down the center of his back. They spread out, each finding their own place to hide. Zach sent Jimbo to the far side of the trail and motioned for him to lay down. Without knowing exactly where he was, he was as well-hidden as any of the men.

Zach saw the charcoal marks on his partner's face and knew that Running Wolf had prepared for battle and was willing to die to protect the children or any of them.

They were all watching the trail, but these Sahpeech warriors were not following the trail. Before they continued on the trail, they were going to make sure there wasn't an ambush waiting for them in the thick trees. None of them wanted to make the same mistake Iron Knife and Crooked Snake had made.

Brave Fox wanted to prove he was a warrior. He had dreamed of making his first kill in battle. As he waited, only a few yards from his older brother, he realized for the first time the men that were coming, were coming to kill them all. Fear shot through him. This was not at all the feelings that he believed going into battle would bring. This waiting was more difficult than he expected. Last night he had not had time to think, he just reacted. But now he knew they were coming, six vicious men were really coming to kill him. He was holding Benny's bow and had a quiver full of arrows. He knew he could shoot, for he had killed countless rabbits, but he had never shot at a man before. He wished he could talk to his brother, but he knew he could not move or make a sound.

Five minutes turned into ten and then fifteen. For Brave Fox and to a lesser degree, Coyote Talker, time seemed to stand still. It felt like they had been waiting for an eternity. Then finally there was movement. What Brave Fox saw wasn't by the trail at all. In fact, it was way off to the side of even where he was standing.

The movement was there again. A warrior, one of the ones that had first taken him. He was coming through the trees right toward him. He knew he wasn't hidden from the eyes of this warrior. Even though he was standing next to a tree, he was in plain sight. If he moved he thought he would be seen, but if he didn't he knew he would be. He knew he must do something for he was now in range of the warriors' arrow.

He watched the warrior carefully place one foot and then another on the ground. Moving so slowly, he wasn't making a sound. Without moving his head, only his eyes, he saw his brother was still watching the trail, not aware this warrior was coming from the side, and getting closer every moment that passed.

Then the approaching warrior froze still. Not a muscle was moving. Brave Fox wondered if he had been spotted, but the warrior was looking past him toward where Grizzly Killer and Running Wolf were hiding. They were well hidden, no this warrior was watching for his own friends, that were coming through the trees as slowly and silently as he was.

Brave Fox, moving ever so slowly edged just slightly around the tree he was hiding behind. He knew he could still be seen, but now he was at least partially hidden.

The approaching warrior stepped behind a tree, and Brave Fox moved again. This time to bring his bow up to full draw. He waited and waited. He wasn't sure how much longer he could hold back Benny's powerful bow. Suddenly there was movement much closer, only twenty yards behind his brother was another warrior. How had he gotten so close without being seen Brave Fox wondered? Without making a sound the warrior slowly stood, drawing his bow and deadly arrow as he did. Coyote Talker didn't even know he was there and Brave Fox knew if he missed this shot it could mean his brother's life.

He slowly moved the iron point of Benny's arrow from where he had it pointed to this new threat. When he was lined up on the warrior's chest he released the arrow. The arrow flew swift and true, heading right for the enemy's chest. The hoop iron point sharpened to a very sharp point, just nicked the side of the warrior's own bow. As it glanced off the hard rawhide covered oak limb of the bow, it cut a deep slice across his shoulder and stuck into a tree just past him.

The warrior cried out a warning to all of his friends. A moment later the thunderous booms of three gunshots rang out. And the forest was filled with the acrid smell and blueish gray smoke of burning powder.

Brave Fox had forgotten about the first warrior he had seen. Suddenly he felt a severe pain in his right shoulder as an arrow glanced off the tree and buried its stone point nearly to the bone. He had forgotten his fear, all he could think about now was defending himself. The adrenalin pumping through his body made the pain disappear. He had another arrow ready to shoot, looking for the warrior that had shot the arrow into his shoulder. Then everything before him became crystal clear. He could see the painted face through a tiny little slot between two trees. He knew his shot had to be perfect. Better than any shot he had ever made before. He released the arrow and watched as it passed through the narrow slot. Missing the first tree by only the width of the arrow's feathers. Although he couldn't see, he heard the solid thump of the arrow hitting the warrior and then the warrior falling to the ground.

He glanced around to make sure Coyote Talker was still safe, then he looked for another target. The woods were now as quiet, as quiet as the death that followed every battle. No one dared move. No one knew how many were dead or how many of the enemy on each side still waited to bring more death.

The vicious growl of Jimbo broke the deathly silence of the forest as he attacked one of the surviving Sahpeech Warriors. There was only a muffled scream that lasted a brief moment. Then the eerie silence was back.

Moments passed, but to Brave Fox it seemed like another eternity. Then a camp robber landed in the tree right above him and squawked out, breaking the silence once again.

Grizzly Killer's voice shouted out from the downed tree he was behind, he was speaking in the language of their enemies. To his left, Benny yelled out, and from the far side of Coyote Talker, Buffalo Heart yelled out, then Running Wolf. Then in his own tongue Grizzly Killer shouted to him and Coyote Talker to let their enemies know they were still well and strong. Coyote Talker howled like a coyote and then Brave Fox screamed his battle cry. A high-pitched shrill scream he had practiced with his friends since he was a child. None of them had been seriously hurt. They all knew the Great Spirit had been with them today. A moment later Brave Fox saw flashes of what he believed were two or maybe three warriors running away through the thick trees.

They all waited, even though they believed the battle was over. Not one of them wanted to be the first to stand and be a target if one warrior had decided to stay behind and trade his life for one of theirs.

Finally, Zach sent Jimbo to make sure all was clear. They found three dead, two Sahpeech and one Piute that was with them. There was a blood trail in the snow leading back to where they had left their horses. One of the three that had escaped was wounded. He was the one that Brave Fox stopped as he was about to put an arrow into Coyote Talker. The other one that Brave Fox had hit was dead. The sharp iron point had hit him half-way between his eye and his ear.

Brave Fox was excited with their victory. It was his first battle and they had soundly defeated their enemy. His older brother was even more excited for him than he was for himself. He knew Brave Fox had saved his life and killed one of his captors. Brave Fox no longer had to dream of becoming a great warrior, he was already one.

No one knew for sure who killed the other two, or if they did, they weren't saying. Both dead warriors had been hit in their chests with the deadly lead balls from rifles. Coyote Talker and Brave Fox took their scalps. They would dance around the scalps of their enemies to celebrate this great victory many times in the near future.

Zach was quiet, as he always was after a battle. Men had lost their lives, and he believed it was completely unnecessary. He would never understand the warrior society of so many of the Indian tribes, any more than they would understand him for not celebrating a great victory. Even Zach's closest friends did not understand why killing a dangerous enemy seemed to make him feel bad. It seemed strange to Buffalo Heart and Running Wolf both that anyone as good at killing an enemy as Grizzly Killer did not ever celebrate his greatness.

They rode back to the small rocky sanctuary. Ely couldn't contain his smile as he saw each of them riding back through the trees. As they squeezed through the narrow opening, they all noticed Willow's eyes light up as Brave Fox came inside. She saw his bloody arm and rushed to him. But it was Ely that pulled the deadly point out, then smiled as he watched Willow bandage his arm. They all believed there was a romance starting between the two of them.

They were all exhausted. No sleep the night before and the brief but intense battle had taken a toll on these hardened men. To survive in the wilderness meant the work never stopped. They had eaten the last of the bear meat and now tired or not, they must hunt or go hungry. None of them would let the little ones go without eating. Zach, Buffalo Heart, and Benny rode down to the willows where they had seen the deer before. They had been gone less than an hour when the sound of a gunshot and then another reached the grotto.

They brought back a yearling buck and dry doe. Ely and Willow had fresh venison roasting over the fire within an hour of them returning. They took two-hour shifts standing guard through the night. Even though none of them believed the Sahpeech warriors would return, they were taking no chances.

Chapter 25

The Spotted Stallion Returns

Red Eagle rode hard, taking the two women to trade for horses. From the south end of the lake he rode into the large, deep valley that lies beyond the high flat top ridge west of the lake. After reaching the creek in the bottom, he turned south. Hoping to find the Piute village along this creek. The storm had dropped only a little snow in the valley, it had saved most of its fury for the high mountains and the valley of the lake.

After riding for several hours, he had seen no sign of the village. They came to where the creek flows into a larger one then cuts its way through another canyon heading further west. Eventually reaching the headwaters of the river that flows past the Sahpeech Village, his childhood home.

They rode down through this canyon, pushing the three horses to their limit and found the village of Broken Lance on the western end of the canyon.

Four Bears had been right, Red Eagle was greeted as a

friend by Broken Lance. The women, one young, the other nearing 35 summers, were a needed addition to the village. They would be taken as wives by two of the Piute warriors and treated as they treated all of their women.

The life of an Indian woman wasn't much different from that of a slave. They worked from daylight to dark seven days a week and had children along the way. But they knew no other life, they lived the way they always had. Other than now they were among strangers, their lives with the Piute's would not really change. They would now have to please different men, but to them, most men were the same.

Red Eagle traded them for three horses each and spent a warm restful night in Broken Lance's teepee. As a guest of the chief, he was given the younger of the chief's wives to keep his bed warm through the night.

Three young Piute warriors asked to ride with him. Fighting a hated enemy and trading slaves to the Spanish sounded much more exciting than spending the winter in the village.

Red Eagle led the three young warriors and six extra horses back up the canyon before daylight the following morning.

They were within ten miles of the lake when they stopped for the night. The steep climb up to the valley of the lake had tired the horses. They would spend the night and continue at first light.

It was just past midmorning when Brave Hunter saw the riders approaching from the south. He and Crazy Hair were by the fire. Laughing Fox was watching the horses. Red Eagle looked around. He saw the slaves were gone, and Brave Eagle was there. Brave Hunter was burned, and Crazy Hair had his shoulder bandaged. Laughing Fox was the only one that wasn't hurt.

Red Eagle and his Piute recruits listened as Brave Hunter told Red Eagle what had happened. They all could see the anger and the hatred in his dark eyes. He vowed revenge, not only to the other warriors with him, but to himself. He would see the white warrior and Ute traitor dead, if it took him the rest of his life.

*****

The next morning the sky had cleared. Zach and his group were riding north, staying in the timber along the west side of the valley. They did not know that Red Eagle had returned and with his Piute recruits their numbers were once again even. They were cautious, although they did not believe they would be followed, Buffalo Heart stayed well behind the others, he would keep a very close watch on their back trail.

As the sun appeared over the eastern horizon, its warming rays were mighty welcome. Willow rode alongside Brave Fox, and the children rode next to Ely. It was just past midday when Zach stopped. He could see a dozen horses running toward them. As they got closer it became evident, they had no riders. Then Zach saw Thunder, the spotted stallion was pushing the horses to them.

Ol' Red brayed, the sound echoing through the surrounding hills. Thunder reared up, striking the air with his hooves. Benny shouted out, "The spotted stallion returns!" Zach could feel Ol' Red was excited to see his friend once again. Benny, Coyote Talker, and Brave Fox rode out to contain the horses since they were scattering in all directions as Jimbo ran out to greet Thunder. The spotted stallion and great medicine dog touched noses then Thunder reared again and whinnied, before trotting up to Zach and Ol' Red.

Together again, they pushed on northward. Over the high ridge where they could once again see the breast like mountain to the north. Ely laughed again as he looked at it, "Yep, that's Molly's Nipple alright." The children kept looking up at him, wondering what he kept laughing about.

They made it all the way to the creek in the big canyon where they camped in a stand of Cottonwoods. The bright yellow leaves of the cottonwood and aspen were now on the ground. The violent storm had stripped the branches bare.

The mountains tops were still white as the sun set, but the October storm had left only a couple of inches in the bottom of this canyon, and it had mostly melted during the day. But the nights were cold, and Zach spread out the heavy grizzly hide for the children and Willow to lay on since there weren't enough really warm robes. When Zach got up a couple of hours before sunrise he smiled, Willow wasn't with the children she was sound asleep cuddled in the arms of Brave Fox.

Running Wolf's arm was still stiff and sore. And the following morning Brave Fox found his wounded arm was much worse than it had been right after Ely had pulled the stone point from the muscle of his arm. He thought about Running Wolf, that arrow had been stuck in the bone. He was determined to be as tough as Running Wolf was, no matter how painful his arm was, he would not complain.

As they drank the last cup of warm coffee, Running Wolf said, "I am not sure we should take the same route home. Not sure I want to get that close to the Sahpeech village now we have killed several of them." They were all silent as his words settled upon them. Zach said, "You think we can follow this canyon to the east and go north along the east side of these mountains staying on this side of the Green River?"

"At least that way, I think we will be a lot closer to friends." Running Wolf continued, then Ely stood up and said, "Well, I ain't never been up this here canyon before. I is always excited to see new country. Whichever way we gonna go, we is a long way from home so we best get after it."

Zach smiled, he too was excited to see new country, but he had a nagging feeling they had not seen the last of Red Eagle and Brave Hunter. As they mounted up for what he knew was to be one of many long hard days on the trail, he looked up the mountain to the south and wondered why the nagging feeling that Red Eagle was behind them would not leave his thoughts. He believed there were warriors on the distant horizon, wanting to rain hell upon them.

Going east the canyon narrowed, in places they had to ride in the creek as it snaked its way through narrow rocky ridges on both sides. In other places, it opened up and they rode through dense juniper and pinion forests.

It was midafternoon when they crested the last ridge and started down the eastern side of the pass at the top of the canyon. That evening they camped in a stand of cottonwoods by a nearly dry wash. It had just a trickle of water, but it was enough for their coffee and the horses to drink their fill.

Jimbo checked in a large circle all around and come back wagging his tail. Their campsite was clear, Buffalo Heart had stayed more than five miles behind most of the day and it was nearly an hour later when he rode in. Zach didn't say, but he didn't need to. Buffalo Heart understood the questioning look on Zach's face. Making sure the young ones could not hear him. He and Zach stepped off to the side and as the strips of venison was roasting on sticks of the fire, Buffalo Heart said, "Grizzly Killer, I did not see any sign we are being followed, but like you, something is telling me they are back there."

Zach thought about Buffalo Hearts' words. He knew if Red Eagle or any of his men were following them, they would eventually catch up.

Zach looked to the north. The land was barren and dry. Slate Gray hills rolled out before them and just a couple miles to their west were the mountains they had just crossed. Zach thought about what to do throughout the night. For his own peace of mind, he needed to know if he was leading Red Eagle or others not only toward Blacks Fork and their families but to the land of the Uintah Utes. Where they once again may try to steal slaves. No, Zach decided, he must know for sure.

The next morning, just before they started out, Zach told them all he would not be riding with them today. He was going to stay behind, if needed for a few days. He asked Running Wolf, "Do you plan on following the Duchesne River up over the top?" Running Wolf nodded and said, "Yes, unless the snow is too deep. Don't think it will be, but if it is, we will have to go back through the Yambow and follow the canyon of many echoes and cross the Bear River then on to Blacks Fork."

Buffalo Heart stayed back and Zach said, "No partner, this may be a foolish waste of time, you go ahead with the others." Buffalo Heart smiled, shook his head and said, "I do not like to go against you Grizzly Killer, but I am staying with you. If there is trouble even Grizzly Killer and the great medicine dog might need a little help. If not, at least you won't have to ride home alone." Zach truly did appreciate Buffalo Heart and his words. But he didn't want to see any of his friends in more danger. The arrow in Running Wolf's arm had weighed heavily upon him. He would rather himself get hurt than see any of his friends.

They stood there by the small fire and watched their friends ride up and over the last distant hill. Zach wondered if they would see them again before they reached their home on Blacks Fork.

They had seen a few deer in the bottom and Buffalo Heart had jumped two small groups of sheep as he rode into the hills looking for vantage spots where he could see for a long way behind them. He found one such place on a ridge only a couple of miles from where Zach had stopped to make this camp. He said, "Grizzly Killer, if Red Eagle or others are following, they shouldn't be more than two of three days at most." Zach nodded, and said, "I think that's right, if we ain't seen any sign of them by the end of the third day, we'll head out."

Buffalo Heart then pointed to a rocky ridge a couple miles west of them and said, "I rode across that ridge before I came in last night. From there you can see a long way back to the west. I think that is a good place to watch our back trail." He smiled and said, "When I crossed it last night, there were a few sheep laying in the shade behind the rocks and we are going to need to make some meat."

Zach smiled at his eager young partner, then stepped up into the saddle. Although he and Running Wolf, and now even Benny tried to fill the void Buffalo Heart still felt after Red Hawk was killed, Zach knew without words being spoken, that he missed his lifelong friend every single day. It was a void that would never be filled. Good friends are with you for a lifetime and beyond, whether they are by your side or not.

The sheep were not in the shadow of the rocks, but they hadn't gone far. The dozen big horns were only a quarter mile north grazing along a hill side. Buffalo Heart slipped off his horse, leaving his rifle in its scabbard and handed Zach his reins. With his bow and arrows with their hoop iron points, he started a slow stalk toward the unsuspecting sheep.

Down in the shadow of the rocks, Zach built a small fire pit. Then he dragged dead branches from both cottonwood and juniper to the edge of what he presumed would be their camp for the next couple of days. He believed if Running Wolf and the others did not run into trouble, like some large impassible canyon, or the like, they should make fifty miles a day traveling through the relatively flat barren land for as far as he could see to the north. He almost hoped for another storm to cover their tracks, but the weather looked clear, and it was warm for being the middle of October.

The whistles and grunts of the bull elk were now silent, their rutting season was over. Now it was the deer's turn, he knew the big bucks necks would be starting to swell in another week or two. November, ezhe'i-mea', the cold moon to the Shoshone would bring the buck deer together fighting for the right to breed just like September and into October had with the elk. Then after the deer rut was winding down, they would be able to hear the vicious blows of the Big Horn Rams as they battered their heads together, showing the ewes who would be the strongest to pass their strength onto the next generation.

Buffalo Heart took a large lamb, and they set up a spit, slowly roasting a haunch over the small fire all afternoon. Zach had found a comfortable place in the rocks where he could see nearly four miles to the west. Looking to the east reminded him of being on the front range of the Rockies and looking forever across the great expanse of the vast prairie. The land to their east wasn't a sea of grass. This was dry and baron land. He could see distant mountains to the southwest but he knew those mountains were many days, if not weeks away. Between them and those distant mountains he could see the top of buttes and castle like rocks that he knew signaled great difficulty for anyone venturing out across it.

The day passed quietly. They ate their fill of the fresh lamb and enjoyed their small fire nestled in the shadow of the rocks. The wind was calm, and the rocks had soaked up heat from the sun all day. There had been no sign of anyone following throughout the day, and now darkness had fallen, and with it the temperature started to fall. Zach added a few more sticks to the fire looked up into the heavens and said, "Thank you lord for keeping us safe today, and please watch over our loved ones, let them know we are safe and will be home in a few more days. And if it ain't asking too much, keep it from storming up yonder for a few more days so we can go over the pass to get home."

That was the first time Buffalo Heart had heard his partner pray. Oh, he knew Zach prayed on occasion, but he usually went off to be alone when he did. He didn't know why it surprised him that Zach was talking with the Great Spirit just as if he was a good friend, but it had. Hearing what Zach said, even made him feel better. He didn't understand why, but he really did feel better.

Chapter 26

Vow of Revenge

The storm had moved east leaving Blacks Fork under clear skies. Grub and the women were once again using the outside fire for their cooking. During the day, Grub had shot another small buck. Although it appeared life was moving as normal in the small village of Grizzly Killer. For those that were there, it was anything but normal. Their men had been gone too long. They all believed they were in danger and Running Wolf had been hurt. All they could do was wait. They tried to keep their troubled minds on their daily tasks.

They worked hard every day. For one to survive the wilderness there were no days off, and the worry they felt for their husbands made their work seem much harder.

They fixed a stew of the fresh venison, using wild onion, camas, sego roots, and cattail shoots. They made biscuits and had fresh coffee. Yellow Bird walked away from the others, as they were busy preparing the meal.

She was pale, the sight of the food made her stomach turn and she was afraid she may throw up. Everyone felt better tonight, even though they did not know why, and they did not notice the pale, worried look of Yellow Bird. They sat around the warm crackling fire and as they ate the sun dropped behind the western ridge.

Although none of them knew why, their mood was lighter as they ate. It was lighter than is had been in many days. They didn't noticed Yellow Bird did not touch her bowl of food.

Although no one spoke of it, they could all feel it. It felt as though a heavy rock had been lifted from their minds. Grub even joked a little and brought smiles all around.

The western sky turned ablaze with color, and they watched in awe of its beauty. The color had not yet faded when the evening star started to twinkle its brightness in the darkening sky. Star sat down between Shining Star and Sun Flower, Shining Star asked her, "Do you remember what Papa taught you about the first star you see?" Her bright blue eyes lit up as she looked up at the star and said,

"Star of wonder, Star so Bright the first star I see tonight.

I wish I may, I wish I might, get the wish I wish tonight."

She then looked up and said, "Papa coming home soon. I wish for Papa to come home, and he is coming." She then turned to everyone and shouted, "Papa coming home soon!"

Star was excited, and that got the rest of them excited too. But what did soon mean? Was soon tomorrow, or many more days? None of them knew, but Star's excitement had been contagious. They went to their sleeping robes feeling much better than they had for many days.

Yellow Bird did her best not to let the others see how she felt. She did not know what was wrong with her. She hoped by morning her stomach would be settled.

Morning brought more nausea to her troubled body. As they prepared their morning meal, she could not hold it in. She rushed to the river and bent over, throwing up nothing but bile that burned the back of her throat.

She turned toward Raven Wing. There was no hiding her sickness any longer. She was pale and felt terrible, but to her surprise Raven Wing was smiling. Their medicine woman did not seem concerned and then turned to the others and said, "It seems our village is growing," then she turned back to Yellow Bird and asked, "How long have you been with child, Yellow Bird?" Yellow Bird stood there in stunned silence. She had seen many women have morning sickness when they were first with child. But had never even considered that she could be a mother, she never had a child with her first husband. Now she thought she was too old to have a baby. Babies were for young women not one of over thirty summers old.

*****

Following the east side of the mountains north, Running Wolf and the others covered over fifty miles that first day. The children, Little Robe and Fawn had fallen asleep on their horses but they did not slow them down.

They made camp that night in thick Junipers, on a ridge before dropping into the canyon of the ancients. This is the canyon they had spent last winter in with the Ute village of Two Feathers. Running Wolf had stopped thinking of the Ute village of his birth as home. His home was now in the village of Grizzly Killer on the banks of Blacks Fork.

Running Wolf told them, "One more day and we will be on the Duchesne River, two more on the Bear, the next we will ride across the big meadow and be home.

It will be hard pushing that far each day, if the horses need more rest it will take longer, for it is a tough climb over the mountains."

*****

Zach and Buffalo Heart watched their trail down the eastern side of the pass, taking turns through the night. In the dark they knew it would be easy to miss riders moving slow and quietly down from the pass. At first light, Zach went down to make sure there were no fresh tracks. He took his time, making sure he left no tracks or sign that he had been there, he left only their tracks from the day before.

The day passed slowly and Zach hoped Running Wolf and the others were making good time. He believed Running Wolf would take the route through the valley of the ancients. Then north to the Duchesne River, follow the river up past Rock Creek and over the high pass under the big round bald mountain and down the Bear River until he reached the trail leading to Blacks Fork. Zach smiled, thinking they could be home in just four or five days, barring any trouble that may lie ahead. Then he looked at their back trail and thought, or any trouble that may find us from behind.

The second day passed quietly. After two days of waiting and watching, Zach and Buffalo Heart were ready to move on. They believed the others would be at least a hundred miles ahead, and there was no sign they were being followed. But Zach could not shake the feeling someone was behind them.

At dusk he mounted Ol' Red and rode back up to the top of the pass. He stayed well off to the side of their original tracks. It was a clear star lit night as he reached the pass, and to his dismay only a mile below, on the west side he could see the flickering light of a fire.

A wolf howled somewhere to the south, and a pack of coyotes started their high-pitched yipping as he stepped out of the saddle. He dropped the reins, knowing Ol' Red would not move. Then a sound made him jump, and he spun around, bringing his rifle up as Buffalo Heart held up his hands and said, "It's me."

Zach smiled a sheepish little smile and then said, "They are down there alright." Buffalo Heart looked over the pass to the west and asked, "Have any idea how many there are?" Zach shook his head, then added. "But, if they're on foot, they ain't gonna be able to follow us very far." Buffalo Heart then said, "If we send them the right message, they may not want to keep following whether they're mounted or not."

Zach reached down and rubbed Jimbo's ears and said, "You have to stay back, big feller. You might ruin our surprise if their horses smell you." Buffalo Heart had heard Zach talk to Jimbo like that many times before. He didn't really know whether Jimbo understood the meaning of each word, but he had no doubt he understood what Zach meant.

The two of them spread out. Staying about a hundred yards apart, they crept toward the flickering light. Jimbo followed behind Zach until they were within a quarter mile. Then, with nothing more than a closed fist, Zach told the big dog to stay. Zach knew if Jimbo was needed, he would cover that distance in mere seconds.

Zach dropped to his belly and crawled, keeping his rifle cradled in his arms when he was about seventy-five yards from the fire. He waited until he was sure how many of the enemy they were up against. He knew Buffalo Heart was doing the same somewhere in the darkness to his left.

Zach was surprised there were six of them, but from that distance looking through brush and trees he could not tell who they were. He crawled closer, finally hearing the horses, as one nickered, he hoped his own scent wasn't making them nervous. The air was dead calm. He knew it did not matter which direction he approached from.

He stopped within easy rifle range and listened to the voices. It took only moments for him to confirm Brave Hunter was one of them. While Zach waited for them to bed down for the night, Buffalo Heart had slowly and carefully circled the camp so their horses were between him and Zach.

The cold from both the ground and the air was making waiting very uncomfortable as the two of them watched from the darkness. Finally Zach saw four men lie down by the fire, another dragged a large log onto the flames that would burn long into the night, then, he too laid down. The last of the six of them were guarding the camp. Zach watched him walk out away from the light of the fire to check on their horses, then a few moments later come back.

As he watched he realized the guard was not going to leave the warmth of fire as he took his turn at guard.

An hour passed, Zach knew he must get into position at the horses, but could he get that close with the horses getting nervous? He knew he must try.

Zach was still fifteen yards from the end of the picket line when the guard stood and added more wood to the fire. As the flames flared with added fuel, Zach could see all six of their horses had their ears forward and their nostrils flared toward him. He whispered softly, speaking Ute. He hoped the words he was using were familiar to them.

He slowly continued, then the dark buckskin closest to him stomped the ground and took a step away as he reached out and run his hand across his withers. Zach's soothing touch seemed to calm the buckskin. He then used his knife to cut through his end of the rawhide picket line. As he cut the braided rawhide, a horse down the line stomped, and another nickered. The restless horses had got the attention of the guard. Zach froze as the guard now fully alert started toward them.

He was holding the cut line so the horses wouldn't move but knew he would be in plain sight of the guard in only moments. The guard, one of the young Piute's that had joined Red Eagle had been staring into the fire and his eyes had not fully adjusted to the dark when he stepped outside the light of the fire and into the dark trees where the horses were picketed.

Buffalo Heart, had moved in so silently that Zach had not heard him. As the guard walked past the first tree Zach dropped the end of the picket rope and stood hoping to stop the guard before he could shout out to the others. At that same moment Buffalo Heart's hand closed around the unsuspecting warrior's mouth as he thrust his knife all the way to its hilt between the Piute's ribs.

The Piute jerked and fought against the shock and pain, but only for a moment. Then Buffalo Heart felt blood running through his fingers on both hands and he lowered the now limp body to the ground.

Taking out the guard had not been as quiet as either of them hoped, and Zach saw another of their enemy sit up next to the fire. He raised his rifle, aligning the sights by the light of the fire. Buffalo Heart, using his bloody knife cut through the other end of the picket line.

Trying not the wake the others, Laughing Fox, who was now sitting watching and listening, whispered out to the missing guard. Zach knew they had but a brief moment, and he knew getting the horses was more important than killing another. In one swift movement he jumped onto the back of the buckskin, as Buffalo Heart did the same at the far end of the picket line. With a scream and terrifying war cry, they pushed the frightened horses up toward the pass. They heard shouts over the pounding hooves of the running horses, and they knew the warriors were running through the darkness after them. Then there was a sound they had both heard many times in the past, the vicious and terrifying growl as Jimbo attacked.

Laughing Fox was the first after them and he was less than a hundred yards behind Buffalo Heart when the two hundred pound dog's powerful jaws bit down on the side of his head and neck, ripping through skin and flesh. At hearing the attack, the others stopped. Red Eagle slowly approached his severely injured friend with knife in hand and wondered. Was it a pack of wolves that ran the horses off? Did a wolf just attack Laughing Fox? He then shouted out, "Where is Black Feather? He was supposed to be watching the horses!" Another warrior shouted back, "Black Feather is dead." Then Brave Hunter said, "Grizzly Killer, it had to be Grizzly Killer and the great medicine dog."

Red Eagle stood there staring into the darkness. The pounding hooves of their horses had faded into the stillness of the night. The hatred he felt for this man he had never even seen, consumed him. He vowed right then he would follow Grizzly Killer, no matter how far, or how long it took, he would find this great white warrior and kill him.

Chapter 27

Home at Last

Zach and Buffalo Heart rode on through the night, pushing the six stolen horses in front of them. Just before light they stopped at a small creek running from the mountains to their east. They let the weary horses rest and drink and graze on the dry grass along its banks while they got a couple of hours' sleep.

Dawn brought with it a high cloud cover and a warm south wind. As they mounted up again, they could both feel a change in the weather was coming. Zach believed there would be another storm within the next day or two.

They rode on, letting the horses walk about half the time and keeping them at an easy lope the other half. They stopped and let them rest for a half hour every three or four hours.

As the miles faded behind them, Zach wondered about the warriors they had left behind. He couldn't help but wonder if they'd had enough or would he have to fight them again someday yet to come. He had delt with men like Red Eagle many times in the past. Although he had never met or even seen Red Eagle he believed he knew him. He was a man consumed by hate, he needed to be in charge but his temperament made only ruthless vicious men want to follow him. He was proud and believed he was invincible. Just like many other warriors that Zach had faced in his time in the mountains, he believed that one day he would have to face Red Eagle again.

They passed where Running Wolf and others had camped, but with a couple hours of daylight left they pushed on. They stopped on the creek in the canyon of the ancients. They had spent the winter before with the Ute village only a dozen miles further down the creek. They had hunted this area many times and knew it well. The horses were all tired and seemed content on the grass along the creek. While Buffalo Heart got a fire going, Zach hiked up the creek to a meadow not far above them and shot a young buck. As the venison roasted, they talked about home and wondered how close Running Wolf and the others were to getting there.

Zach was tired of the trail. He wanted to be back in the warm embrace of his wives. He wanted to see the smiling faces of Star, Jack, and Little Moon. He wanted to know Running Wolf's arm was alright. As he laid down next to the fire, he was as tired as he could ever remember being. The wind was still gusting, and it was warmer now than it had been in many days. As he drifted off to sleep, he could almost feel the naked bodies of Sun Flower and Shining Star lying next to him.

A light rain awakened them. Dark, heavy storm clouds had moved in during the night. Although it was light enough to see the canyon walls, Zach didn't believe the sun was up, but he wasn't sure with the dark thick clouds setting so low in the canyon.

Buffalo Heart picked one of the horses that he liked and they used it as a pack horse, putting the deer, and their bed rolls on it, then headed out again into the light rain. Knowing the canyon would provide everything the horses needed through the winter, they left the others there in the canyon of the ancients.

*****

Two days later, at midday, Luna bounded across Blacks Fork and ran across the big meadow. As fast as she took off, everyone watched as she disappeared over the low ridge on the west side of the meadow. Raven Wing knew her husband was coming, and she too crossed the stream and started running across the meadow when a dozen riderless horses came over the ridge. She stopped in shock as the horses, pushed ahead by the spotted stallion ran toward the other horses in the big meadow.

Star watched across the meadow, just like the others. They were all expecting the men to come riding over the ridge at any moment. No one noticed Stars bottom lip was quivering, or the tears that were in her eyes. She knew her Papa wasn't coming, at least not now. She knew he was alright, she could see him and Buffalo Heart on the trail leading a pack horse in her mind. But he was not going to be there to throw her in air and spin her around and hug her.

Shining Star knelt down beside her and when she saw the look on Star's face, panic shot through her body. In that instant, she too knew Grizzly Killer was not coming. But unlike her daughter, she did not know he was alright.

Tears filled her eyes as she feared the worst. Her whole

body was trembling as she held Star tightly against her. She feared she would never see or hold him again. Sun Flower saw the reaction of Shining Star and she could feel her own heart beating hard and fast as she too felt the panic of the unknown. Before she could say anything, Running Wolf rode over the ridge across the meadow. Raven Wing ran toward him and Luna pranced alongside his pinto.

Little Dove and Yellow Bird ran across the stones of the river and across the meadow, running to their husbands. Morning Song waited for Buffalo Heart to bring up the rear. He was normally the last one on the trail, but he didn't come. Panic shot through her as well. She fell to her knees, tears streaming down her cheeks. She felt the same fear she had when she feared he had been lost in the great avalanche a couple of years ago.

Then Star said, "Mama, Papa and Jimbo and Buffalo Heart stay behind. They stop the bad men from coming." Shining Star was still trembling as she asked, almost afraid of the answer, "Is Papa alright?" Star got a strange look on her face, like, why would you ask that. She said, "Papa is always alright, he is Grizzly Killer, but he isn't coming home today." Then, with a shaky voice, Little Dove asked, "And Buffalo Heart?" Star looked at her and said, "He with Papa, and Jimbo."

Gray Wolf had run after his mother and Running Wolf jumped off his pinto and was hugging Raven Wing and Gray Wolf. Little Dove and Yellow Bird were just reaching their husbands as Grub said, "Guess we best get a couple of haunches on the spit. Gonna be a good time tonight."

Brave Fox and Willow, along with the children, Little Robe and Red Fawn, watched with joy the reunion of these men and women. Running Wolf saw his sister and knew she must be worried. He picked up Gray Wolf and set him up on the horse as they moved on across to the small six lodge village.

He told Shining Star, Sun Flower, and Morning Song he expected their husband would be another two or maybe three days.

A light misty rain had started to fall, but within an hour it stopped. Two Flowers had taken Red Fawn and Little Robe into her and Grub's teepee and cleaned them up. With the warmth and loving care, both children were asleep within minutes. It had been a brutal and exhausting experience, especially for the children.

Coyote Talker was expecting Growling Bear to be there and was extremely relieved to find he had recovered and left several suns before to return to their village.

Raven Wing mixed bear grease and several healing plants together to soothe the young one's tender wrists, and for Coyote Talker and Running Wolf's wounded arms, she examined them both she was pleased. Their wounds were healing just fine.

Coyote Talker watched as Grub and Ely met and hugged one another. He could see the bond the two men had. He understood that bond, it was the same way he felt toward his brothers. Ely was proud of Coyote Talker. He felt the young warrior had matured tremendously in a very short time. When he introduced him, Brave Fox, and Willow to Grub, he said, "Pard, I want ya to meet three of bravest people I ever met." Everyone around could see the pride on their faces.

Although nothing was said, Raven Wing could tell Running Wolf was concerned about Zach and Buffalo Heart. He did not know whether they were being followed or not. But he trusted his partner's instincts, and Zach thought they were being followed. If they were, he knew Grizzly Killer and Buffalo Heart could be in a mighty dangerous situation, and he was more than just a little worried about them.

Star insisted her Papa and Uncle Buffalo Heart were coming home, and although she didn't give any details, her positive attitude made them all feel better.

Grub laughed at his partner. He had never seen Ely so happy. The thought of Ely becoming a father made them all smile, but for Ely, it was more than that. He had always loved his life as a trapper, explorer and mountain man. He truly did think his life couldn't be any better. Then he married Yellow Bird and now she was going to have a baby. Ely felt he was going to explode with happiness. He'd never realized what he had been missing.

Coyote Talker watched everyone in the little village as they waited for Grizzly Killer. He was amazed that different people could live together and be as happy as these people were. White men, Ute, and Shoshone all together showing love and respect for one another as though they were family. He still did not understand why these men had done what they had for him, a complete stranger. But he would always be grateful they had.

The last three weeks had changed Coyote Talker's life. He could feel the change in himself and hoped he would become not only as great of warriors as these men were, but as honorable as well.

Coyote Talker knew he and Brave Fox had another seven or eight suns before they reached their own village, and heavy winter storms could make that time even longer. They needed to leave, but he would not leave before he was sure Grizzly Killer and Buffalo Heart made it back safely.

Late in the afternoon, on the third day after their return, Luna once again ran out across the big meadow. As they all turned to watch, they saw Jimbo greet her half-way across. A moment later the long ears of Ol' Red and then Zach's wolverine hat appeared over the ridge. Star, Jack, and Little

Moon started to jump up and down with excitement. Then Star turned to Coyote Talker and with a big smile said, "That is my Papa."

Morning Song had tears streaming down her checks as Buffalo Heart stepped out of his saddle. Sun Flower and Shining Star both waited silently until Zach had picked up his three children, threw each one in the air and spun them around, just as he did each time he returned. He then turned to his wives and with an arm around each of them. He breathed a deep sigh of relief. He and all of his friends were home, and all were safe.

The next morning Coyote Talker, Brave Fox, and Willow prepared to leave. Willow's village was just south of the great lake of salt. She believed Red Fawn and Little Robe's village was just around the mountain from her own. They told them all they would take the children back to their families before following the great lake of salts eastern shoreline to the north.

Zach gave Brave Fox and Coyote Talker each four of the horses Thunder had stolen and told them both that great warriors needed extra mounts. They both beamed with pride at such a compliment from the great Grizzly Killer.

Red Fawn ran to Ely and hugged him tight for a long time before finally saying, "Goodbye, Grandfather." Yellow Bird leaned into him as his eyes filled with tears. She knew he was going to a great father.

They all stood on the bank of Blacks Fork and watched the two young warriors with the children following ride west across the big meadow. Ely said, "It will be a long hard trip, but they is gonna make it just fine."

The following morning Zach climbed up to the small clearing above the lodge. It was the clearing he'd dreamed of, the grizzly changing into his Pa, and his Pa's warning to beware of the man riding a spotted horse. It was a place he had been many times. A revered place for him to think and pray. From there he could see the wilderness he so loved. He could see his loved ones at the lodges below. He thanked God for helping them all return safely. He then laid back and watched the clouds move across the deep blue sky.

He saw the blue eyes of his daughter staring back at him from high above when the cry of an eagle broke through the serenity of the moment. Then, from out of the blue, streaked a large eagle, its wings were tucked in as it streaked from the sky. The morning sun was reflecting off its golden feathers and made the eagle look red, almost blood red, and it was diving straight toward his children.

Zach jerked his eyes wide open. He hadn't even realized he had closed them. He looked at the lodges below, making sure his children and Gray Wolf were safe. He scanned the sky from horizon to horizon and all was clear. Was this just a nightmare brought on by their ordeal of the last three weeks? Or was this a warning, was Red Eagle now a threat to his family? He knew only time will tell.

Note from the Author

Grizzly Killer: Hell on the Horizon, is the twelfth edition of the Grizzly Killer Series. It is a work of fiction, coming solely from my imagination. The settings of the story are real, and I described them in the book without using their modern names as best I could. Following is the route they followed as they trailed the renegade band of Sahpeech Ute Warriors through the length of Utah's Wasatch Mountains.

Heading west from their home on Blacks Fork in the Uintah Mountains of northeastern Utah, they travel through Chalk Creek canyon turning south (Present day town of Coalville, Utah) following the Weber River into the present day Kamas Valley, what the Ute People called Yambow. They continue south reaching the Provo River, (Named for Etienne Provost, the trapper and explorer that is credited as the first to explore this area of Utah) and follow it into the Heber Valley, (Heber City, Utah). Following the route of US Highway 40 southeast into the Strawberry Valley, (Strawberry Reservoir) and then turn southwest to

US Highway 6. They follow US 6 to present day Thistle Junction. From there the trail leads them through Sanpete County along US Highway 89. That is where the San Pitch River runs into the Sevier River near the present day town of Gunnison, Utah. Following the Sevier River south about ten miles is the town of Redmond, with its salt mines of an ancient, mineral laden salt deposit.

From the Redmond salt mounds the trail leads them south along the Sevier River to Salina, Utah, and from there they follow Salina Creek back to the east along the route of Interstate 80. Turning south once again they follow the Gooseberry Road (Forest Service Road 038/040) as that road winds its way up and over the nearly 11,000 foot high, Niotche/Lost Creek Divide. Then south along Forest Service Road 640 they follow Seven Mile Creek to where it flows into present day Johnson's Reservoir. They follow the Fremont River (Named for John C. Fremont, the first man to map a route through the Rocky Mountains to California.) upstream to Fish Lake.

I placed the Sahpeech Ute renegades camp where Twin Creek runs into the west side of Fish Lake. Today the Fish Lake Lodge sits in that location just south of the creek. The Fish Lake area and the National Forest named for it has been used for thousands of years as a place to hunt, fish, and spend the summers, and it still is today. It is truly a beautiful place. It is a place very dear to my heart, I was born only fifty miles from the lake in Richfield, Utah. Some of my fondest memories are of fishing with my father and uncle at Fish Lake and the surrounding areas.

Sanpete County, Utah and the San Pitch River are named for the Sahpeech band of Utes. The meaning of Sanpete, Sahpeech, San Pitch, means Tule or Bulrush, named for the extensive marches that once existed along the river through the Sanpete Valley.